MW00772372

BY LINDA HOLMES

Evvie Drake Starts Over

Flying Solo

Back After This

back after this

Back After This

a novel

Linda Holmes

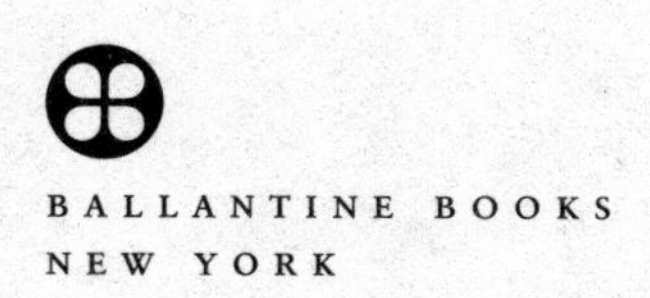

BALLANTINE BOOKS
NEW YORK

Published in the United States by Ballantine Books, an imprint of Random House, a division of Penguin Random House LLC, New York.

LIBRARY OF CONGRESS CATALOGING-IN-PUBLICATION DATA
Names: Holmes, Linda (Radio talk show host) author.
Title: Back after this : a novel / Linda Holmes.
Description: New York : Ballantine Books, 2025.
Identifiers: LCCN 2024059136 (print) | LCCN 2024059137 (ebook) |
ISBN 9780593599259 (hardcover ; acid-free paper) |
ISBN 9780593599266 (ebook)
Subjects: LCGFT: Romance fiction. | Novels.
Classification: LCC PS3608.O49435456 B33 2025 (print) |
LCC PS3608.O49435456 (ebook) | DDC 813/.6—dc23/eng/20241210
LC record available at https://lccn.loc.gov/2024059136
LC ebook record available at https://lccn.loc.gov/2024059137

Printed in Canada on acid-free paper

randomhousebooks.com

9 8 7 6 5 4 3 2 1

First Edition

For Jessica, Mike, Hafsa, Liz, Rommel, Candice,
Nick and Lauren, Jess, and Mike again

Author's Note

This is a story about people who love audio. I think it's only fair to the people I work with to be perfectly clear that it is not a story about my own career, nor is it a veiled exposé. I know a lot of audio people, but the ones in this book are truly and fully fictional, even if the difficulties of navigating the media landscape are soberingly real. (There are things you can do to make it less terrifying. If you choose to be in an employment relationship, get a union. Stuff like that.) So nobody in the book maps directly to anybody in real life, and Palmetto Media is not based on any real place in particular.

How much work goes into your favorite podcast, however, is the absolute truth.

back after this

PROLOGUE

2:00 A.M.

The trick was not to be noisy. Slowly, as slowly as I could manage, I turned my head until I could see his face in the blade of streetlight that came in between the bedroom curtains. His eyes were closed and his mouth was slack and open (which was both how he slept and how he kissed), and he was not quite snoring. I moved inch by inch, sitting up, removing my weight from the bed bit by bit and waiting to make sure he didn't stir. Then I tiptoed out into the living room and opened my laptop.

We had finished an edit before we went to bed. It was an episode about a woman whose car was stolen, and when she went shopping on Craigslist for a replacement, someone tried to sell it back to her. I had done all the interviews—with her, at her cramped apartment in Columbia Heights; with her sister, at the bar where she worked; with a cop, at a diner; with the seller, at the sketchy lot where he swore to me that he'd had no idea it was stolen when he bought it.

I had written the intro: *There's something about having something stolen from you that is just . . . infuriating.* That's my stuff, *you think to yourself.* How can you take my stuff, that's my stuff,

I paid for that stuff. *It bugs you. It nags at you. It makes it hard to concentrate on anything else. Even if what you lost isn't worth that much, how can anybody believe that they can take what's yours? Today, I'm going to introduce you to Casey, a woman who felt exactly that helpless, and then, somehow, it got worse.* I had written it, but he had tracked it.

We didn't use my voice on the podcast. At the station where we both had day jobs, I'd done only a handful of things on air, and I'd started to avoid it so I wouldn't have to get a bunch of emails about what was wrong with the way I talked. I'd once spent about fifteen minutes retracking a single line in a studio because the veteran editor in the booth insisted my voice was frying on the last syllable. I read it again and again; he didn't get any happier. I told him, "I think that's just my voice," and he sighed, "I guess it is."

So Justin was the host. He was the voice. I did most of the research and interviews. We split the producing, although he was usually satisfied before I was. I'd say I thought the episode needed one more pass, and he'd say it was fine, and I'd say okay, and then I'd do one more pass on my own.

This is why I had crawled out of bed. We wanted to publish tomorrow morning, and we'd run late with the edit. It was my last chance. I put my headphones on and brought up the episode on the laptop. I was pretty sure that the problem was in the middle, around the transition into the interview at the sales lot. I played the same minute back four times.

It started with Casey saying, *I needed a car. I couldn't be without a car. And I was in a rush, and that's probably why I went there in the first place.* And then Justin's voice: *When Casey says "there," she means Smithson & Son, the lot three blocks from her apartment. What it lacked in customer satisfaction, it made up for in convenience.* And then Doug, the car salesman: *I pride myself on making things easy for the customer. You need something, we're right there.*

I didn't like it, but I couldn't figure out what I didn't like about it. After four listens, though, I heard it. We didn't need Justin's second sentence: *What it lacked in customer satisfaction, it made up for in convenience.* I snipped it out and cleaned up the edges of the cut. When I played it back, the rhythm was much better to my ear. I saved it and closed the laptop.

In the bedroom, he hadn't moved an inch. I lowered myself onto the bed ounce by ounce, and just as I slid in beside him, he took a big inhale, stirred a bit, but didn't wake up. For a while I lay there facing him, looking at the bar of light on his cheek. I knew he was the only person who could ever understand why I would get up in the middle of the night to cut 4.63 seconds from a twenty-two-minute podcast episode that we were making out of our apartment. Not that I was going to tell him unless he brought it up.

That was before I lost the guy, lost the apartment, lost the show—I even lost the bed. But I was right about that cut.

CHAPTER ONE

The Pitch

In Studio D, I was trying to record a short intro that should have taken less than fifteen minutes. The board in front of me was lit up, the mic lights were green, my headphones were on, and the host was in the chair on the other side of the glass. I pressed my talk button. "Tell me what you had for breakfast."

"Well," Miles began, leaning intimately toward the microphone, as if I were really asking. "I had an omelet. Four eggs, goat cheese, and arugula. Oh—and a diced tomato." He knew that one purpose of this exercise was to make sure his P's didn't pop unpleasantly at the poor public, but he managed never to eat anything for breakfast with P's in it. No potatoes, no pepper, no prosciutto or pancakes.

"I've never known anybody who eats as many eggs as he does," Julie muttered from the chair next to me in the booth, firing up her laptop. "I'm never sure whether he actually smells like eggs, or whether I just think he smells like eggs because I look at him and I can't stop thinking about eggs."

I pressed my button again. "I need to hear some P's, Miles."

"Oh!" he said, always freshly surprised, months into production. "Peter Piper." I heard Julie moan in the corner.

"A few more than that, please," I told him, "and back off the mic about an inch, you don't need to swallow it. As we've talked about before." I looked over at Julie. "Too much?" I asked.

She nudged her glasses up on her nose. She must have gotten a late start with her daughter and not had time for her contacts. "Nah. I think it's charming how every day is like the first day. He's like a newborn baby."

"Pizza!" he said. "Pickles, popcorn. Sergeant Pepper. Yellow Submarine."

How had he gotten lost over the course of seven words? "Right," I muttered. I fiddled with the sliders and talked to him again. "Okay. Go ahead on the intro, please."

Miles had come to audio from one of the biggest newspapers in the country, where he'd won the biggest awards in journalism for reporting on the biggest corruption scandal in the history of his state. My boss, Toby, had been perched atop a mountain of investor money, jonesing for respect after getting Palmetto on the map with a pulpy true-crime podcast and an addictive series of marital-infidelity confessionals. He was trying to keep the place on track after Rob, his co-founder, who had recruited me, cashed out. Toby had snapped Miles up like a blue-ribbon hog at the state fair, bidding and bidding until the competition threw up its hands. The paper could, after all, hire three young reporters (or twelve interns) for what it would cost them to keep Miles, which was easy math for people who now worked for venture capitalists. So Miles Banfield became a podcast host, interviewing newsmakers, presenting some of his own reporting, and delivering commentaries that Julie and I would cut down from seven or eight minutes to a tight two and a half.

He was very bad at it. He made mouth noises—tsks and gulps and smacks of all kinds—while other people were talking. He would overlap the first few words of the next question with the final few words of the last answer, which signaled his impatience and rattled guests. He asked the same question in different ways four times in a row. He refused to read any of the research Julie stayed up late creating for him and then told Toby we hadn't prepared him. He would spend most of a half-hour interview asking a prolific author about the dedication in a single mid-career book, ignoring our efforts to interrupt, sometimes pointedly taking off his headphones. He clattered his watch on the table every time I didn't remind him to take it off. He hummed tunelessly while I was trying to solve technical problems. I couldn't get him to improve his active listening past an obnoxious "oh-oh-oh-OHHH," which he occasionally unleashed ten times in the same interview. A former senator emailed me once and complimented me for editing his interview with her to the point where you couldn't hear him making "that car alarm noise." I told no one.

And now, as he spoke, I heard his mouth clacking and sucking, like an octopus playing with a wheel of cheese. He was three sentences in when I hit the talk button again to interrupt him. "Hey, did you by any chance drink Mountain Dew before you came into the studio again?"

He paused. Looked at us through the glass. Shrugged. "So what?"

I silently turned to Julie, who chuckled and looked determinedly at her notes. "Oh, boy," she said. "Just remember, it could be worse. It could be the true-crime guy with the big glass of milk."

I leaned on the desk, flattening my palms against it on either side of my script so I wouldn't raise my voice. He had already told the boss—his and mine—that he did not like it when I raised my voice. So I inhaled deeply, puffed out air several times until my lungs emptied of what Toby called my *tone,* and spoke again. "Do you remember when I told you drinking Mountain Dew makes you sound like your mouth is sticking to itself?"

"No."

"Well, I did. A couple of times. There's a bottle of water right there. Take a few sips. And please don't drink Mountain Dew when you know we're tracking. It doesn't help you sound your best."

Looking away from me, down at his phone, he said, "It's journalism, Cecily. The audience is smart. I don't think they care what I drank with lunch. Let's not get distracted by the small stuff."

"Well," I said. "Your smart audience has things to listen to that don't sound like they were recorded inside a Saint Bernard's mouth." I heard Julie snort. "The microphone you are talking into cost as much as my first car. You're in a room designed to make sure that the sounds that come out of your face are the one thing that everyone is one hundred percent guaranteed to hear. Right now, that means it's picking up every time your lips pry themselves off your gums. So again, please stop drinking Mountain Dew before we track."

I could hear Julie take a breath. "Oh shit," she whispered.

Miles turned and looked at me, hard. I raised my eyebrows at him. Tilted my head. He rolled his eyes, then held up one hand in my direction. He put down his phone. "Let's take it again," he said. "You wrote 'debut' in here, and 'introduction' will sound better."

I had written "introduction" originally. Over email, he had changed it to "debut."

It took Miles thirty-two tries to get through the seventy-two-second intro, interrupted by multiple water-swishing breaks. Halfway through, I had a Slack from Toby: "Can you come by when you're done? Have great news to share." I promised I'd be there soon, and after I saved the tracks and shut down the board, I turned to Julie and said, "I have to go see Toby."

She scowled. "What's he want?"

"No idea. He says it's good news."

"Oh no," she said.

"I bet he wants to tell me something about promos." Toby had Slacked me throughout the previous day about fifteen-second promos versus twenty, because he said he couldn't decide. He'd added a GIF of a cat following a tennis match with its eyes.

"Better than talking about his divorce," Julie said. "I'll do a first pass on this and you should have it by the end of the day."

"Oh, blergh, what if it *is* about his divorce?" I asked.

"Well, then at least memorize everything. I'm morbidly curious." Toby was a middle-aged skinny-pants-wearing, hip-haircut-sporting, nerd-glasses-affecting overachiever who loved to talk about investing and eating paleo. He'd recently split from a funky ceramicist who, just before they met, had spent two years following a jam band around the country. Their union had made no sense to me. If he'd followed anybody around for two years, it would have been a productivity guru who sold unregulated protein powder out of the trunk of his car.

"Pray for me," I said, and I threw my body against the heavy studio door.

Palmetto was open-office (a wild idea for audio, I thought, but nobody asked me). Everybody wore headphones at their desks, whether they were listening to anything or not, and only the sounds of phone calls and hushed bitch sessions created a low murmur. The décor had been described as "industrial" in a couple of magazine articles about our early successes. This mostly meant you could look up and see pipes and ducts zigzagging across the ceiling, and some of the walls had wide expanses of reclaimed wood. The floors were a light gray laminate, and bright pops of yellow showed up in chairs and sofas in our break rooms. Potted palms rested in corners like the afterthoughts they were, and modest succulents were grouped on conference tables.

The wall outside Toby's office was host to an enormous black-

and-white photo, probably five feet by three feet, of Toby and Rob laughing in their chairs while speaking on a panel at a tech conference. It was from five years ago, when business had been better.

Toby's door was open, and he was at his standing desk with his back to me, looking at what seemed to be a selection of coats on sale. "Hey hey," I said.

"Oh. Get in here," he said with a grin. He persistently thought it was endearing to talk to me like I was a voice-commanded robot vacuum or a border collie, and to save time, I ignored it. His office had inspirational art on the walls—no actual slogans or quotes, just a photo of a guy scaling a cliff without ropes and another one of Muhammad Ali. All the awards that Palmetto had won in the last ten years, none of which had Toby's name on them and several of which had mine, were lined up on two floating shelves, and the overflow extended to the top of a cabinet I knew held smoothie ingredients in its drawers instead of files.

He sat down, rolled over to his other desk, and gestured toward a low lime-green chair. Of the many things I dreaded about my trips to his office, the chair was in the top five. It was not a good chair. It was a *cool* chair, a *modern* chair, and sitting in it made me feel like my ass had a manufacturing defect. I dropped into it anyway, and before I could even ask what was up, he was upon me. "So you know how valuable you are to me."

I hesitated. He had a townhouse in Georgetown. Once, after he invited a bunch of us over for cocktails, Julie and I looked it up on HouseStalker and found it valued at $2.3 million. I lived in a one-bedroom apartment with a leaky kitchen faucet. "For the purposes of this conversation," I said, "I'm going to say yes."

He laughed and nodded. "Right, right. You get me." I didn't. "What I want to talk to you about is that I think we have a show that you would be perfect to host. In fact, it's a show I think you're the *only* right person to host. And to help build from the ground up, if you're willing."

After working for Toby for six years, I didn't think he could surprise me. He'd never let me create a show myself. I had pitched idea after idea, and he had rejected them all.

Well, all but one. All but *Clothing Line,* a series on fashion history that was my personal hobbyhorse for about a year, and that I wanted to host. He loved the idea. He praised me for it, he thanked me for it, and then he took it. He set it up with Daphne Flood, a former food blogger he'd hired at a high price. Two projects he'd planned for her had already collapsed, and she was threatening not to renew her contract, meaning they'd get nothing for their investment at all. So I didn't host it. I didn't produce it, either, because at the time he needed me to throw myself at a deeply dysfunctional two-man chat show where one host was dating the other's ex. I helped them hit deadlines and not strangle each other. *Clothing Line* had won one or two of those awards on his shelf, and it had kick-started what was now a successful audio career for Daphne. I got a "special thanks" credit for my trouble.

I stared, caught off-guard by him as I rarely was. "Really?"

He nodded more. "Really. It's going to be our first-quarter tentpole next year. And it's very secure, because we already have advertisers interested. Just so you know, we have more interest for this than we had at the same point when we were developing *Cheats.*" *Cheats* was the show where people talked about the affairs they'd had. It had been the second hit Toby and Rob had made after *Otter Tail,* the true-crime sensation with the deceptively zoological name. It involved dead people and camping and the mishandling of DNA evidence, but no otters. "You want to hear about it?"

"Of course." I started to think before he started to talk. This was a way out of Miles's lip-smacking and ranting and watch-clacking. Miles wouldn't like it, but he'd go along with it, because he'd never want to admit he needed me for anything.

"Well," Toby said, "it's about *women* . . . and how they make *the big change.*" He emphasized each word by slicing the air with both hands, like he was making a stump speech.

"Like . . . menopause?"

"No."

"Because 'the change' usually means menopause."

He shook his head impatiently. "The idea is women making big changes to their own lives. We want to really get intimate about what it's like out there. On your own, trying to better yourself." He took a dramatic pause. "Aided by a whole industry that might—or might not—be trying to help."

Toby had been making scattered noises for half a year about wanting to make more shows for women. I had been ignoring a gut feeling that it would wind up being something exactly like this, a goofy product in a pink box. "So it's self-help?"

Toby smiled. "And self-*care*. And not for just anybody. The thing is, we want it to be about you. Your own path. Single woman gets it together."

I felt like my whole forehead pressed itself into a tiny dot between my eyebrows. "Gets what together?"

"You know, life. Big dreams. Relationships."

Now a wave of deep concern, blended with a dash of panic, washed over me. "Relationships? You want me to talk about dating?"

Toby looked wounded, but strategically so, like he had a plan for this conversation and it was on track so far. "Can I just pitch you before you say no? We want it to be about this collision between business and personal. The industry of happiness. In this case, we want to talk about life coaches. People who get hired to give women advice about how to fall in love and get it together, all that."

"Please stop saying 'get it together.' "

He held up his hands in a reflexive non-apology. "Don't take it the wrong way. You're the most together person I know in a million different ways, you know that. We think you're in a unique position to open up this door in a way that anybody could relate to and understand. You're single, you had a breakup—"

"Not recently." In the four years since Justin dumped me, I hadn't been on more than four dates with anybody, which I didn't bring up with Toby, since I didn't think it would exactly help my cause.

"Sure. But you're still looking, right?"

Truthfully, I was still looking for a person to be with in the same way I was looking for a bigger apartment: longingly, daily, and around the edges of all the other things I had to do. I would look at dating apps and townhouse listings, become utterly defeated, and forget about it for another day. "I am, but . . . Toby, no."

"Cecily, yes."

"Why would anybody listen to a show about me trying to get a date?"

"For the adventure. For the journey. Think of it like this: The audience is the tour group, and you're the guide."

"Really? Because it sounds more like I'm the attraction. It sounds like I'm sharing an exit off Route 66 with the Blue Whale of Catoosa, and you're going to put up a billboard of me frowning in a bathrobe with a pint of ice cream under the words 'Five Miles to the Old Maid,'" I said.

"Oh, come on," Toby protested. "You know I'd never make you look bad. The woman we have who's going to take you through the whole process, I guarantee you're going to love her. Positivity is her whole thing. You might learn something."

I watched his eager little eyes behind his bright green frames. He was counting downloads in his head. He had probably been doodling promo art while he was on the phone. "Go ahead," I said in my most level of voices.

"She's a dating coach, life coach, influencer, whatever. Her name is Eliza Cassidy."

I had heard of her, vaguely, in the same way I'd heard of a lot of companies that sold stylish luggage and stretchy bras on Instagram. "What kind of influencing does she do?"

"She started out in beauty, she expanded into lifestyle, she's done some health and wellness, and now she's starting a consulting thing in relationship coaching."

"A consulting thing," I repeated.

"Right. She wants to change everything about how relationship advice is given. She wants to make it less sexist, less nasty, less judgmental, more upbeat. Never settle, you're enough, girl power, that kind of thing." I didn't realize how not eager I was to hear Toby say "girl power" until right then.

"But she isn't trained to do this," I said. "She's pivoting from how to find your perfect foundation match."

"Now, don't be a snob," he said. "She has a lot of experience connecting with audiences. The people who follow her absolutely love her, and they trust her. She has millions of followers on YouTube. Millions on Instagram. Millions on TikTok. She's probably got millions of followers on something you and I have never even heard of. How's that for a built-in audience?"

"But why are they going to care about me?"

He shrugged. "They're going to care about her taking you through this approach she has."

"Toby, I'm not a good candidate for this. I am a dork who spends most of my time in headphones. Nobody is going to believe I'm going to meet a prince because I live the truth of some kind of listicle about dating. It's not going to convince anybody."

"You don't even know what she's going to say."

I did know what she was going to say, because I knew what these people always said. People paid the women who wrote *The Rules* an ungodly amount of money to tell them to make men pay for dinner and not to return phone calls. And, of course, not to talk too much, and people had been telling me that for free since I was in first grade. "I hate dating advice," I said.

"Perfect, so does she. That's why she wants to shake things up. Wisdom with . . . with reinvention."

"How old is this wise person?"

"She's thirty-three, I think."

"That's a year younger than I am."

"Well, my doctor is younger than I am, but I still take his advice about my cholesterol. Besides, she's very happily married, so maybe she knows something."

"A lot of people are married, Toby. Serial killers are married. To people who marry them *because* they're serial killers."

He forged ahead. "Well, she's not a serial killer. She does video, she wrote a book, she speaks at events."

"Oh, I see. Events."

"What's wrong with events?"

"An event could be anything. A raging fire is an event."

"She doesn't speak at raging fires."

I shifted in that terrible chair and tried to get my spine to line up with itself. "What would she do to me, anyway?"

"For crying out loud, she's not going to *do anything* to you," he said. "She's going to work with you for a few months. She wants to set you up on twenty dates."

"Twenty?" The idea of going on twenty first dates in front of an audience with the ability to provide feedback sounded like a level of humiliation that would outstrip any underpants-up-the-flagpole nightmare middle-schoolers could conjure.

"Twenty. You do everything she says, you see what happens, we get tape. Tape of these dates, tape of your coaching sessions, lots of storytelling directly from you. No-holds-barred, totally honest portrayal of the experience. I won't interfere, you can tell the absolute truth. It's going to be a killer show."

"Who would produce it?" I said.

"Well, we're working on that, but one possibility is that Julie would."

Julie Nazari had come to Palmetto after I met her at a conference and we became texting friends. I'd recommended her to Toby, and she'd been the assistant producer on a bunch of projects I'd headed up since then, including Miles's show. "It could be an opportunity for her to move up to the next level. Abby and Charlie will help." Toby leaned toward me. "It's going to kill. Come on, I'll get you a dream team."

I'd heard this before, the way he'd hedge about letting Julie be in charge of something if only I would do him this one favor. I did love Abby and Charlie, who were best friends and had come to us from the same local station in Minneapolis. It was hard for me to believe they would be interested in this, but maybe they would? "Toby, this is self-help. I'm terrible at self-help. I am allergic to journaling. I don't have a love language. And I'm only highly effective when you don't bother me."

"Learning new things is what you're good at," he countered. He folded his hands on his desk. "Listen, I can't make you do it. I mean, I can, but I won't. But I'm telling you, this is an opportunity to break into being on mic. I think you'd be great."

"And what do I get if I do it?"

"What do you mean? You get to do it. You get to be a host, which I thought you wanted."

"But I'd be a host of *this,*" I said. "Which is not what I wanted. As you know." For the last year, I had been pitching, hard, a series about the mothers of famous men. I'd sketched out six episodes. I'd done preliminary research for two of them on my own time. I wanted to build it. I wanted to host it. He kept saying maybe, he kept having meetings with me, he kept asking for more, and then he kept doing absolutely nothing. He was sitting on pages of proposals he probably hadn't read, prep work that I'd polished and perfected and then hurled into the void of his office. "If I do this one for you, can we go back to my thing?"

"I can't say for certain," he said. "But if you do this and it's successful, you become a personality. And I can't sell a history show unless it's built around a personality. So if you want to go forward, then yes, this is a way that we could do it."

Dating. A *dating* show. Everyone would learn about Justin dumping me. Strangers. People listening at the gym while they climbed thousands of steps to stay in the same place. People who just wanted something to keep them company while they fell asleep. People Justin and I had worked with. People who knew us both, who might think he was too good for me or I was too good for him, either of which they might say in public, and either of which would be mortifying. And oh my God, *Justin* would hear it. He would hear me trying to learn how to find a boyfriend *and* trying to learn how to be a host, and what if I failed at both, and he got to listen to me do it?

Toby could see me continuing to squirm, and it wasn't only because of the chair. "I don't know," I said.

Just then, there were two quick knocks, the office door opened, and Brick DeWitt poked his head in. "Oh hey," he said. "Is this a good time?" Brick was one of the ad guys. Brick, Duncan, Tucker, and Joe. It was like they wrote the gospels, if the gospels were about dynamic ad insertion.

"Perfect, actually," Toby said, pointing to his other chair. "Cecily, I asked Brick to come by. He's just been feeling out advertisers. Obviously, everything is still tentative, but since this idea came from somebody on his team, I wanted him to explain how strong the enthusiasm has been about the version of this pitch that we've shared with them."

"The idea came from the ad guys?"

Brick put up both hands defensively. "From partnerships. Eliza's team reached out. All we do is mention opportunities."

I nodded. "Okay. So, tell me all about the enthusiasm."

Brick didn't so much sit down as lean his ass on a low cabinet, twirling a pen in his hand. "Fitness West," he said.

"The *gym*?" I said.

"It's not a gym," he said. "It's very innovative. They partner with a lot of wellness start-ups to provide services on-site. They're looking for growth with single professional women between thirty and forty, and they're really excited about doing something in relationships. We're still trying to lock it down, but we're close. We think they're going to wind up making a major investment."

I looked at Toby. "So it has to be me because of their demographic? Why can't it be, I don't know, Abby?"

"She's too young."

"Kyla."

"She's a contractor. I'd have to write a new contract."

"Marissa."

"They're looking for somebody who wants to date men."

"How about the new one, Alessandra?"

"Somebody who wants to date men, not somebody who's already engaged to one. Cecily, you are it. So let him explain."

"Fine," I said. "It's going to be sponsored by going to the gym. And?"

"We have interest from a bunch of places," Brick said. "We've had a lot of meetings."

I believed it. In fact, I wasn't always sure what the ad guys did *other* than meetings. "Specifically what interest?"

"Well, beverage companies are big business right now, particularly specialty drinks and mail order. I'm talking to a place called Wine 4 One." He held up four fingers and then one, and I nodded. "You tell them how many glasses of wine you drink and how often, and you take a quiz about what you like. And they send you what you need for the month in individual, vacuum-sealed servings. Recyclable packaging. It's green because there's no waste."

"Uh-huh," I said. "What else?"

"Well, of course, you know how big meal-prep boxes are, but they're moving to more niche stuff, more specific populations. We're talking to a company that does meals especially for single people."

"Isn't that just Lean Cuisine?"

Brick ignored me. "It doesn't require you to scale up or down, and it doesn't leave a lot of leftovers. They call it Just Me."

I narrowed my eyes. "Like in a restaurant. When they ask you how many are in your party. And you say, 'just me.'" I had eaten in enough restaurants when I traveled for work that I was very familiar with the look they give you, like you're the gnarliest, ugliest rescue dog at the shelter.

Brick ignored me again. "They've got great ingredients, good sourcing, really starting to pick up speed, and they're looking to connect, you know, *deeply,* with exactly the kind of intelligent, high-end audience we know this project is going to attract." He grinned.

I didn't smile. "Is that it?"

He pointed at me. "Oh—pets are huge with direct response, right? People spend all kinds of money if you tell them it's going to make their dog like them. Subscription boxes and specialty foods are the traditional angles. But a lot of the action has been happening in those food and treat spaces, and the one we're talking to is evolving more in amusement, in the amusement arena. And rather than focusing on dogs, where the market is so saturated, they're more pertaining to cats, which they think is a neglected market."

I nodded. "So they're in the cat amusement space."

"Exactly."

"Anything else?" Brick looked at Toby, so I did too.

Then I turned back to Brick. He appeared to be thinking, which seemed like trouble. "I mean, nothing firm," he said. "Nothing definite."

I didn't take my eyes off him. "Understood. But how about what's *not* definite?"

Brick twirled the pen faster in his hand. "Oh. Well. There's a company, really new, does a lot of exciting things in the financial planning world, but it's, you know, they specialize in independent professional people? Affluent clients who are just, you know, making sure all the loose ends are tied up?"

I remembered the first time I met Brick a year and a half ago. He'd come in with his fancy new phone and his Bluetooth earpiece, and he'd put a green Tupperware container full of quinoa and vegetables in the fridge, which he ate in the break room that was mostly used for lunchtime gossip. After eighteen months of trying to sell ad space to every conceivable weird-ass start-up and creating promo codes for everything from wearable bug zappers to erotic-themed bedding—not to mention surviving several new show launches both successful and not—he now regularly ate Chipotle at his desk.

"Loose ends?" I asked. "What kind of loose ends?"

"Just general . . . generally loose ends. Any ends that . . . that are loose."

"So," I said to him, "it's estate planning. Bequests. Burial plots."

Brick glanced at Toby again, then back at me. "I mean, sure, yeah, I guess, but not exclusively."

"What's the company called?" I asked.

People going into gum surgery look more excited than Brick looked at this moment. I once saw a radio host have to run to the bathroom immediately-as-in-immediately during a live broadcast, and he seemed happier about that than Brick was about this. Brick finally scratched his head and said, "They call it Finally. You know, 'Finally: the last item on your to-do list.' But there's no A. And they're both capital L's. FinLLy."

The room was still. Brick looked tentatively at me, tentatively at Toby, then hungrily at the door. He wanted quinoa, Chipotle, hemlock, a stab in the throat, anything.

"Can I have a second with Toby?" I said, and Brick practically left a Brick-shaped puff of smoke behind as he beelined out the door, pulling it shut behind him. "So," I summed up. "You want me to host a show where somebody teaches me how to get a boyfriend. And it's going to be sponsored by eating alone, drinking alone, dying alone, and cat toys."

"That's very glass-half-empty."

"Toby."

He laughed. "Don't forget the gym!" he said. "Look, I get it. Just think about it, would you?"

I could imagine the promo art, which would be something like a woman reaching for an engagement ring that was just beyond the tips of her fingers. I could imagine myself trying to explain this show to my sister, who saved pets' lives for a living. I could imagine Justin laughing as he fired up the first episode. "Oh, Toby, why are you doing this to me?"

"Listen," he said, "you know things are tight. You know what's happening with ads. This is a critical piece of our strategy, and there aren't a lot of people I would trust with it. We don't have a lot of chances to bring in anything as big as what these discussions with Fitness West could mean." He took a breath. "I'm not going to lie to you, Cecily. I need a hit." He looked past me through the glass wall of his office. "Everybody who works here needs a hit." His eyes came back to me. "Take a day and think about it. You don't have to answer me right now. Sleep on it, and we'll talk tomorrow."

"Toby, I—"

"Tomorrow. I'm not hearing 'no' until tomorrow." I got up, freeing my ass from his uncomfortable chair, and as I got to the door I turned back to him. But he was already at the standing desk with his back to me. "Tomorrow," he repeated, and he reached his hand into the air and waved goodbye without turning around.

I closed the door behind me. "Cat toys," I muttered as I headed back to my desk. "What is happening to my life?"

CHAPTER TWO

Happy Hour

"Does it count as ironic that we spend happy hour complaining?"

Julie thought about the question, plucking a pretzel from a shallow dish. "I think it's pretty common." She popped it into her mouth.

Every other Tuesday, much of the staff of Palmetto slid onto stools and into booths at a bar called Ruckus, where the restroom was sometimes out of order and it smelled a little like feet, but the drinks were cheap and it was quiet. We'd dribble in whenever we were done with work, until the last stragglers sat down with the last lingerers and had the last beers. I'd made it earlier than usual, by 5:30, and Julie and I had found seats at the bar. She had a fondness for chardonnay that I didn't understand. I preferred to nurse a cheap whiskey, particularly when I was feeling defeated, which was increasingly common.

Her phone was face down on the bar, and we both jumped when it buzzed. She turned it over and set her jaw in a way that usually meant one thing and one thing only. "Oh, no," I said. "Chris?"

She put the phone down and nodded. Only her ex got this reaction. "We're in this *thing*. Bella wants to go to science camp next summer," she said. "Chris says a six-year-old should climb trees like he did, and climbing trees is free."

"Wow. It takes a special kind of dad to be against science camp."

"He's not against science camp. He just hopes my parents are going to pay for it. He doesn't understand that the Bank of Grandma and Grandpa is closed since my dad retired."

Julie's parents were both college professors who had immigrated to southern California to study and then taught there. Her father was Persian and specialized in medieval art history; her mother was Spanish and specialized in tree rings. I'd had dinner out with them and Julie a couple of times when they were in town, and they were among the kindest, loveliest, and most intellectually imposing people I had ever met. Dr. Amir Nazari had retired a year ago; Dr. Camila Nazari planned to follow soon. In the ladies' room after a luscious dinner of tandoori lamb chops the previous fall, Camila had thanked me for looking out for Julie and Bella. It was something I would have tried to do anyway, but after that, I tried even harder. I was confident that if Julie asked, they would still pay for science camp, but I got where she was coming from.

"How much is it?" I asked.

She looked at me sideways. "You are not paying for science camp."

"I didn't say I was!"

"You were going to. It was going to be the play kitchen all over again."

"That was for Christmas!"

She shook her head. "I have months to work on her father to pitch in before we have to register. That's why I started now. Keep your wallet in your pants, Aunt Ceci."

I put up both hands. "Fine. I don't even like science."

"Besides, she's got enough distractions for now. My mom gave her a bunch of my old Barbies. Apparently, they've been safe in a plastic bin since I abandoned them."

"Oh, nice," I said. "Does Bella like them?"

"She pulls their heads off," Julie said. "I think she's genuinely disappointed every time there's not gore in there."

"Well, hopefully she will not do the same to Mickey Mouse." In two months, Julie and Bella were heading to Walt Disney World.

"Yeah," she said, "Unfortunately, I'm not sure if that's happening anymore."

"No! Why?" She just looked at me. "What?"

"I mean, Miles's contract is up next summer."

"Yeah."

"I don't know if you expect that job to continue, but I don't." She ran her finger around the top of her glass. "And there's all this talk about layoffs. If I don't find something else to do, I don't know if Toby is going to keep me around."

Talk about layoffs never really went away anymore, it just rose and fell by degrees—a little more when another shop was going through it, a little less when we were launching something we were excited about. I wanted to tell her not to worry, but I spent more time thinking about Julie losing her job than I did thinking about losing my own. I'd recommended her three years ago when Toby asked me to run a series we did about Al Capone and asked if I knew anybody who would be good for an associate producer job. The fact that she was tethered to Palmetto as it struggled was my fault.

"I don't think that will happen," I said, knowing that I mostly meant I could not stand to think about it happening. "He knows you're good at your job."

"I'm very good at my job," she said. "Which is irrelevant."

I wished she were wrong. We spent a lot of time trying to figure out why Toby did anything, why he green-lit this show and not that one, or kept this person and let that one go, or why he would suddenly get very passionate about video or social media and then lose interest right after everybody spent a lot of time trying to meet his curiosity with options.

"There's no way," I said. "I would never let that happen."

"I love you," she said, "but I don't think there's a lot you can do. We're all going to find out together."

"Ugh," I said.

"Well, *you're* going to be fine," she said. "You're his favorite."

I was not Toby's favorite, but I spent a lot of time cleaning out the figurative junk drawers of his business. Help with this edit, brainstorm with this team, write a presentation for him to give at this conference, smooth it over between him and this on-air douchebag he was overpaying. "Jul," I said, "he will have to physically fight me if he wants me to work there without you. I'll carry you out of there like *An Officer and a Gentleman*. We'll make our own company. We'll join the indies."

Right then, a pair of arms wrapped around my neck and squeezed, and I smelled cigarettes. "Mel," I said, putting my hands on her hands and then turning to see her face beside me.

Melissa was only twenty-four, and she'd just finished helping produce an eight-episode season about sharks. She grinned, her spider clavicle tattoo peeking out of her shirt. "Hey, Mom; hey, Jul." She leaned in toward the bartender and ordered a Blue Moon.

I rolled my eyes as she wedged in between me and Julie. I was only ten years older than she was—I was a disconcerting number of years older than a disconcerting number of our producers—but I could not shake the nickname. "Yeah, yeah."

"You know I love you," she said, knocking me with her shoulder. "I have to give you shit *because* I love you."

"How are things?" I asked.

"Oh, *fabulous*," she said. "My whole table over there is trying to game out who's going to get canned." She gestured at a corner booth where a little knot of young producers huddled around their drinks, looking somber.

"See?" Julie said to me. "Everybody knows it's coming."

"It's just this feeling," Melissa said. "You know, the astronomy show didn't go, and then Toby was trying to land that YouTuber for the gaming thing, and that didn't go, and then they changed the toilet paper."

I put my drink down. "They did what?"

She nodded. "I was talking to Izzy, and she asked me if I'd noticed that we used to have great toilet paper in the bathrooms, and now it's this stuff that's like, all scratchy. I think it's one-ply. And I realized—I hadn't thought about it, but my ass knows it's true. The toilet paper sucks now. Benji says the first sign that a company is really in trouble is when they switch to cheaper TP."

"I'm not sure that's an ironclad rule," I said, even as I realized that *my ass also knew it was true*. "A lot can happen. The industry is just sort of chaotic at the moment."

Melissa leaned in toward us conspiratorially. "Speaking of which, I assume you heard the Justin thing?"

I looked over at Julie and knew instantly that, unlike me, she had already heard the Justin thing. "I didn't," I said. I didn't really want to hear industry news about my ex, but it was better to hear it from Melissa than from one of the several guys in dress sneakers I knew were in this bar somewhere at this very moment, probably gossiping about this same thing.

"He's making a new show with Paul Casper," Mel said. "Fancy, huh?"

My heart seized inside my chest. "What?"

The world of audio was a pyramid of nerds who were moderately famous only to other people within that pyramid, and Paul Casper was one of the few at the tip-top who poked up high enough to pass into the realm of being famous to regular people. He'd been profiled on *60 Minutes,* and about half the white guys I knew who were hosting podcasts sounded suspiciously like they went to the Paul Casper School of Minimal Enunciation. Even for Justin, who was already doing annoyingly well, this would be a leap.

Melissa nodded. "I don't know exactly what it is, but it sounds like there's going to be an announcement within the next few weeks. They're recruiting. They tried to poach Abby, that's how we found out." The network of producers was a smart, benevolent mafia. What they lacked in official power, they made up in the practical capacity to complicate the lives of their enemies.

"Well, that's great for him." I pulled a good swallow of my drink and felt it burn my throat.

Melissa looked at me. "I've only met him a couple of times, but I've always thought he seemed like a jackass, for the record."

"I appreciate that."

"Tell me if you need me to say it again," she said.

"If I do, are you going to call me Mom again?"

"It's affectionate!" She took in my squint. "Okay, fine. Fine. I won't call you Mom."

"Thank you."

"You're welcome." The bartender slid her beer across the bar and she nodded at him. "Hey, before I go back to those guys, do you have two Advil?"

"Sure," I said. I took my big black tote from the hook under the bar—my sister called it the Beast—and dug through it. I shook two pills into my hand and offered them to her.

"While you're in there, we're going to do trivia, do you have a pen?"

I handed her a blue fine-point.

"Can I have five dollars?"

I got my wallet out. I had it unzipped before I froze. I looked up at her. "You are such an asshole."

She was laughing, and she threw her arms around me again. "Love you, *Moooom,*" she said. "Bye, Jul." And she was gone.

"Boy, you walked into that," Julie said.

"Yeah, no kidding." I went back to my glass, tapping at the edges restlessly. "Paul Casper," I muttered.

Julie looked over at me. "I know. I didn't want to say anything. But I mean, truly, who cares what he's working on? He already has a show. He makes a new show, what's the difference?"

"Nothing," I said weakly. "I just don't understand why he gets to be cool."

"He is not cool," she declared. "He tattooed his own voice on his arm. So he will be very uncool forever."

This was, regrettably, a true story. Justin had a tattoo that ran down the inside of his forearm. A jagged soundwave copied from a recording of his own voice saying, *Hi, this is Justin Dash*. I should have broken up with him the day he got it, because there is a very particular kind of guy who would do that, and although I told myself at the time he didn't seem like that type, it turned out he was exactly that type.

Still. *Still.* His was a name you heard at the beginnings of shows; mine was a name you heard at the end. Or, more likely, mine was one you didn't hear at all, because you had turned it off when the credits started. And now this? Of everybody, Paul Casper? I knew where it would probably go from here: Justin would expand his little production company. It would grow until he could sell it to a giant conglomerate, suck out the value, and retire. He'd probably devote the rest of his life to collecting his goddamn whimsical boxes of defunct breakfast cereal. Urkel-Os and Sir Grapefellow stacked up next to his awards cabinet.

"I hate this," I said.

"Okay, well," she said. "Then while you're already mad about this, I'm just going to tell you the other thing I heard, because I don't want you to hear it from anybody else."

I turned to her very slowly. "Oh, no. What?"

"Well, Clarissa."

Clarissa was a producer who had been at Palmetto for a while, but then Justin had hired her to help with a project he was making. She'd moved to New York, and now they were dating. I suspected she was unofficially helping him with the very same show he and I had started together years ago, which would be exactly his style. "What about her?"

"I guess they're engaged," she said. "My friend saw her in New York last week, she had a ring, and . . . I guess they're engaged."

"Wow," I said, trying to ignore the feeling that my head was going to spin off my neck. "Mel kind of buried the lede, huh?"

"I'm sure she doesn't know. I don't think a lot of people know yet. Obviously, all these nerds are going to be a lot more interested in the fact that he's making a show with Casper than in the fact that he's getting married. I know you probably feel differently. Although maybe you don't."

"This is astonishing timing," I said. "Because I haven't told you yet what Toby wanted when I went to see him in his office."

"Please tell me he doesn't want you to report on Justin's wedding."

The fact that this wrung a laugh out of me was a tribute to Julie's quickness. "No. It actually might be more mortifying than that."

"I'm impressed."

I stopped nursing my drink and threw the rest of it down my throat. "He wants me to host a show about self-help where I work with a dating coach who tries to find me a boyfriend."

Her eyes widened. "You hate self-help."

"That's what I said! And, Jul, you should have heard the ad roster. It's like Miss Havisham's Amazon wish list. I told him no. Or I'm going to. Or I was going to."

She nodded slowly. "Okay. I mean, I'm not going to lie, it sounds sort of fun to me, because I like self-help, but I'm not sure I'd expect *you* to do it."

"If you were a little older, I'm sure he'd have asked you. He seems to be stuck with me," I said. "I can't say it wouldn't be great to have something of my own."

"A show or a person?"

"Both, maybe," I admitted.

"Well, I mean, if you don't want to do it, you shouldn't."

"He wants me to talk about how long I've been single." I shuddered. "And I'd rather ride the Metro naked at rush hour. The red line."

"Well," she said, "if you say no, I'm sure he'll offer you something better next time. And we'll work on it together. You and me, no Miles. And Justin can hear all about *our* big project." She shrugged. "Even if it sucked, it would be fun."

I didn't sleep very much that night. I worried about Julie losing her job and imagined her mother frowning at me disapprovingly in a restaurant ladies' room. I worried about Melissa and her table going back to Ruckus on some awful day yet to come to commiserate about some terrible announcement from Toby. I even worried a little about myself. When Justin and I first broke up, I'd moved in with my sister and her husband; I didn't think I had the strength to do it again if I lost my job and my apartment and every atom of my stability.

I turned over and lay on my other side, and I worried about Justin growing his empire until he was a dot in the distance and people wouldn't even believe me if I said I knew him, let alone dated him. I thought about the press he would do, the profile with the photo of him sitting at his desk, staring gravely into the camera, with some of his cool-guy hair hanging in his face. They would say he was the future. They would recite some figure, some number of millions that he'd socked away to fund his beautiful life. Nothing would make it not terrible unless I became so wildly successful that someday it would be *me* pretending not to remember *him* at an industry event.

I had thought he was going to propose to me once. It wasn't one of those slapstick sitcom things where I found a ring that wasn't meant for me. We just went away on a trip, and we stayed at a B and B in the Blue Ridge Mountains, and he kept telling me how much he loved me. We went for a hike on the last day, even though I'm not much of a hiker, and we kept stopping to look at the sky as it turned pink, then orange, then red. And I had the overwhelming feeling he was going to ask me to marry him, which we'd talked about only in this kidding-but-not-totally way that you do when you want to marry somebody but you're not ready to say you are. I even looked at his pockets, trying to see if he was carrying anything. But it didn't happen. We got back, and we had dinner, and we were happy, and I forgot about it until he broke up with me six months later and went back to New York, where we'd met.

I rolled onto my back and felt the emptiness of the bed. I would have loved to be able to say I was only feeling lonely because he was engaged, or I was only feeling lonely because being offered a dating coach made me feel like a loser. But really, I had felt lonely already, and those things were just pressing down on my chest and making it seem much more urgent.

Wouldn't it be funny if this turned out to be the right answer? Wouldn't it be funny if a dating coach found me a guy? Really *funny*? I reached out with one hand and thought about someone lying there sleeping, a chest rising and falling next to me, the sound of breathing, being awakened in the morning by someone's breath on my neck.

CHAPTER THREE

The Deal

The next morning, I set down the Beast at my desk and went directly to Toby's office. When I got there, the door was closed. I could see through his glass office wall that four people were in there with him already. Why were all these *dudes* in there?

Toby looked up and saw me through the glass. He waved me in, but I hesitated and mouthed that I could come back later. He shook his head, waved me in again, and I opened the door. There, positioned around Toby's desk, were Brick from ad sales, Carl the business guy (whose official title I never remembered), Kevin from marketing, and a balding man with a gray-and-red tie.

"Hi," I said. "I didn't mean to interrupt."

"Not at all, we're wrapping up," Toby said. "And this involves you, so I wanted to introduce you to somebody." He indicated the gray-and-red-tie man. "This is Vance, he works for Fitness West."

Vance leaned over two other guys to hold out his hand. "I'm assuming you know us."

Oh boy. "I've never been, but I've been hearing about it." Fitness West advertised themselves as "wellness for every woman." I looked at that slogan every time I rode the Metro for what felt like months. The ad showed a woman in purple yoga pants and a matching sports bra, extending one leg behind her while standing on the other, and reading a book at the same time.

"Cecily, I'm going to let these guys go, and I'll give you all the specifics myself. Tons more good news." *Oh no,* I thought. *Again with the "good news."* Toby had once told me he had good news, and it turned out that I had to write a manual for new employees about how to navigate our complicated proprietary system of saved audio files so they would know exactly where every backup was, exactly how to publish or republish finished shows, and exactly how to lock and unlock whatever they needed to work on. I was the unofficial Keeper of the File System, which meant people had sent me emails for years with subject lines like "AAARGH HELP ME." So it hadn't, in fact, been good news.

"Gentlemen," Vance said, standing, "I have a meeting on Capitol Hill. I'm looking forward to working together. And with you, of course." He nodded at me. They all filed out, the entire Office Bullshit Club, and I sat across from Toby. "You didn't even wait for me to say yes."

"I knew you were going to. I had faith in you."

"Well, I have conditions," I said.

"Conditions for what?"

"For this. For doing this show."

"Okay, go. I'm ready."

"Number one: I want to meet Eliza off the record first. I'm not making any promises until I've talked to her."

"I was going to suggest that anyway. She's at the ready."

"Okay. Number two: I want you to agree that after I do this, you'll let me make a pilot for my show. You don't have to commit to making the whole thing, but you have to let me make a pilot. You have to give me two good producers and a good editor and enough time."

His face was unreadable. "Okay," he said tentatively.

"Number three: Julie has to produce, period," I said. "If you back out of that, the deal's off." He looked concerned. "Look, I know how things are. And everybody out there? Your twenty-four-year-old PAs who have a hundred thousand dollars in student loan debt and are living with four roommates in Petworth because they hope you understand the future? They know how things are, too. Practically every other shop has already had layoffs this year."

Toby hesitated, but then he nodded. "There's no question we may have some tough times ahead. As I told you yesterday, it would help to have a hit."

"Right," I said. "Right. And I'm assuming my job is safe because you work me like a mule."

"Are you kidding?" he said. "You're my best producer. I want you to train everybody who ever works here. And of course, if you're a team player, that's only going to be a stronger conviction on my part."

"Okay," I said. "Then if we do this, Julie is the lead producer. She's the only person I trust to keep this from being everything you have promised me it's not going to be."

"She has less experience than some of the other people at her level."

"But she's better at her job."

He would have loved to disagree, but I knew he couldn't. "So that's number three. That, and your word that after we do this, you find another assignment for her, whether she wants to work on my pilot or not. I can't ask her to take this on if it means she's going to get lost in the shuffle at the end."

He screwed up his face. "Is that it?"

"One more," I said. "You have to promise me this will not be bullshit. If this woman wants to coach me, that's fine. But if I'm doing it, it has to be real. If I like the people she sets me up with, I'll like them. And if I don't, I don't. You have my word that I'll go in with an open mind, and I'll listen to her, and I'll go on her dates. But you have to give me your word in return that if I don't hit it off with anybody, that will be the story we tell. Because if this is all an ad for her company, I can't do it. The show has to be the truth. That's the deal," I said. "Those are the conditions."

He sat back in his chair and folded his hands over his middle, which was taut from the stationary rowing machine he talked about so much. "All right. You have a deal," he said. "I accept your conditions."

"And all this holds whether the show is a success or not."

"Yes. As long as you do your part and you take it seriously."

"I'll do my part."

"And take it seriously," he repeated. "You don't have to fall in love, but you have to try. You can't do it to make fun of it. The advertisers will riot. And Eliza has this business manager, her name is Marcela, and Marcela terrifies me more than the advertisers. She terrifies me more than my mother. If you don't cooperate, I think she'll burn down the office." He held out his hand to me. "But we can shake on it, and your job and Julie's job will be just as safe as I can make them."

Toby knew me. He knew I really loved Julie, and it gave him an advantage when negotiating, because he didn't love any of us. I shook his hand. "Deal."

"Look happy!" he said. "Be excited. Eliza says doing the work makes people their best selves."

"You know, every time I hear something like that, it makes me want to quit all this and go be a cheesemonger."

"Why a cheesemonger?"

"For the cheese."

"Ah."

"I can't believe you're making me do this," I said.

He shrugged. "I'm not making you. We have an arrangement."

"And by the way, please keep the arrangement part between

us," I said. "Julie would kill me." If she wouldn't let me chip in for science camp, she certainly wouldn't allow this. He nodded. I would just tell her I decided it was worth it to get a chance to host something, and to work with her. Which, in part, was true. *There's nothing wrong with the fact that you're not cut out to be a host,* Justin had said. *You're a born producer.* He was not right. He was too much of a jerk to be right. "So what now?"

"Okay," he said. "The thing is, the schedule is a little bit tight. We want twelve episodes, and the finale needs to drop on Valentine's Day."

Of course he wanted it to be Valentine's Day. Of course he did. I looked down and counted months on my fingers. "So we have to premiere at the end of November or something."

"Well," he said, "we're going to put out six, then take two weeks off for Christmas and New Year's, then put out six more. So actually, we need to get the first one out in the middle of November."

I went back to my fingers and counted weeks this time. "That's, what, eight weeks from now?" It wasn't something we *couldn't* do, but it was going to be a sprint.

"Nine," he said brightly.

"Oh, a cakewalk, then."

"Well," he said, "the thing is, Fitness West has a new program starting in the middle of October that's especially for singles. That's part of what they want to promote. I told them there was no way we could ask you to start putting episodes out in a month."

"Thank you for that, at least," I said. Maybe he did understand what he was asking.

"But we wanted to offer them something." Nope. He didn't. "So Brick had an idea, kind of a new promotion model. We want to hit the day of that launch of theirs on October . . ." He looked down at a list on his desk and jabbed at it with one finger. "October 16—we'll run a preview that day. Like a preview episode. We introduce you, introduce Eliza, we start getting the buzz going. We'll drop it as a bonus in all the feeds we have, so it will get lots of ears. And by the time your show really starts a month or so later, you'll already have subscribers lined up."

"So technically it's thirteen episodes."

"No, it's twelve. And a preview. I know it's a little bit of a time crunch."

"A little."

"We're not asking for outside research or outside voices, though; it's mostly going to be the two of you and the people who are involved in your story. We're trying to make it low-touch."

"Low-touch" was a phrase Toby generally used to suggest that he expected me to do four people's jobs for six months and be rewarded with all of eight hours off before I had to start the next thing.

"Once the show really launches in November, we'll have two episodes a week. One is for everybody, one is boncon for subscribers. Second one, you don't have to worry about. It's just Eliza answering listener questions and giving advice." Palmetto Premium cost $6 a month. You got ad-free episodes, occasional videos of hosts showing you around their offices, and then the prized bonus content, which Toby was trying to get everybody to call "boncon." I generally stayed out of the boncon business, not because I didn't like money as much as the next person, but because at Palmetto, it was also the extra work business.

"Is that it?"

"Well, the reason we're trying so hard to accommodate Vance is the other reason he was here," Toby said. "As it turns out, our friends at Fitness West have decided they'd like to be premium sponsors."

I had never heard of a premium sponsor at Palmetto before. "What is that? Is it something besides money?"

"It's just a sponsor that your show has a special relationship with."

So it was a lot of money. "Oh," I said. "Are there push-ups involved?"

"No, no," Toby said. "No, they just want to partner with you, because the show really fits their vision."

"Which is what?"

He looked back down at the notes on his desk. "'Supporting women in all the aspects of their lives.'"

So I had missed the part where Toby, Brick, Kevin, and Carl the business guy all got together to talk to Vance about supporting women in all the aspects of their lives. Perfect. "Okay," I said. "What's that look like?"

"Show art will have a little logo in the corner. We're still workshopping it, but something like *You Go Girl by Fitness West* would show as the title." He looked at my face when I heard those words. My face, as always, probably looked exactly the way I felt, which is why I tended to be a bad diplomat. "Relax, it won't literally be called *You Go Girl,* it's a placeholder."

"So was *The A-Hole Chronicles,*" I said, dipping my chin to glare at him. Two years earlier, Toby had put a show into production where each episode was about some woman's bad boyfriend. All through production, he called it *The A-Hole Chronicles,* and I kept telling him to name it, and he kept saying it was just a placeholder, and then all of a sudden it was launching in six weeks, and do you know what it wound up being called? *The A-Hole Chronicles*. Which kept it from being covered by half the outlets our PR team pitched to, and which kept me from telling my mother I had even worked on it. It flopped. "And what does the premium sponsor need from me?"

"Just some extra announcements and a couple of collaborations for social, things like that. It's just more support. It's a good thing."

"I don't have to run laps?"

"Nah," Toby said. "They're not *exactly* gyms anyway, he calls them wellness hubs. You'll love it. They're anti-gyms, really." He handed me a thin spiral-bound information packet of some kind, and when I paged through it, it showed treadmills, spin bikes, free weights, people doing yoga, and a smoothie bar. But there was also some kind of classroom where it looked like a woman was pointing at a whiteboard and teaching a lesson on stress reduction. To me, this did not quite qualify as the anti-gym. The anti-gym would be, say, several rows of vending machines with nothing but Doritos in them. And maybe a supersized couch with a lot of pillows, and giant glasses of wine and Homer Simpson–style donuts brought by on trays every few minutes.

"Okay," I said.

"We're going to get you a membership," Toby said, "and they'll set you up with some social opportunities and things." This was careening toward "doing push-ups on Instagram" territory. But an opening was an opening, and hosting was hosting. Besides, if they wanted me on social, that could mean only one thing: I was turning into a personality. That was one of the steps I was supposed to be taking.

"I'm so proud of you for doing this," he said.

"Don't be proud of me until I meet her."

CHAPTER FOUR

The Influencer

I went back to my desk in our open-plan office and looked up Eliza Cassidy. Her Instagram bio called her "your partner in getting to your future—get going, mama!" Her hair was a dark blond, shadowed at the roots, and in almost every picture, it was exactly the same: smooth on top, wavy at the bottom. My sister, Molly, actually referred to this style as "Instagram hair," best achieved with direct-to-consumer tools that cost hundreds of dollars. Or, of course, with a blow dryer and a round brush from CVS.

Eliza had sponsored posts in her feed featuring, just in the last few weeks: a skincare line, something called "adaptogenic vodka," a $400 smoothie blender, a fragrance "inspired by human pheromones," and a company with whom she had released a set of workout leggings that said "ECFitness" across the ass in gold script. "MY COLLAB HAS ARRIVED!!!" she had announced in an unboxing video. I was pretty sure Molly could have made the same thing with her cutting machine and some glitter vinyl, just like she did with my WORLD'S BEST SISTER mug, but who would pay $80 for that?

No cat toys. No ethically sourced cemetery plots. Eliza was on the right side of something that I had found myself on the wrong side of.

She was photogenically married—a TikTok highlight showed them running into the ocean in their wedding clothes—to a guy named Cody with dark, slightly scruffy hair who wore band T-shirts and always looked like he didn't *entirely* want to be in whatever picture was currently being taken. She looked like an artificial intelligence image result where the prompt was "attractive white lady," and his prompt was maybe "guy who likes to play Halo but not *too* much." She hashtagged all their photos #myman and #codycassidy and #reallove and #findyourreallove.

On her YouTube channel, there wasn't much about official relationship coaching just yet. There were a lot of videos where she reviewed eyeshadow palettes or cleaned out her makeup drawers or tried TikTok's favorite concealer tricks. Sometimes she reviewed clothing brands or hair products or fifteen funny things she got for under ten dollars on some garbage e-commerce site. Sometimes she answered questions from her viewers. Once, she tried out skincare products for men on Cody. There were a few videos where she talked about their wedding, which had been about three years back. She had given a tour of a snazzy and roomy new house in Bethesda a year or so ago. Bethesda meant she really was making money.

Her TikTok was similar, but shorter. Her Instagram was similar, but more photogenic.

I was surprised she even had a regular website—who needs one?—but she did. It was in pure white with modern gray lettering, and there were light blue accents, like you were about to squeeze her from a fresh tube of minty organic toothpaste. She did seem well-positioned for self-help, since I suspected that once you took out protein powder and pickup artistry, an overwhelming percentage of self-help was marketed to straight women, which seemed to be her deal as well.

Eliza's history, as told by her website, went back about seven years. She'd been sailing along as an influencer until a couple of years ago, when she'd done a TikTok from her apartment kitchen in which she announced that any woman who wasn't married by the time she was thirty would never get married unless they took some kind of drastic action. This had gone viral and led to a back-and-forth I vaguely remembered among people who thought she was just telling the truth, people who thought she was up to her perfected hairline in internalized misogyny, and people who thought she was just saying it for attention, which they gave her. She started doing live chats where she gave advice to her fans, who would write in with relationship questions and other personal problems.

Since then, she'd been steadily rising. A year ago, she had been on morning television. Not *local* morning television, *national* morning television. She had a book out called *Get It Together!* Her second, called *Get It Together! Again* was set to go on sale "soon."

She had even very briefly tried making a podcast of her own called *Get It Together: The Conversation,* but it looked to be on hiatus. She'd published episodes—or someone had—irregularly for three months or so and then given up, which put her about two months and two weeks ahead of the average podcast when it came to output. As Julie always said, Apple Podcasts is figuratively littered with the bodies of people whose last words were "How hard can it be?"

I was fully engrossed in her TikTok when my phone rang. The number came up as "CASSIDY PRODUCTIONS LLC."

"This is Cecily."

"Cecily! This is Eliza Cassidy. How are you?"

I am trying to save my friend's job by documenting my humiliating efforts to offer myself up to an indifferent buyers' market like a Beanie Baby on eBay, how are you? "Eliza, hi. I'm well, thanks, how about you?"

"Amazing. Is this an okay time to talk?"

It was as good as any other time was going to be, so I closed my browser window. "Sure."

"Great, great. So, Toby just texted me and told me that you're ready for us to meet."

"I guess that's right."

"You don't sound excited; I want you to be excited." She sounded . . . not high, exactly. She sounded like she was on camera, in front of her ring light, wearing her single gold bangle. Even over the phone, I knew exactly how her hair was positioned as we spoke.

"Oh, I'm fine, I'm just now figuring all this out, that's all," I said, hearing my own nervousness, which was generally not the way to have the most interesting conversations with people, so I dug deep for some enthusiasm. "But yeah, let's do it, I'm game." *Julie, Julie, Julie,* I thought. *Projects, projects, projects. Pilot, pilot, pilot. Money, money, money. Suck it, Justin; suck it, Justin; suck it, Justin.*

"Okay, love that. Do you want to meet at Sophie's in like an hour? Have you been there?"

Sophie's was a coffee shop that had just opened at the site of a defunct tea shop, which had been built on the site of a defunct coffee shop. Whoever Sophie was, I had to admire her optimism. "I have. That would be great."

"What are you wearing? So I can recognize you?"

I looked down. "I am wearing . . . gray jeans. And a gray sweater."

"Oof. What's your bag look like?" she asked.

Did she just react to my description of myself by saying, "Oof"? *Oof?*

My eyes went to the tote that was under my desk as I tried to think of an answer besides *It looks like I bought it at Target maybe four years ago and whatever it's made of is flaking off and quite possibly poisoning me*. Finally, I told her, "Black shoulder bag."

"Great, great. I'm sure you know what I look like."

My eyes started to roll, because what kind of a person announced first thing that she was sure you had already gazed upon her glorious visage? On the other hand, though, how many people did Eliza meet in a business context who *didn't* already know what she looked like? What her bio said? What Cody looked like and what their hashtags were? Had I not, in fact, gazed upon her glorious visage? Was I not guilty of having engaged in first-degree felonious glorious-visage-gazing from the minute I had gotten the chance? And so I just said, "I'm sure we'll find each other."

I had only been to Sophie's maybe twice; I was a person who made coffee at home in the morning, drank that, made more, put it in a steel green thermos, and threw it in my bag with the snacks and the flashlight and the recorder and the lip balms and the tissues and my wallet and my keys and my charger and my iPad and my headphones and all the stuff that collected at the bottom of the bag—a padlock, a little screwdriver, a pair of knotted wired earbuds I rarely wore, my sister's birthday card. I did not typically wander out in the middle of the day for coffee.

Sophie's had an array of two-person tables within a few steps of the counter where you ordered, and most were occupied by people on laptops or pairs of people passing short break times until they returned to laptops awaiting them elsewhere. At the table in the corner, closest to where the counter was, a thin woman with her hair pulled back in a ponytail tapped away at her phone from under a ball cap pulled low. The air seemed different around her, as if molecules were slowed. I walked closer until I recognized her. "Hi!" I said, in a clanging chirp, way overshooting my goal of sounding friendly. I did this *all the time* in my job. I talked to strangers, I used my normal voice. Surely, I could do it again.

She looked up from her phone. "Oh, hi hi hi!" she said. She

stood up, revealing a loose aqua sweatshirt that dangled off one shoulder like in *Flashdance* and a pair of black yoga pants that I suspected, but could not see to verify, said "ECFitness" on the ass. I don't know exactly what I was expecting, but she extended one hand, and we shook. I had been afraid she was going to hug me, and I was not in a guru-hugging mood.

"Well, geez," she said, "you look fine! You're doing a tone-on-tone thing. I thought you were going to look like a rain cloud! You undersold yourself. Never undersell! We'll make that lesson one. Do you want to go get a coffee at the counter? I'm working on a green tea latte."

I might have looked like a rain cloud, I might have been in gray, I might have been carrying a bag of detritus, and I might have been about to sell my privacy and my dignity, but by God, I would not sit and occupy a table in a bustling D.C. coffee place and not buy anything. Even a flawed and teetering society is still a society. I fetched a vanilla latte, and when I got back to the table, Eliza had pulled off her cap and was sliding her phone into a pocket in the thigh of her leggings. I sat across from her and ran a hand over my hair. "Thanks for doing this," I said, putting on my interviewing tone in case it helped at all. "You picked a good spot."

"I love it here. When I'm in the city, this is my favorite place for meetings or just sitting and working."

"So you don't live in D.C.?"

"My house is in Bethesda," she said. I pretended not to know, and not to be impressed. But truly, you couldn't unfold a chair in a closet in Bethesda for a price I would be able to afford. "Cody grew up there, his mom and dad still live there. But we also have an apartment in Manhattan, and he works remotely, so we divide our time. We take the train. Like I always say, I really live in three places—the house, the apartment, and the Acela. Where are you?"

I described my neighborhood to her, feeling the whole time like

I was auditioning to play myself. Did my one-bedroom apartment sound right? Was I single enough? Established enough? What was she going to make of me? What was she going to ask me to make of myself?

"Okay," she said after I had described my neighbors and their pets to the best of my ability. "So you're established, you're independent, you have friends and this great job. What's missing?"

"I don't know that anything is *missing*," I said.

"Are you interested in a relationship?"

"Yes. I guess I just haven't quite . . . stumbled on the right person."

"Well, no wonder, right? The only thing you stumble on is obstacles. The right person is something you go and find." I had a feeling that by mentioning "stumbles," I had accidentally set her up, like one of those old "It's sooooo hot"/"How hot is it?" jokes.

I nodded tentatively. "Okay."

"Okay. Perfect. Now, I want to make this work for you, for your life. Tell me how to make you comfortable with me. Your team told my team you had some concerns."

I had a team? Her team was probably this Marcela; was my team just Toby? "My skepticism isn't personal," I said. That was maybe fifty percent true. I would probably not have trusted any dating/life coach operating on the internet. But she did give off vibes that made me suspect she would want me to do squats and exfoliate until I got to the point where I was abrading my skull directly. "I'm just not sure I'm the right candidate for this."

She smiled. "I get it. Everybody is afraid of the possibilities." Her teeth were *really* white.

I tried to match her smile without looking like a happy clown. "Oh, I'm not afraid of it."

"Everybody worries that they're not up to what I'm going to ask of them."

"It's not that either." After all, I had a belt sander I could use if the exfoliating *did* get that far.

"You think I'm going to tell you that you're not attractive enough."

Did she hear me gulp? Did the rest of the *coffee shop* hear me gulp? Did I just gulp, or did I say the word "gulp" out loud, and was there now a cartoon balloon floating next to my head that said "GULP"? As I was coming to suspect was her habit, she kept going. "You are attractive enough. You're quite attractive. Like I told you, you're just underselling. You told me you were wearing a gray sweater and gray jeans. It makes you sound dull, which you aren't. That's probably exactly the vibe you've given when you've had a dating profile. I'm assuming you've had a dating profile before."

I had two as of this conversation. And when I had to go to a wedding by myself or something else happened that convinced me the world was simply too hostile to exist in as a single person, I'd go back and use them again. I'd look for four weeks here, six days there, each time right up until I realized I was never going to say yes to anyone because none of them used punctuation and too many of them, at least around here, described their work in ways that made them sound like lobbyists or spies. "I have, yes. Wait, how was I supposed to describe a gray sweater and gray jeans?"

"Well," she said, "since I'm a woman, you should have told me, maybe, that you were wearing a gunmetal cashmere pullover and steel gray skinnies."

"Oh, it's not cashmere."

"Doesn't matter. It's soft-looking. You're not making an inventory for your insurance, you're just getting the general idea across."

"And the general idea would be different if I were talking to a man."

"Oh, of course. If I were a man—like a man you were interested in dating—you would tell me you're wearing, maybe, a V-neck dove-gray sweater and slim-fit pants."

"But this isn't dove gray, and dove gray isn't the same as gunmetal."

"Oh, straight men won't distinguish between grays. That's just a fact."

I wondered exactly where that research had been done. Presumably the University of Unsupported Hunches, where I was guessing she was a tenured professor. "It's also not a V-neck," I said. "It's a scoop neck."

"Sure, but men haven't heard of scoop necks. They think a V-neck sounds like something low-cut and dove gray sounds soft, but you can't say cashmere to them because it makes it sound like you have expensive tastes, and that might freak them out. Before the first meeting, you're just trying to make the sale."

"What am I selling?"

She looked at me like she was waiting for me to get it, and I wished she would just accept that I was never going to, because it would save us a lot of time. "You're selling the first meeting." She fiddled with her bangle bracelet. "Speaking of which, I'm guessing you need new pictures taken. What pictures are you using?"

I took out my phone and opened up a folder where I kept a few pictures of myself that I liked. I handed it over to her and she scrolled through them. She held the phone up, comparing the pictures to my live human form. "Oh, yeah, you're way better-looking than these." She frowned. "These are a no. We'll get you good ones."

"And those are for . . . dating apps?"

"They could be, but for now, they're for me, for when I arrange dates for you. So new pictures are going to be early on the to-do list."

I had technically not agreed to do this yet. But I could see the train pulling out of the station, with me hanging on to the caboose. I took a long sip of my latte and sat up straighter. Back to reporter voice. "Speaking of steps, what do you do, exactly? Your website is a little nonspecific. And it doesn't say what anything costs."

She smiled. "Pricing is flexible. We customize everything, so the prices don't make any sense outside the context of the specific plan that we come up with for every person depending on her situation. In your case, what we're putting you on is a version of what's called the Platinum Goddess Package."

"What is that?"

"What does it sound like?"

"It sounds like a gift basket I get for ovulating."

"Ooh." She reached into her pocket for her phone. When she started typing, I peered at her. "What are you doing?"

"I'm writing it down." She kept typing with her thumbs. "It's an interesting idea, an ovulation subscription service. We could work with a cycle-tracking app. Heating pad, tea, journal—"

"Postcard from the department of health asking whether you're pregnant." She stopped typing. "I don't know what people would write in an ovulation journal anyway, besides, like, 'light mittelschmerz.' It's not much of an experience."

She tucked the phone back into her pants. "I'll think on it. *Anyway*. Platinum Goddess! What that means is that you and I will work directly together for twelve weeks, give or take. Your situation is unique, obviously." She looked down at her phone, seemingly referring to some kind of schedule. "We do a couple weeks of prep, and then you go on twenty dates."

"Yes, Toby said that. It sounds like a lot to me in a short time, I have to admit."

"It's not that many," she said. "But I think it gives us an excellent chance that somebody will pan out. You'll go on more dates with the people you like, some spark will *definitely* catch, and we'll even have time to go through the first stages of seeing a new person. Then I'll set you free and you'll fly away into your future. That's it. Platinum Goddess."

"What happens if I meet somebody the first week?"

"Well, *that* won't happen, because you won't meet anybody for a little while except your dummy."

"My . . . dummy?"

"Not a *dummy* dummy," she said. "A dummy date. Don't worry, he'll still be somebody great. But in this case, we'll record that, and I'll listen back to it, and I'll talk to him after, and to you. It's like a placement test."

"But what are we testing?"

"Your approach. How you make conversation, how you talk about yourself, how you present." She probably saw my face changing color. I envisioned it as a greenish gray. "It's not going to be bad," she said, reaching out and putting one hand on my arm. "It's going to be fun. People don't learn how to date, because they don't go on dates with themselves. This is like a date with yourself."

I had never been on a date with myself, it was true. I wasn't sure I wanted to know what that experience was like. "Okay," I said slowly. "Then what? After the dummy date, what's between that and the big man-binge?"

She laughed. "Well, we work on you," she said. She saw me flinch. "Not on changing you, just on getting you ready to be successful. You get ready to get out there, we get your photos, we talk about your past experiences, we clear the decks, we make sure you're in the best headspace. Because that's the way we make sure that when you do the twenty dates and you meet somebody, you are in the best position to succeed. Hashtag . . . year of Cecily," she concluded. "You're going to love it."

"What if I meet somebody on my own? What then?"

She raised her perfectly shaped eyebrows. "I mean, is that really going to happen?"

I'd had dentists show me my X-rays with less unvarnished candor. "It's not impossible."

She smiled, and then un-smiled, and then smiled again. "How do I explain this? Okay, do you take the Metro? Like, to work?"

"Bus, actually."

"Of course. And there's part of you, probably, that thinks that you're going to be walking to the bus one morning and a hot superhero is going to come by and ask you for your number. It's a nice idea, and a lot of people are carrying it around, but that's not a thing that happens in real life. And furthermore? Even if it did happen? That will end in tears."

"Tears," I repeated.

"Well, look," she said. "From everything I already know about you, you wouldn't pick a job because somebody came up to you on the street and offered it to you. And you shouldn't pick a relationship that way either. Not without a plan for what you're looking for."

"A plan," I repeated.

She leaned closer. "A plan. You've been picking for yourself for what, like, twenty years? How's that turned out?" I didn't answer. "My point exactly," she said. "Take three months off. Relax. Exhale. Stop looking. Let me help, and see how you feel about it."

"What happens if it doesn't work?"

She shrugged. "Make a podcast about how relationship advice is a fraud." She must have seen my eyebrow go up. "I'm serious, Cecily, cross my heart. If you try this, if you do what I say and you really think it's nothing, then go ahead. Make your show, do your exposé, prove that I have no idea what I'm doing. Prove I'm not qualified."

"I mean, *are* you qualified?" I asked.

"I majored in marketing," she said immediately. "And while I was in school, one of my two jobs was at a clothing store where I got treated like absolute trash by rich women every single day until I cried in the bathroom. And my other job was taking customer service calls for the pharmacy section of a health insurance company, where I learned that all people want is for somebody to listen to them. A few years later, I went to Riviera Maya with some of my girlfriends, and I noticed that one of them was obsessed with this woman who reviewed swimsuits on Instagram. And I thought . . . *That seems like more fun than sitting in meet-*

ings with boring men who want me to tell them how to get nineteen-year-old girls to buy bottled low-alcohol, low-carb, low-sugar cocktails."

I knew she had probably told this story to a hundred podcasts already. But I, too, had clothing-store experience. I'd once worked for a fast-fashion behemoth, folding and refolding hundreds of black tees. If I had, at that time, seen my friends going gaga over somebody talking about clothes on Instagram—instead of what actually happened, which was that I became obsessed with that one podcast that everyone always pretends was the first podcast ever, you know the one—I might have done the same thing.

"By the way," she said, "I went back to Riviera Maya this year, everything was comped, I treated all my friends, and we were living *la isla bonita.*"

I tipped my head. It was possible she was a Madonna completist, but I suspected she knew it from *Glee.* "I think you might be thinking of *la vida loca.*"

She rolled her eyes. "Whatever, right, *la vida loca.* By the way, one thing to work on? You don't have to be so smart all the time. I know you didn't think I would know what 'mittelschmerz' is. And you're surprised that I do."

She was right.

CHAPTER FIVE

The Great Dane

I knew about the groundhog and the six more weeks of winter, and I knew about the black cat and the bad luck. But I can't say anyone had ever told me that if a dog with a head like a cinder block crosses your path, you are about to have a fateful meeting.

The morning after my coffee with Eliza, I came out of my building and let myself out of the security gate. I was at the top of the steps that led down to the sidewalk when I saw movement to my left and looked over to see an enormous dog trotting at a good clip down the pavement, past the building, down toward the next corner. He was black-and-white and massive, and I figured him for a Great Dane, since my only other thought was "marauding escaped cow." His purple rope leash bounced uselessly along the sidewalk with nobody at the other end.

A few seconds after the dog passed, a man ran by, evidently in pursuit. He was in jeans and a white tee, very ordinary-looking, except that a cape flapped from his shoulders. It wasn't a fashionable cape, if there is such a thing, it was brown with white block print, like what they would wrap around you at a hair salon, and it crinkled when it shifted in the air. He had long legs and arms, and you could almost have frozen him in space and drawn him into a comic strip, floating, elbows and knees at right angles, cape extended straight back. You'd draw little lines to emphasize his speed, and in capital scribbles, you'd write next to him, *WHOOSH!* He didn't even seem to see me.

I followed, obviously.

I was wearing my most comfortable black flats, so I settled into a purposeful stride. Near the next cross street, the dog—whose name was Buddy, according to the urgent shouts of Captain Haircut—stopped near a tree where countless dogs had preceded him. He stuck his nose close to it and began, presumably, to index them. Captain Haircut caught up to him, then paused nearby and leaned over to catch his breath, putting his hands on his thighs. He was still in this position when I got there.

"Do you need a hand?"

He stood up, looked around as if I might be talking to someone else, and then nodded, hands on hips. "Yeah, that would be great, actually." He had dark curly hair and dark eyes, and he was tall enough that the dog almost made sense beside him. "I've been chasing him for ten blocks. Every time I get any closer than about like this, he takes off again. I think he's taunting me."

"He does look calculating," I said, watching the dog bite off a mouthful of grass and gum it halfheartedly.

"Maybe I can get out ahead of him." He started to gesture back and forth between us. "If we work together, maybe we can surround him."

"It's worth a try," I said.

For a moment, we just watched Buddy, who began to sniff a fire hydrant. "A fire hydrant, seriously?" Captain Haircut said.

"Fine line between a cliché and a classic," I said.

Buddy paused and hoisted his meaty hock—my first thought was that it was what a velociraptor drumstick must look like—and began to empty the tank. It went on. And on. "He could put the fire out without the hydrant," I said, awed. Captain Haircut laughed, and I laughed back. He motioned for me to stay where I was while he tried to creep closer. He traced a wide arc in the grass on the other side of the sidewalk as Buddy finished up and went back to his determined sniffing.

But just as Captain Haircut started to pass him, Buddy turned left and headed up the street. We swore simultaneously and followed him past a couple of houses, at which point he started sniffing a low patch of flowers next to the sidewalk. "Okay," Cap said. "I'm going to try to get in front of him again."

"Act casual," I said. He nodded.

Cap walked past Buddy on the sidewalk as Buddy turned his attention to some nearby ivy. "Good morning," he said in a low voice, like an airport gate announcer. "The first thing we're going to do is get hold of your leash. Just eat those flowers, take it easy, and understand that there is a plan."

"I don't think he's going to understand the importance of the agenda," I said as he got far enough that Buddy was between us.

"I'm trying to make him comfortable." He pointed at me. "You said to act casual."

"Yeah, casual, not *business* casual."

He did not smile at this. He did not chuckle or chortle. Instead, he doubled over and let his arms dangle so his hands brushed his Chuck Taylors, and he laughed for a solid three seconds before he stood back up. "I like that." He collected himself. "Okay, cover me. Tell my mother I love her." But as soon as he took a step, Buddy turned and trotted across the street, settling into a whole different row of plants. "Ah, dammit," he muttered.

"Why is he being like this?" I said.

He turned and looked at me with his eyebrow cocked. "See? I told you he was taunting me, and you didn't believe it." He put his hands on his hips and looked around. "Do you see any rope lying around?"

"What for?"

"I was thinking I'd lasso him."

"You want to *lasso* him?" I said. "Like lasso him, like 'yippie ki-yay'? Do you have any kind of lasso experience?"

"No," he admitted. "Do you?"

"No. I mean, my sister watches *Yellowstone*. And I saw *City Slickers* on DVD when I was a kid. Oh, and there's an episode of *The Brady Bunch* where they have to get the key—"

"Off the wall of the jail," he said. "Right." He considered this thought as Buddy considered disrespecting a DRIVE LIKE YOUR KIDS LIVE HERE sign as he had the hydrant. "It doesn't seem that hard." He turned to me. "I feel like, you know, you just . . ." He traced circles in the air with his hand. "You just need a little finesse."

"I admire your optimism, but honestly, I think it seems very hard."

He made the air circles a couple more times, then he put his hands back on his hips. "You're probably right. Maybe we're thinking about this wrong, maybe we need to figure out how to get him to come to us."

"It won't work to call him?"

"I've been calling him for ten blocks," he said. "I'm pretty sure I could yell at him for hours, and all he would do is eat plants and run."

"Oh, wait," I said. "Eating. Eating is the idea." I reached into my bag and pulled out a jar of chunky peanut butter. Walking slowly toward Buddy, I unscrewed the lid. "Do you want a snack?" I asked. I dug two fingers into the jar, pulling out a golf ball–sized glob. Behind him, Cap watched.

Buddy looked up from the ivy. He saw me, saw the peanut butter. Saw me, saw the peanut butter. I waved my fingers in a figure eight pattern, in case I could get the scent to waft in his direction. He began to close the distance between us, one cautious step at a time, as I did the same. When we met, he gently touched my hand with his velvety muzzle, which was like being tenderly caressed by the bumper of a Humvee, but when his fat tongue emerged and started to pull at the peanut butter, it wasn't that different from feeding a baby. Or, from how I supposed feeding a baby would be, given that a baby can bite you on the boob at any time. I reached out and took hold of Buddy's purple leash, and Cap walked up to us. "That was riveting," he said, crossing his arms across his chest. "You should have a TV show where you feed animals peanut butter exactly like that. I would watch ten seasons of it."

I held the leash out to him. "Nah, I'm not ready to go pro yet. I want to hang on to my Olympic eligibility."

"Hey, truly. Thank you," he said, taking the leash from me.

"You're welcome. I'm just glad everybody is safe. I guess you have to hold on pretty tight to a guy this size, huh?"

"Oh, he's not mine."

"He's not?"

"No, no."

"You chased him all the way here and he's not your dog?" I screwed the top back on the jar and shoved it down in my bag, pulling out a cylinder of wet wipes and cleaning the peanut butter off my fingers.

"No. I was getting my hair cut at this place up on Rhode Island. You know, where the chairs face the big front windows?"

"Sure."

"I was kind of people-watching, everybody's going by on their way to work, and I see this woman walking with him." He pointed to Buddy. "And right as they pass the window, a guy goes by on a scooter. Just some dude, khakis and a messenger bag and the . . ." He gestured at the center of his chest.

"Lanyard."

"Lanyard, exactly. Anyway, he practically runs into her, but he keeps right on going, total prick. The dog barks, she tries to keep her balance. But, well, do you know how the sidewalk goes up like a little A-frame house when there's a crack in it, like—"

"Right, I turned my ankle in Dupont Circle that way, right in front of the bookstore."

"Oh, the hell with ankles," he said sympathetically. "You know, one of mine still puffs up when it rains because I messed it up practicing backflips in the backyard with my brother when I was ten."

"Yeah, I messed mine up practicing looking at my phone while I was walking."

"Ouch." He shifted Buddy's lead in his hand. "Anyway, anyway, the lady fell, and she dropped the leash. She was on the ground yelling, 'Buddy, Buddy, come back.' So I figured somebody had better get the dog. If he got lost, it's not like he was going to call her later and tell her where to pick him up. And his legs are really long, so he covers a lot of ground."

I looked at Cap. I could see now, up close, that the right half of his dark hair was neatly trimmed and the left half was longer. He looked like a one-man before-and-after picture. "And you got up and ran out the door?"

"Yes."

"Of the hair salon."

"Yes."

"Did you say anything?"

"Like what?"

"Like, 'I'll be right back.' Or maybe, 'I have to go catch that dog.'"

His eyes narrowed. "You think I should have?"

I nodded. "It probably doesn't happen every day that somebody jumps up in the middle of a haircut and runs out the door with the cape on."

He reached around his back and felt for it. "Oh, damn, I forgot I even had that. They probably want it back, huh? And Buddy's mom is probably wondering whether I ever caught up to him. I hope she's not too worried."

"Hey, you still did your good deed for the day."

"Well, I was just running after him until I ran into you." He looked down at me. "Imagine if he'd run down some other street? What would I have done?"

"Chased him all the way to the Capitol, I guess." I pointed up ahead of us. "I get the bus up on Fourth. Near your hair place."

"Oh, great," he said. "I'll walk with you."

We fell into a slow stroll, with Buddy pausing every few steps to stick his face in something new. "So I followed Buddy, and you followed me," he said. I nodded.

He leaned over to peek into my bag. "Peanut butter, huh? You always that prepared?"

"Yeah, I work late a lot. I get stuck at my desk. I always have peanut butter in my bottom drawer, and crackers, maybe half a cookie or something. And a couple of squares of dark chocolate for late at night."

"Ooh, yeah, you've gotta have that night chocolate."

"Exactly, night chocolate. Like, the kind so dark it's a little bit punishing? Your mouth rejects it, but it's so good? That's what keeps me going when I'm editing at three in the morning. Oh, and I should say, there's always an apple, although it's usually old enough that I don't want to eat it, I just think about how I *should* eat it."

"You look at it."

"Right, it's aspirational."

"What do you edit?" he said.

"I edit audio," I said. "Podcasts and stuff."

"Oh, cool," he said, in exactly the way people do when they are wondering whether you work for a noxious political show or a rich celebrity who gets paid a million dollars a year to try to be interesting, which are the two kinds of podcasts I am commonly asked about.

"How about you, what do you do?" I asked.

"Little of this, little of that," he said. With my luck, it was probably a little murder for hire and a little light environmental pollution.

We passed my gate, where two women who lived down the hall from me were just coming out, and they waved at me as they passed. "That's my building," I said. "Do you live near here?"

"I live by Harris Teeter, on that block with the little coffee shop and the big coffee shop."

"Oh, by the store with the glass lamps and wall hangings and stuff."

"Yep."

"Okay, I have to ask you. Do people ever go in there and buy things? I don't think I've ever seen anybody going in or out, I just see fancy stuff in the window."

"No, you're exactly right. I was telling my sister the other day, I think it's money laundering. There are probably seven guys in the back, putting cash through those automatic bill-counters, you know, *ftt-ftt-ftt-ftt.*" At the sound, Buddy turned briefly before continuing up the street. For all his dawdling and wandering, it occurred to me that Buddy was a well-behaved leash walker, which was a good thing, since he could have pulled Cap off his feet just by leaning the wrong way.

"What do you think this dog weighs?" I asked him. "Hundred pounds?"

Cap looked down at Buddy. "Oh, way more than that. I bet it's a hundred fifty. I know how much my girlfriend weighs, and he's a lot bigger than she is." Of course. "Or my ex-girlfriend, I guess." He narrowed his eyes at the dog. "She walks on two legs, though. And her head is smaller."

"Would you rather fight one Great Dane–sized ex-girlfriend or a hundred ex-girlfriend-sized Great Danes?" I asked. And then I suddenly had the horrifying sense that I had stepped off a conversational cliff and was about to hold up a sign that said HELP. And so I hastily added, "I'm sorry, it's a weird internet—"

"No, I know, with the ducks and the horses, a horse-sized duck or a hundred duck-sized horses. I know the thing, I just got this picture in my head of myself dancing with Buddy at my cousin's wedding, and it's really . . . vivid."

"Are you both in tuxes?"

"Just me. Buddy's in Meredith's green dress, strapless, with the laces in the back."

"I bet it looks great on him. The perfect complement to a fifteen-pound tongue." It was time for me to turn left to get the bus. "I go this way," I said, jabbing my thumb down the street. "This was fun."

He was suddenly holding his phone. "Hey, can I call you or text you or something?"

"Why?" I knew why. Why did I say "Why?"

"Well, I like talking to you." He grinned. I might have asked why, but he knew I knew why.

"Oh," I said, using all the powers of articulation that made me a good editor.

"But, you know, also . . . I feel like I should let you know that Buddy got back to his mom okay, right?"

I nodded slowly. "I do think that would make me feel better."

"Besides, what if next time I'm running after a monkey and you have a banana in your purse? I gotta have your contact info."

It obviously wasn't anything, he was just going to tell me about the dog. It was business. It was kindness to animals. So I gave him my number. We did the thing where you trade phones and you add yourself as a contact, and maybe you use your real name, and maybe you use your real number, and maybe you don't. And I put in "Cecily," and he put in "Will," and they were both our real names, and they were both our real numbers, and that's how we met.

. . .

I thought about him and the dog all the way back to the office, and when I walked through the door, it was like I'd been whomped in the face with my own choices. Because despite this serendipitous meeting, an entire project, involving a good number of people, was now taking shape, wherein I would meet men via the least serendipitous method ever devised by humans.

My progress through Eliza's program would stay a few weeks ahead of what was airing, but it still made me terrifically nervous that we'd start airing the season without knowing the ending. Toby kept telling me it would be okay, people made shows this way all the time. I bit back the urge to tell him they were shows I often ended up not liking.

Later that day, as Julie and I waited for Miles so we could retrack something where he said "Chernobyl" instead of "Three Mile Island," she took out a notebook. "Oh, I meant to fill you in on the production meeting you wisely didn't attend." She adjusted her glasses. "You want the details on the schedule?"

"Sure."

"So you know this part: The preview is the sixteenth of next month. First episode is November fifteenth. We'll run six episodes, then we're on pause for Christmas week and New Year's week. And on top of not having episodes come out, that's when Toby wants everybody to take whatever vacation they want over the next five or six months, and Eliza's going to Hawaii for New Year's anyway. So I think we'll be . . . not totally dark for those two weeks, but that will be our break, and then we'll do the final push to Valentine's Day." She looked up at me. "Good?"

"Good. Did they say what these episodes are actually going to be?"

"Yeah." She looked back down at her notes. "After the preview, we'll have two that are background, one on you and one on Eliza. Then we figure we can probably cover twenty dates in six episodes, so that means we'd have four left. And what happens in those would depend on . . . what happens, I guess. Hopefully they're all about you going on second and third dates with some really awesome guys. And presumably we come up with some kind of ending."

I rubbed my eyes and said, "Self-help."

"I know."

"I'm better at help-help. I help-helped save a dog this morning."

"How did that happen?"

"I walked out of my building, and there was this giant dog running down the street, and this guy was running after it. So I helped. He returned the dog to its owner, and all is well."

"What did you do?"

"Fed him peanut butter off my fingers."

"The guy?"

"The dog."

"Oh. What did he look like?"

"The dog?"

"The guy."

"Oh," I said. "I don't know, I'm terrible at describing people, you know that."

"Well, what famous person does he look like?"

"Why does everybody have to look like a famous person?" She just stared at me. "Okay. Okay, imagine a very, very good-looking celebrity. Like, someone who's famous for being extremely handsome, light shines from his eyes, eerily symmetrical face, all that."

"Well, you have my attention," she said.

"You know how you sometimes see a photo of somebody like that, and next to him is another guy? And like, he's handsome, but he's a normal amount of handsome. And you find out that this guy is the celebrity's brother. And you think, yes, this guy is exactly the right amount of handsome to be an unmanageably handsome man's brother. You know what I mean?"

"Oh, sure."

"There you go. And I helped him, and now an enormous dog is safe because we went and stopped him before he could become a menacing stray knocking over trash cans with his head."

"Well, I'm proud to know you," she said.

"I'm just here to help the gargantuan-dog community," I said. And we went back to waiting for Miles.

CHAPTER SIX

The Sister

My sister, Molly, was two years older than I was and four inches taller. When she invited me to her pretty Silver Spring house for dinner, it was always in the same form: a day of the week, the meal her husband was going to make, and a question mark.

Tuesday, lasagna?

Saturday, chicken mole?

Wednesday, that spicy pork thing
with rice?

This time it had been Friday, spaghetti?, and I had said yes. That was before I knew that I would be trying to prepare to have my romantic innards exposed to a wide audience, and my plan was to work up to telling her about it. Of course, once she opened the door, I lasted about three minutes before I started spilling the whole thing to her and Pete.

The three of us were in their small kitchen. He was looking

after a boiling pot of pasta, Molly was pouring me a glass of wine from the bottle I'd brought, and I just said, "They want me to make a show about dating."

"But you're not dating," Molly said, handing me the glass. "Wait, *are* you dating?"

"Well, the idea is that I would be," I said. "I have to go on twenty blind dates."

Molly literally squeaked. "That sounds like a nightmare, why would you have to do that?"

"I'm supposed to learn from it. Someone would . . . coach me."

Pete turned around from the stove to slice a loaf of Italian bread on the counter. "Like a sex coach?" he asked. He was tall enough that he often looked like he might bump his head on the range hood, but he navigated their kitchen with a lot of style. I envied him, as someone who did not cook. And I envied her, as someone who did not have a guy who cooked living in my apartment.

"No!" I said. "Not like a sex coach. I think she's more like a life coach. Tries to help you be your best self or something."

"Oh," said Pete. "So it's like a makeover."

"I hope not. I don't want to have to get veneers for a podcast." They quizzed me about the things I'd expect them to: whether I really wanted to do it, whether I was *sure* I really wanted to do it, and whether I thought Toby would stick to our agreement. Molly was not a big fan of my boss. "I think he will," I said. "I guess we'll find out."

I offered to help finish setting the table, and she brushed me off, as always. Just then, my phone buzzed. It was Will: Update! His name isn't Buddy, it's Gideon. She just calls him Buddy. And he's not her dog. She volunteers at a rescue and was walking him. But he's back to her safe and sound.

I texted him back: Glad to hear he's okay. And then I typed and deleted three or four different sentences before I settled on a pair of emojis. A dog's paw and a thumb pointed up. I put the phone away.

"What's up?" Molly asked.

"It's just this guy I met the other day. I helped him catch this huge dog that had gotten loose." I told her the story, from the haircut to the peanut butter to the fact that we traded numbers.

Her eyes widened. "You gave him your number! That's a development."

"I mean, not really, it doesn't count, he wasn't *really* asking for my number."

"If he asked you for your number," Pete said, pulling out a noodle and peering at it, "then he was really asking for your number."

"He just wanted to tell me that things turned out okay with the dog," I said.

"Hah!" Pete barked without turning around to look at me. "Maybe you do need a coach."

"Either way," I said, "it doesn't matter, right? I'm doing this other thing. I just wanted to know the dog is okay. And he is. This guy took him back to his rescue, and now the dog can freely use his head to knock over walls."

We ate around their kitchen table, and the conversation turned, inevitably, to the fact that, as had been the case almost continuously since they bought their house five years earlier, large sections of floor were torn up and several interior walls were down to the studs. The people they bought from had owned the house for fifty years, and it hadn't been updated in ages, which was the only way they could afford it. I had helped paint three of the rooms so far, but it wasn't clear to me whether it would one day be finished, or whether this was just how they liked it, living inside a constant list of projects to be accomplished.

"It's coming along," Molly said. "We're about eight weeks behind on the upstairs hall bathroom, and the contractor just told us that he bought the wrong size bathtub for our en suite, so we're going to be waiting a little while for those things. Your brother-in-law is trying to talk me into a double oven for the kitchen."

"I want the double oven," Pete said, gesturing with his salad fork. "Business in one, party in the other. Chicken on top, cheesecake on the bottom."

"I don't think we need it," Molly said, "but as you can see, I'm having a lot of trouble talking him out of it."

"Hey, you got the big tub," he said. "A big tub for a double oven, that's a fair trade." He raised his eyebrows at Molly. "And you're the one who's going to get to eat the cheesecake, baby. You can eat it right in your big tub."

She smiled. "Right answer."

When we were finished eating, Pete went off to watch the Nats on TV in the basement and Molly and I parked on opposite ends of the living room couch. "Have you talked to Mom?" she asked.

"Not for a couple of weeks. What now?"

"She's meditating in Sedona."

"Of course," I said. Our parents were hardly ever around in person, as a result of near-constant spiritual quests and personal growth experiences they'd engaged in for most of our lives. I considered it a minor miracle that they'd never wound up in anything that qualified as a full-on cult (yet), but they never met a guide they didn't want to pay for a weeklong or monthlong retreat to explore their inner selves. It was where most of their money went, which remained a source of low-level stress for us, given that we secretly suspected that at some point when they couldn't travel and had spent themselves broke, they'd expect to move in with Molly. They hadn't even seen this house, in part because Molly and Pete didn't want them to know how much space there was. I suspected the endless construction was covertly intended to discourage them in their golden years.

Starting when we were about twelve and fourteen, they would go off and leave us on our own, because neither of us ever had the slightest interest in any of these adventures. They did seminars, weekends, mountaineering, orienteering, whitewater rafting, marriage-improvement retreats (six times!)—and they trusted us to take care of ourselves.

Molly and I would stay home watching movies and trying to get homework done. It never occurred to us to have parties, because we just would have had to clean up after them ourselves. We would divide up the chores on a chart on the refrigerator, and our sole act of rebellion was that beginning when Molly was seventeen and I was fifteen, we would each have one shot of whiskey on the last night before they got back. They weren't really drinkers; they didn't realize the level on their massive jug of Jim Beam was dropping bit by bit. We added water when we thought they might get suspicious.

Now that they were retired, Mom and Dad traveled separately most of the time. She was still deeply into wellness culture, while he liked to pick up new hobbies and go somewhere to pursue them fervently until he reached the limits of his abilities. He'd been to two tennis camps, a ski camp, a surfing camp, a rock and roll camp, and an adult space camp. We caught up with them between trips, or whenever they decided to call. I loved them, they just weren't around. The role that a lot of people's parents played in their lives, Molly played in mine.

"Well, hopefully, meditating in Sedona will give her everything she didn't get from meditating in Vermont this summer."

"New Hampshire."

"Whatever. Anyway, tell me about *your* trip." Molly and Pete had just gotten back from a getaway in Ocean City, so I made her tell me about every day they were gone, every walk and every meal. I asked her about the weather, I grilled her about what they saw on the boardwalk, and I nailed down every detail of their hotel room from the windows to the rug to the cat who lived in the lobby. I wanted to tour her happiness and run my fingers over the corners and the edges.

I found contentment in general very reassuring. As the news

got more and more depressing, and I got older, and the work I so loved was swamped by stories about murder and shows where L.A. comedians invited friends over to talk for three hours about nothing, the idea of simple good days had started to seem implausible to me. I'd started to think about real happiness as not just precious but owned, kept, borrowed, shared, stolen, divided, and sacrificed. When I was around it, I wanted to *eat* it, almost, like a cupcake. Happy kids, happy dogs, happy crowds, they were irresistible.

When she had told me everything she could remember, she said, "Okay, now I want you to tell me something. You're sure you want to do this dating thing?"

I smiled. "I am."

"Because of the job? The boss?"

"Sure," I said. "But for me, too. I really am tired of being alone."

It was hard to say exactly why there hadn't been anybody since Justin, since the night he explained in a very matter-of-fact way, while I was doing the dishes, that he didn't think he loved me anymore. Out of all the details of that agonizing memory, my brain had held fastest to the fact that he said this to me with his phone in his hand, as if it were normal, as if it were just an opening salvo for a conversational serve-and-volley and not the relationship equivalent of "you don't have to go home, but you can't stay here." And so although he didn't say the words "I want to break up," I moved out that night. He kept the apartment; I kept walking. I walked until I got to the Metro, and I took the Metro to Pete and Molly's, carrying my tote, my laptop, my recording kit, and a suitcase.

"It's just so much to *tell* people," she said. "Everybody listening to your business, don't you think it's going to feel creepy?"

"Maybe. But I mean, I ask other people to do it all the time," I said. "I ask them to talk about horrible things that have happened to them, embarrassing things, really private things. I would be a total hypocrite if I refused to do it myself. Maybe this will make me better at it."

"They're not going to, like, record you, are they?" she said in a scandalized half-whisper.

"Of course they're going to record me."

"No, no," she said. "Like, *record* you." I still just looked at her. "*Record you* doing things on dates." She shimmied her shoulders up and down and bit down on her lower lip.

"Are you asking me if there's going to be a podcast of me having sex?"

"I'm just trying to understand!"

"No," I said. "Nobody wants to hear that. I mean, that's not true, obviously *some* people want to hear that, but they're not going to hear it from me."

"Good. I love you," she said, "but I don't want to hear your noises."

I turned and put my face in the couch cushion. "*I* don't want to hear my noises. I don't acknowledge that I even *have* any noises. There are no noises."

"Okay. I just wanted to make sure."

I turned back toward her. "I want to get it in gear, Mol. My goal is to learn from this woman, who is happily married, how to meet people. Ideally, I'm going to master it, tackle it, and be so successful at it that I never, ever, have to do it again."

"Amazingly positive attitude," she said. She had the most beautiful gold-hazel eyes; I had envied them endlessly when we were kids. When she'd turn them on me back then, it could flood me with admiration and frustration that mine weren't the same. Now that look always just made me feel pierced by her constancy, by how long I'd been counting on her, even when I was half-prepared to buckle under the weight of her expectations. "If you think this is the way to go," she said, "then I hope it works."

"I do too," I said. "I'm meeting Eliza at her house in Bethesda. Sunday morning pastries."

"Fancy. And you're already working on the weekend, so that's a . . . sign of something."

"She also has an apartment in Manhattan."

"From *this*? God, maybe I should have been an influencer," Molly said. "I'm sure I have some kind of wisdom to pass along. Do you think people would watch TikToks of me eating peanut butter off a spoon at midnight after drizzling it with chocolate syrup? It's the best idea I've ever had."

"Self-care comes in many forms," I said. "I could probably get you sponsored by a funeral home for cats."

CHAPTER SEVEN

The House in Bethesda

There is a kind of house in and around D.C. that is very nice, very well kept, spacious, fully updated, and gorgeous from the street, but carries a horse-chokingly high price that still seems impossible to justify. When Molly and Pete had been looking, sometimes an app would send her one of these houses as a suggestion, and she would send it to me with a series of exclamation points under it.

Eliza Cassidy lived in this kind of house.

It wasn't convenient to public transit (they often aren't), so on Sunday morning, I took a cab. When the driver pulled into the driveway, he said, "House looks haunted." I tipped him, thanked him, and climbed out with my kit and my bag.

It did not look haunted to me, except maybe by capitalism. It was a great big colonial with a wide garage at the end of the driveway and a porch that spanned the front of the house and surrounded an elaborate entrance. The landscaping was all trimmed as precisely as a prize poodle, with a stretch of red flowers planted along the walkway to the front door. A black door knocker in the shape of a heart was surrounded by a dried-flower wreath. I knocked.

Eliza opened the door, and she looked the same as the first time I saw her, except without the ponytail and the cap. Yoga pants, slouchy sweatshirt, perfect makeup, instant smile. "Hi hi hi," she said. "Good morning! Come on in! Take off your shoes!"

This was the whitest house I had ever seen. Her entry and kitchen floors were white. Her walls and her fireplace were white. Her rugs were white. Her couches were white. Her accent color, used on a few pillows and a chair, was gray.

On one of the walls of the entrance hall, there was a wedding photo the size of a movie poster. On the wall opposite, she'd hung framed copies of three magazine covers on which she was featured. It was her very own Museum of the Self, an exhibit of her successes—greatest among them, her marriage. I suppose if you had a business based on your ability to, say, bake cakes, you might decorate with a picture of one of your towering creations covered with buttercream flowers and sculpted fondant.

"Let's sit in the nook," she said. "It's sunny in there." I had seen houses with breakfast nooks before, but I wasn't sure I'd ever heard anybody call one "the nook." We passed through her enormous kitchen—white, white, white, and white with white trim—to a light wood table with a bench on one side and chairs on the other. It was the nookiest nook I had ever seen, with giant windows that really did pour sun through the whole space. She picked up a remote, and a translucent blind whirred halfway down until we didn't have glare in our eyes. "Cool, huh?" she said with a little grin. She already had a French press of coffee sitting on the table. "Have a seat, I'll get some milk and stuff."

She came back and set down a little pitcher. "It's oat, I hope that's okay. I love oat milk. I used to like soy, and then I switched to almond, but I think oat is my favorite. Do you like oat?"

"Anything that makes it beige is fine," I said.

"I like your flexibility," she said as she poured two mugs of coffee and pushed one toward me. "So."

"Your house is really beautiful," I said. "I couldn't keep a house this clean if my life depended on it."

"Oh, I couldn't either," she said. "We have a team. They come in as soon as we leave for New York and they do everything, so by the time we get back, I feel like we're checking in to a hotel. I love it."

"Is it hard to keep everything like this? The white couches and stuff?"

She laughed and pushed her hair behind her ear on one side. "No pets, no kids, no shoes. And we don't drink anything in the living room but clear liquids. Only white wine indoors." She pointed at a wine fridge built into the kitchen island. "Red wine is only for outside on the deck."

My mind went to the time I had tripped in my own living room while holding a glass of merlot and a takeout container of baked ziti, both of which I then spent an hour cleaning out of the upholstery and the carpet. Was this how other people did it? Were they just made this way? It was hard to believe she had ever tripped over anything, with or without wine in her hands. "Well," I said, "it's all gorgeous."

"Thank you. Are you excited to get started?"

"I am," I said. "I'm nervous, but I figure you can't do any worse at this than I'm doing."

She nodded. "I'll tell you what I tell every client at the beginning of the process. I'm in your corner, I'm on your team, I'm with you. There's nothing wrong with wanting love. We all want love. I'm no different. I wanted love, and I worked hard to get it, and I did. I found somebody who shares my goals and affirms me and wants the same things out of life that I want."

Like a perfectly white living room that requires you to drink broth and apple juice like you're prepping for a colonoscopy, I did not say.

"People want to know what makes me the right person to do all this," she went on. "I just tell them: look around." She paused. She actually looked around. "And they get it. That's why I post a lot of pictures of me and Cody. It's why he's in my videos. That's why I'm everywhere on my site. We all are walking demos of whether what we're doing is working. And what I'm doing is working. Like I said, I'm not any more special than you are. You're a special person, I can tell. So I know it can work for you, too."

I could see over her shoulder into the hall. I could see her wedding picture. She was standing on the beach barefoot, her head thrown back laughing, lifting her skirt above the sand. Cody faced her, leaning toward her laugh, grinning with a champagne flute in one hand, ready to splash bubbles onto the ground. They weren't touching, but they looked joined by the laugh and the smile. I could see to the refrigerator, where more photos of them were hung with magnets—they were at dinner, they were at a party, they were with a bunch of other, less glamorous people. He was working out, she was working out, they were embracing.

"I'm ready," I said. "Let's do it." When I looked down at my coffee, I saw grounds floating on top. But nobody is good at everything.

As she led me up the wide staircase, she told me the house had five bedrooms, and I counted them in my head. There had to be a large primary suite in a house like this; a stand-up shower and double sinks, maybe a soaker tub, too, and probably his-and-hers skincare fridges. There would be a guest bedroom, although if I ever stayed in this house as a guest, I would have to wear a hazmat suit the whole time to avoid smudging anything. There had to be a gym. There had to be an office, a place she could park a laptop and go over sponsorship deals. That left one, and of course, it was the content studio.

It was a big room, bigger than the bedrooms in any house I'd lived in. The walls were a warm white, and on two sides they were covered in gray foam acoustic panels. Ring lights and softboxes were on stands in one corner, flanking a fat blue sofa I recognized from her YouTube videos. Over the sofa was a light-up sign in script that said CHOOSE YOU. A white desk sat near a window, with another set of lights nearby. There was a set of shelves behind the desk that had room for plants, a plaque she'd been sent for having so many followers, and a framed ECFitness logo. "I don't record everything here," she said. "I also sometimes use a studio over in Silver Spring. But I can do a lot without even leaving the house."

One corner was closed in with room dividers, and when I peeked in, there were two chairs. Two mics on stands. "That's the podcast studio," she said. "That's where I made mine when I had it," she said.

"But you stopped?"

"Yeah, it was Nowheresville compared to video, video's the future," she said flatly. "No offense."

"Oh, none taken," I said. "I wouldn't have lasted a week in this job if I got offended when people thought it was Nowheresville." Troublingly, Toby often said similar things, that video was the future, and I feared that this meant I would eventually be transported over to the blue sofa against my will. Away from my comfortable home in Nowheresville.

We settled into the tiny den. She had good mics that were sitting unused, so I plugged them into my recorder, put on my headphones, and checked our levels. She was much better at levels than Miles; she might have been a relative newbie, but she'd had enough experience with some real producer somewhere that she claimed to have had pizza, a parfait, and a shamrock shake for breakfast. I stopped talking and stopped breathing, and I turned up the volume in my headphones to make sure I couldn't hear a refrigerator, or an air conditioner, or a hum or a buzz or a whoosh or a hiss. I started rolling.

"Tell me your name and what you do." This was my go-to first question for anybody who was going to talk to me about their work. I wasn't sure what she would even list as her job until the words "I'm Eliza Cassidy, and I'm an author, a content creator, and a romantic life coach" came out of her mouth. It made her sound like she consulted on Valentine's Day gifts or planned dates for *The Bachelor.* Or, honestly, like she really was a sex coach.

"I'm not sure people know exactly what a romantic life coach is," I said.

"In my case, I work with women who want more love in their lives. I give them support and training to be the best version of themselves, and then I arrange some dates for them to help reset their idea of what kind of person might be right for them."

"Where do you find the men you arrange these dates with?"

"I have a network," she said. "That's where most of them come from. People I know, people I've worked with, people I meet at events. But I'll sometimes walk up to guys I see at the gym or while I'm out around the city. And then once I have the lead, I vet people before I do anything. They're all screened personally by me."

"And what are you screening for?"

"Qualities," she said. I kept looking at her, waiting for her to continue, name a few of these qualities. But she didn't. Instead, she said, "Now tell me who you are and what you do." It was effortless the way she turned it, like she was flipping a fish filet.

"My name is Cecily, I'm an audio editor and producer, and I live in D.C."

"Are you in a relationship?"

"I'm single."

"When did your last relationship end?"

"I broke up with my boyfriend about four years ago. I know that's a really long time. We'd been together for about five years. Since then, nothing I'd call a relationship."

"How about not-relationships? People you went out with more than once. When was the last time?"

"April. April fifteenth." Possibly I shouldn't have had that date at the very top of my mind, but there it was.

"And how did it end?"

Ben and I had been set up by a friend of his who worked at Palmetto. We'd gone out four times. He took me to an axe-throwing bar on our first date, and he was very good at axe-throwing, which I suppose impressed me, because you never know when you might need a guy who can kill a monster in a cartoon dungeon. Every time we went out, it was benevolent but weapons-adjacent—we played paintball with his friends, he tried to teach me archery, and we went to an exhibit of historical swords. I sensed a theme that wasn't quite right for me and was about to pull the plug, but on April 15 he announced that he didn't think we were well suited to each other. It was tax day, and he said paying his taxes always made him think about the future.

Here is what I said to Eliza: "He took me axe-throwing, and then he said he didn't think we were well suited to each other."

"Okay. Tell me about another one."

Keith, another one I had gone out with four times. This was a short story: He happened to catch me at a very stressful time at work, and I bored him to death talking about podcasts. The ones I worked on, the ones I didn't, the ways they should be better, the ways that the economic model was broken, the future of the industry. He had noticed, he said, that one of my main interests seemed to be discussing shows that would be better if I worked on them. I maintain, by the way, that every show I told him I could have improved, I in fact could have improved. He ghosted me. It's my fault I know how to cut interview tape?

I told her, "He was put off by my attachment to my job."

"Okay, who else?"

Molly had set me up with Logan. He had gone to college with

Pete. He was kind and smart, he was attentive and had interesting things to say, and we went out four times. But then we had sex, and I didn't enjoy sex with him at all. It wasn't some specific move that I was getting or that I wasn't getting. It was the whole thing; it was not sexy. I felt dutiful. Molly pleaded with me not to give up quite yet; she thought maybe I wasn't turned on by him because he was so nice, and if I gave it time, I'd get over my unmovedness. But I don't really believe in bad sex. If choosing to have sex with someone should give them confidence in anything, it should be that you are happy about it.

"I ended that one, just incompatibility," I said. "They're all like that. Just little things, things that don't work. It's happened a bunch of times."

"Okay. I get the gist. Tell me about the boyfriend."

I pretended to search my mind, like I barely remembered it.

When I was working in radio at a station in New York after college, Justin had the cube next to mine. We were both production assistants who had started as interns, and I would hear him on the phone trying to book interviews for pieces reporters were working on. He'd swear in frustration while he was cutting tape, which we all did, but he did it very softly and very creatively. One day he was having trouble with an edit, and I heard him say, "Oh, smack a wet turtle." I laughed, and he heard me from over the cube wall and apologized sheepishly. I called out that it was no problem, and then we were friends.

He'd come by my desk and linger, asking for help with his time card or our buggy digital publishing system. Or, as time went on, he would bring me a problem he was trying to solve in a story. Who to call, how to get them on the phone, how to recover a file he thought he might have lost. In my first real job, my one retail job, I'd been the only one who knew how to fix the register tape.

Now I was the only one who knew how to repair his corrupted files so he could import them.

It's tempting to say, in retrospect, that this was why he liked me or why we started dating, that he was taking advantage of me and letting me do his work for him. But we were well-matched in a way I'd never been with anyone. He was at ease with strangers, which I wasn't. I was detail-oriented and organized, which he wasn't. He wanted enormous things for himself, master-of-the-universe stuff I wouldn't have even been able to visualize. And back then, I knew how to put one foot in front of the other to get the next apartment, the next assignment, or the next ticket to the next show in a way that he was too impatient, too eager to stomp on the gas pedal already, to work out. And at the time, whatever we could hear in headphones was the whole world, to us both.

One night after work, we went to dinner, we got a little tipsy, I went back to his apartment, and then we were a couple. We were the same obsessives as always. We went to talks about the future of audio in the evening, we went to networking events, and we went to listening parties and launch parties for new shows, where he'd work the room while I stood by the bar and checked my phone.

When my lease ended, he asked me if I wanted to move into his apartment, which he complained constantly was too expensive and only getting more so by the day. I said yes. We both ended up getting laid off about a year later, and by then, Rob and Toby had started Palmetto down in D.C., and Rob recruited me. At around the same time, one of the D.C. news operations was ramping up its podcasting, and Justin managed to get a job with them, so we left New York and came down and got an apartment in Logan Circle.

One night when his brother was in town, the two of them were talking about how they couldn't get their dad, who was bored and in his late sixties, to give up his obsession with his police scanner.

He would sit for hours just listening to it, and whenever his sons called him, they'd end up hearing a series of tales about this neighbor who had a break-in, or this chase that went down the middle of the street near the bank.

After his brother had left, I was brushing my teeth in our bathroom while Justin played something noisy on the PS4, and I said, "I wonder if that's a show. The police scanner." And so we bought one.

Our idea was that each episode would spring from our own listening at our apartment. We would use something we heard as the beginning, and then we'd spin from there. We'd do it on our own time, so we could control it. And so we started, just the two of us, doing everything ourselves.

The more unimportant the story seemed, the more we loved finding the curious details. We split the work pretty evenly at first, but then he was promoted, and his day job took up more time. So I worked the most brutal schedule I'd ever worked in my life, doing a lot of the reporting on evenings and weekends, crisscrossing the neighborhoods of D.C. and Maryland and Virginia, talking to people about bar fights and domestic arguments and break-ins.

I hated my voice at the time. One voice coach wrote to me after I did an on-air story, insisting she could fix several things she said were wrong with it. In all the time I was working with Justin, nobody ever said anything about his voice at all.

So when we got serious about writing scripts and turning all the reporting for *Scanner Stories* into a show, we decided that he would be the host. *Scanner Stories* became, to the people who heard it, *Scanner Stories with Justin Dash*. And that was how it began. "This is *Scanner Stories*, I'm Justin Dash." It came out at the precise moment when the right combustible combination of audio weirdos and media nibbles could launch you into a surprising level of admittedly niche success, and that's exactly what happened. A year after we started, he was interviewed by *The New York Times*. I was not.

I feel compelled to explain how very much I loved him, and how very happy I was living with him, and how very confidently I assumed that we were going to get married and become the first couple of independent podcasting. Because if I don't explain that, it's impossible to explain why I allowed him to say in the credits, "Produced and edited by Justin Dash, with production help from Cecily Foster." He thanked his buddy who wrote the music, he thanked our friends who threw in a little bit of extra editing advice or engineering. And he thanked me. When I first saw his script, I wanted to tell him he could not say, "production help." I needed to be listed as the editor, not to mention a reporter; it had never occurred to me that I wouldn't be.

But I loved him very much, and I believed, in that way that you sometimes do when someone has nursed you through sickness and cheered you up on your worst days, that our successes inured to the benefit of us both. I believed we were standing together inside a small circle, and the benefits of this labor of love would puff into the air like flower petals and blanket us equally. There wasn't any reason to make a fuss about it.

The show grew. I wanted to take it to Palmetto, see if they could do anything with it, but Justin was adamant that we keep control of it. So we stayed independent, and we did about as well as you could do that way. By the time the third season started, Justin had created a new company called Dot Dash, complete with new business cards and a new logo made from two interlocked *D*s. But I was long gone by then, because it was at the end of making the second season that he had said, "I don't think I love you anymore."

I was numb when this happened, I was empty, I was lost. I felt like I was made of dried leaves that would crumble if touched. I wanted to get away from him, never think about him again, never remember him.

About a week after I moved out, he released a new episode we'd been working on. Published it by himself, put it out there, and that was it. And there was no part of me that had either the will or the ability to challenge his assumption that the show would go with him and not with me. We had no formal arrangement. I had kept working a day job to support us after he quit his job to concentrate on it. He had signed the contracts. He knew the business guys. To me, it had always been ours, but to him, it had always been his, and when it couldn't be ours anymore, I had lost before I even knew there was a fight to have. I was deleted from the best and most successful work I had ever done.

"Well, my longest relationship was with somebody I worked with. We were together for about five years. But it just didn't work out. We had worked together some, and that's always hard. But I'm not sure I have a specific explanation."

She nodded and clearly did not believe me, which admittedly was to her credit, since I was not telling the truth. "How did the end of that relationship affect you?"

"It was very difficult." There was a long pause that I resisted the urge to fill.

"Okay. Maybe we'll come back to it. Are your parents still together?"

"Mm, they're together-ish," I said. "They travel a lot. And these days, a lot of the time, it's not to the same places. But they end up back at home every time, so yes, I suppose they are still together."

"In terms of what's right for you, what are you looking for in a relationship? What does love look like?"

"I think I want a lot of the things that everybody wants, which is part of what makes it so hard. I want a sense of humor. Intelligence. Kindness. Some concern about the world. Some sense that he's passionate about things." *And not too much interest in weapons. And no self-referential tattoos. And don't get mad at me because I think about my job in the middle of the night.*

"Nothing for you?" she said.

"What do you mean?"

"Well, I asked you what love looks like to you, and you described a person. You said he would be funny, smart, kind, and passionate about things. But you didn't describe the relationship itself. You didn't say how he would treat you, or what being together would look like. Do you see what I mean? You described a person you see yourself loving, but not what it would look like for them to love you."

Well, hell. "I guess I want someone I can talk to," I said. "Someone I like spending time with who's interested in at least some of the same things I am."

"Okay. But that's also how you'd describe a friend, right?"

"In some ways."

"So how, specifically, do you want romantic love to feel when you're together? How do you want it to make *you* feel?"

I shifted in my seat. "Sexy."

"Okay, good start. What else?"

"Special. Happy."

"Safe?"

"Of course."

"Treasured?"

I winced. "That is a weird word. Valued, maybe."

"What's wrong with being treasured?"

"There's nothing wrong with it," I said. "It just makes me feel like a . . . shiny thing."

"You have a sister, right?"

"Yes."

"Would you say you treasure your sister?"

"Yes."

"Does that mean you're treating her like a shiny thing?"

"Well, no."

"Why is it okay for her to be treasured and not you?"

This—not just that she said it, but that I felt splayed open like a dissected frog and I was tempted to thank her—was the moment when I understood why Eliza Cassidy had a five-bedroom house in Bethesda and an apartment in Manhattan.

I left her house with about an hour and a half of tape, which I sent to Abby, who had worked on *Otter Tail* for Toby and knew all about what he was looking for. Two hours later, she wrote me back in the way only a terrific producer can: *She's great. It's boring in the parts where she's trying to get you to talk and you're stonewalling her, but she knows her stuff. Great talker. Looking forward to more.*

The next morning, I was on the bus to work when I saw a headline: *Is Audio Dead?*

It was just a clickbait headline, I told myself. It was an overreaction to normal amounts of contraction that followed any boom. But as I skimmed it for names I knew, I crashed into one sentence like a train into the side of a mountain. *Rumors of layoffs are particularly loud at Palmetto Media, which produced the very popular* Otter Tail *and* Cheats, *but has been struggling lately. "We desperately need a hit," said one Palmetto exec, noting that hopes are high for a project coming in the spring aimed at a younger female audience.*

Inside my head, a siren started to wail.

CHAPTER EIGHT

The Shopping Trip

I got to work.

Over the next week, I met with Eliza four times, with the producers three times, and with Toby twice—one of those was the meeting where we broke the news to Miles that Julie and I would both be gone soon. As I expected, nothing was more important to Miles than his uncrackable confidence that I did nothing but push a couple of buttons, so although he complained and grumped, he ultimately maintained that it was fine, he'd be fine, whoever Toby brought in would be fine. When it came time to let us go, his lack of respect for us worked to our advantage.

I got tape of every time Eliza and I met. I was a little relieved that Toby was too cheap to send a producer to follow me around everywhere I went at this stage, so I did the recording myself. We would chat in her little studio, or she would take me on a field trip. Despite her repeated reassurances that in no way was I getting a makeover as if I were a recently hatched ugly person or a prom-bound teenager in a movie, she did tell me she wanted me to "explore how I see myself." And to make that happen, we went shopping.

My budget was limited. I'd told Toby that whatever I bought was coming out of his pocket, so we ended up in one of the nicer department stores not far from the office. She'd told me that I should ask for more so we could hit up City Center, but given that the one-ply toilet paper felt harsher by the day, I didn't think the Kate Spade bag she wanted me to carry "for confidence" was in the cards.

"So," Eliza said as we started to wander through the racks, "what's your favorite thing about your looks?"

"Oh, yuck," I said. "Don't ask me that."

"Terrible answer," she said, skipping her fingers through a series of thin sweaters. "You have to know that's a terrible answer." She pointed at a mannequin wearing leather pants and a sequined top. "What are your thoughts about that?"

"I think the pants are still a couple of steps away on my particular journey."

She shrugged and went back to her rack. "Okay, try again. Favorite thing about your looks. Don't think about it. Don't qualify it. Just tell me."

"Well," I said, glad the recorder wasn't on, "I guess it's my eyes."

"Okay." She sighed. "But everybody says eyes. Everybody says eyes because it's just so neutral, you know? It's an eyeball. An eyeball is an eyeball. What's your second-favorite thing? Or wait—favorite thing from the neck down? Spit it out."

I looked down at myself. I lay one hand against my hip. "Hips," I said. "I like my hips."

"There you go," she said, looking over at me like I'd just won the school spelling bee. "That's a good answer. And I agree with you. You have a great shape. Very good proportion between your waist and your hips." I moved my hand over my belly, not realizing I was doing it until I'd already done it. "Tiny waists are overrated," she said. "You have a regular waist, but you have great hips. I want to show all that off." She plucked a deep green top and came over to me, holding it against my torso. "Good color for you," she said. "But it's too conservative."

"I would usually just wear maybe dark jeans and a nice sweater on a first date," I said.

She rolled her eyes until they almost disappeared into her skull. "I know."

I couldn't help it: I laughed.

She rejected a couple of things I chose, and since the real dates were going to take place in the last week of October and the first three weeks of November, I nixed everything without sleeves. But we finally agreed on a loose top that fell off one of my shoulders and a pair of pants that had just enough stretch to accommodate my newly emphasized hips without making me look and feel like a vacuum-sealed pork shoulder ready for a sous vide bath. Eliza looked great in precisely this kind of get-up, relaxed but sexy, giving an impression of perhaps having sung a tune while having her clothes maneuvered onto her body by a group of especially muscular cartoon bluebirds. I was less confident that I could pull it off.

We bought a pair of modest heels and a thick cuff bracelet, and that used up all the money I had. I was now bewitched, bothered, and bedazzled, and she pronounced me ready to start with the "dummy date," which she had arranged for early the next week.

We headed back to her house in her black SUV, and she took me upstairs, told me to wash my face, and sat me at the makeup table in the content studio. "So," she said, "I'm going to show you a basic look, and I want you to try to replicate it on your date. All these products are new, so I'm going to give them to you when we're done, so you'll have everything you need."

I hesitated. "This is really sneaking right up on makeover territory, you know. When I am the 'she,' I fear she will never actually be 'all that.' "

Eliza just sighed dreamily. "Ohhhh, I love that movie. My older sister was obsessed with it. She must have made me watch it a hundred times."

"Mm, this is all starting to make sense."

"Is there anything you want to talk about before this date next week?" she asked.

"Dummy date," I said. "Before this dummy date."

"Well, don't say that to him," she said. "To him, I said it was a practice date. Maybe you'll like him. Maybe he'll like you. It's fine if you hit it off. I just want you to think of it as practice, because it's going to take the pressure off. He's just the first pancake."

I frowned. "Clarify."

"You always have to throw out the first pancake. Right into the trash."

"Who throws out pancakes?"

"I'm making a point. You deserve the best," she said. "Don't settle. Throw out the pancake. The next one will be better."

"How bad do you think first pancakes are? Wait, do you even eat pancakes? Not paleo pancakes or whatever, but real actual pancakes made of food?"

"Okay, fortunately I need you to close your mouth, because I'm going to work on your face." She smoothed things over my cheeks. She puffed me with powders. I had to close my eyes, open them, look down, look up. When she was finally done, she put one finger under my chin. "You look gorgeous," she said. And then she clapped her hands. "Oh my God, come with me." And she got up and ran out of the room. I had no idea what could be urgent at all, let alone this kind of urgent, but I followed her out of the studio, downstairs, and through a door into the kitchen that led into the garage. She'd left it standing open, and when I found her, she was standing in front of ceiling-high shelving that was packed with cardboard boxes. She'd flipped on an overhead light and was scanning them, looking for something.

"Where are we?" I said, looking around.

"Swag room," she said. "Companies send me stuff."

"Stuff" was beyond an understatement. I walked over toward the shelves and saw package after package she'd gotten from makeup brands, clothing brands, booze bottlers, TV networks, movie studios, and even a sports-car manufacturer, who'd sent her a squishy plastic envelope with a red convertible printed on the outside. "There's not a car in there, is there?" I asked, pointing.

She looked over and shook her head. "No, that's their athleisure stuff. They did a collab with whatever that company is that does the shirts with the holes and the . . . anyway, it's clothes." Eliza seemed to find what she was looking for, and she pulled out a box, tore off the packing tape, and swung the flaps open. Inside was a luscious black leather bag from a brand I had never expected to own in my life. I was pretty sure this bag alone, sitting in its packaging, was worth something like two months of my rent. She pushed it toward me. "Here, this is perfect."

"Oh, I can't," I said. "I'll worry the whole time about returning it with hummus on it or something."

"Well, you're not returning it," she said. "It's yours, enjoy."

I stared down at it. "You can't give me this, Eliza, it's way too much."

"Sure I can," she said. "They just sent it to me. I have one almost exactly like it, so I don't need it. I'll take your picture, and when the episode comes out, I'll post it on my Insta and talk all about how I knew this bag was perfect for your big night. Which is true. They'll be thrilled, believe me."

I touched the soft sides of the bag. Opened and closed the zipper by its not-subtle branded pull. "Thank you," I said. "This is really nice of you."

"You are so welcome," she said. "Thank you for taking it off my hands."

I knew she probably could have sold it secondhand or something, but for reasons of her own, she wanted me to take it, carry it, maybe see what it felt like to be the woman who belonged to this bag.

I put it on my shoulder, felt the weight of it, nodded. "Any final advice?" I asked.

She shrugged. "Just be open. And don't blow it."

CHAPTER NINE

The Dummy Date

Eliza had instructed me to show up at 7:36 for a 7:30 date ("You are not a flake," she had said, "but you are not instantly available"), so I met Julie outside Madeline's, the quiet bistro where this date was scheduled, right at 7:30 for our pregame chat.

Toby had agreed to pay for a car, and as I got out, I heard Julie whistle. "You look great," she said appreciatively. She reached out with one finger and tapped my exposed collarbone. "Va-va-voom." I crinkled up my face in response, and she laughed. "Oh, for God's sake, learn to take a compliment, would you? Thank you for wearing something with pockets." She clipped the lav mic to my neckline.

"I wish we weren't doing lav mics," I muttered. "I hate the sound."

"It's not ideal," she acknowledged. "But this is what we're doing, unless you want me to sit there with my headphones on directing a footlong shotgun mic at the middle of your date. Or were you planning to interview him with a handheld like a sideline reporter at the Super Bowl?" She ran the wire down my shirt.

She connected it to the transmitter, which I slipped into my pocket. "We're making it work. It's going to be fine." She stopped cold and touched the bag I was carrying.

"Is this real?"

I nodded. "Gift from Eliza. You should see the free stuff she gets. I saw a collection of lipsticks so big they sent it in a cardboard suitcase. She hasn't even opened it."

"Must be nice," Julie said. "Okay, Andrew's waiting, and he's already wired." She slipped on her headphones, and we checked levels. "Okay, so how are you feeling about this date? Are you optimistic?"

"I think I'm mostly curious. I have no idea who Eliza thinks is the right guy, but I guess that's what we're going to find out."

"Are you worried that he'll be the wrong guy?"

"Uh . . . yes."

She asked me a few other basic questions, and I answered them as naturally as I could with a microphone attached to me, and then she said, "I think that's all we need. You ready?"

"Yes. You're rolling?" I said. She pointed to the bag over her shoulder. "You're going to be listening?" She pointed to her headphones. "What if—"

She raised her eyebrows. "What if what?"

"What if he doesn't like me?"

Julie put her hand on my elbow. "Well, then, he'll be the star of an episode about what a goober he is. Just go have dinner."

I walked into Madeline's. We didn't just have a reservation, we had a table Julie had prearranged so the recording would go smoothly. The quietest spot they had, by a wall and far from the windows, which could bounce the sound and make the recording sound hollow. Julie was set up a couple of tables away, doing her best to be inconspicuous.

A woman in a smart white shirt and a black skirt walked me to a table in the back, where a man in dark pants and a pale blue button-down was already working on a glass of red wine, with the bottle on the table. He had the facial symmetry and the perfectly shaped dark hair of a Lego prince. He stood as I approached.

"Cecily," he said in the enthusiastic timbre I felt like the city was full of: the eagerness of the real estate agent or the representative of the American Association of Toe Surgeons. "It's so good to meet you, I'm Andrew." He leaned over and kissed my cheek, which made me very self-conscious about just how loud that tiny smooch was in the mic.

I breathed in and said to myself, *Be open;* I breathed out and said to myself, *Don't blow it.* "It's good to meet you, Andrew." I sat down across from him. "What are you drinking?"

"Cabernet," he said. "I tell myself the antioxidants make it healthy." And he winked. One significant limitation of an audio presentation of a blind date was going to be the inability to expose a prodigious winker.

I briefly considered saying, out loud, *That's a nice wink you have there,* but of course, I didn't. *Be open, don't blow it.* "Have you been here before?"

He shook his head. "Nah. It's nice, though. Wine?" I nodded, so he poured me a little less than what was in his own glass, to which he then added a little more. This was a man pouring wine someone else was paying for.

"So obviously, you sort of know what I do," I said. "What do you do?" I hated this question. Everybody hated this question. But everybody asked it.

"I work for GAZ-3; I'm in sales."

I was glad that I had my glass in front of my face, because it offered me at least a little bit of cover. What I knew about GAZ-3 was that mostly it ran ads on podcasts I didn't like. I understood it to be a manufacturer of supplements that did things like "sharpen your productivity" and "build muscle" and "provide energy so you can go all day." They weren't supplements like "your erection will grow by leaps and bounds" or supplements like "the heavy metal toxicity is how you know it works" or anything like that. They were just supplements. And he sold them to people.

"Oh, cool," I said as I picked up the menu and looked for something not overly expensive that I could eat neatly. Eliza had a whole thing about eating neatly. *Nobody wants to watch another person eat pasta on a first date,* she had said. *I can't tell you how few people know how to eat spaghetti without looking revolting.* We'd been out for lunch when she told me this, and I was eating spaghetti. And so, of course, she added, *No offense.*

I was just trying to picture myself knife-and-forking a club sandwich when a voice came from beside us. "Are you ready to order?" I looked up at him. He looked down at me. "Oh," he said. "Hi."

"Hi," I said.

"You know each other?" Andrew said.

"We do," Will picked up. "Cecily and I live in the same neighborhood."

"That's right," I said. "Andrew, this is Will." I paused. "He rescues dogs."

"Oh, that's great," Andrew said. He turned to me. "You know, I'm allergic to dogs. Have been since I was a kid. We had a golden retriever, and I broke out in rashes constantly. Come to think of it, that's how I got started on echinacea."

I didn't hear the rest. I was looking up at Will, who was smiling, not unkindly. It was and is my firm belief that most men look very good in a clean, pressed white shirt, and he was, it turned out, the rule, not the exception. The man with half a haircut I had first seen running after a dog with a plastic cape flapping over his shoulders was now close-shaven, with his curls in perfect order. His shoulders broke precisely at the seams of his shirt. I realized suddenly that I was gazing at him, and gazing at someone else while on a date was bad. Even I knew that. I would not like it if a guy did it on a date with me. *Stop gazing,* I told myself, while still doing it.

Andrew broke the spell himself. "I'm going to have the chicken breast, but just poached plain, please," he said. "And with a side of the broccolini and a side of spinach. No salt." It sounded like hospital food without the hospital, and I wondered if he had a medical thing, until he handed his menu to Will and turned to me. "Salt destroys compounds," he said. Oh boy.

"I'm going to have the spaghetti Bolognese," I said, handing over my menu as well. I might as well order what I wanted, given that it was already quite clear that while I had never in the past been the type of person to throw a pancake in the trash, there was a first time for everything.

It was only as Will was walking away that the full significance of this settled on me. He'd not only walked up on my date, but he'd walked up on my date while Andrew and I both had microphones strapped to us, which Julie had probably already explained to him as part of her prep.

The next part of the date was a blur. I tried to dig my smile out of the recesses of my personality. I tried to concentrate, for the sake of the tape I wanted to get. But mostly, I tried in vain to find anything Andrew wanted to talk about that I also wanted to talk about, and I failed over and over. I tried all the basics and some of the conventional icebreakers Eliza had endorsed—favorite book, favorite movie, last vacation you took—but nothing stuck.

Mostly, Andrew wanted to talk about deals he was closing, YouTube channels he liked for finance advice, and the gym. At one point, he whipped out his phone and showed me a picture of himself, shirtless, standing in front of a weight bench. In the time I had spent on various apps, I had seen probably a hundred photos exactly like it. "Ah," I said when he showed it to me. "Sure." What else was I supposed to say? He also showed me pictures of himself on a sailboat with some of his friends, all of whom looked like the guys you might see on TikTok downing energy drinks with dragons on the labels and complaining about feminists and seed oils.

Will walked up with our plates and I lunged for mine, eager to stuff food into my mouth and even more eager for Andrew to stuff food into his. "Do you need anything else?" he asked.

"No, this looks great," Andrew said.

It made for a long dinner, learning quite that much about Andrew's gym routine. It didn't get better when he shifted gears to his opinions about crypto—he was a skeptic about it, which I later realized surprised me mostly because of his hair. Unfortunately, his skepticism was no more interesting than evangelism would have been. I fell asleep behind my eyeballs as soon as I heard the word, like I had been hypnotized to cluck like a chicken when someone said "long division." I nodded, I smiled, I ate. I watched Will walk by and waited for him to walk by again.

Once dinner was over, I wanted to discuss the epic flop that was Andrew with Julie, but she had interviews to wrap up. I didn't even get a chance to tell her that Will was the dog guy. She told me to go home and have a drink, and she'd do the wrap-up interview with Andrew and whatever else she thought would help. Tomorrow, Eliza and I would debrief at the studio. By then Eliza would have had a chance to hear the tape, and she would give me my . . . grade? Evaluation? Action plan? She would give me whatever she was going to give me. I handed Julie my mic, she tucked it into her kit, and I walked home in my uncomfortable shoes.

The next day, I met Eliza in the studio at Palmetto. She told me that I hadn't done as badly as she thought I might, based on the tapes, and she acknowledged that Andrew and I didn't have a lot in common. She insisted she hadn't really vetted him, so the twenty other dates would be better, and she already had some of them lined up. She also promised that it was a coincidence and not some kind of undisclosed synergy that he worked for GAZ-3; she didn't even know they did podcast sponsorships when she picked him.

When we were finished, I sat next to Julie at a desk in one of the editing rooms. She pulled up a document on the screen. "So this is my skeleton of a script for this early promo Toby wants," she said. "You said you want to write the intro. Let's say that's ninety seconds. Then you have your open, 'This is Cecily Foster, this is blah blah blah,' we'll fill in the name of the show when Toby figures out what it is. The first segment will be you and Eliza from when you were at her house. I want to use her talking about her job, you talking about some of your history."

I nodded slowly. "Right. Okay."

"That segment is, what, five minutes, probably. Then we'll have a break. Then we have some more about Eliza, who she is, what she does. Abby's been getting that tape from some people who know her, a couple of her clients. She talked to the husband."

"Oh, how was that?"

"She said 'shy but nice.' Anyway, that's probably another five. I'm going to assign Abby to help with your script, although obviously you can do as much of it yourself as you want. Then another break, and then the last ten minutes or so will be about the date with Andrew. We have the pregame we did with him and the one we did with you, then the date itself. Then we had Eliza record comments while she listened back to it, so we have that, and then obviously the conversation she had with you this morning. We're aiming for twenty-five-ish minutes total." A few years ago, Palmetto would have put one break in an episode that long; now we were more likely to have two if the ad guys could sell the space.

"It sounds like a plan," I said.

"Good." She leaned back in her chair. "I think it's going to be great."

"Of course it's going to be great," I said. "We're going to make it great."

"Now we just have to do the 'make it' part," she said.

We only had about three weeks before the preview episode

was supposed to go out. With everything else we were doing, it would take a few days to write a final script. A couple more to track it and lay it up so people could listen to it. A couple more to send it around to Toby and to whoever else's ears Toby wanted to hear it. Then legal, and partnerships, and probably Marcela, too. There would be notes. Then we'd have final edits, and it would be what it would be. It wasn't nearly as much time as I would have liked, but people made things work with less.

For the next ten days straight, weekends and weekdays alike, I was at my desk by 7:30 in the morning. I did my regular work until lunchtime—whatever Toby had emailed about or dropped on my desk or tapped me on the shoulder to ask for, because it wasn't as if my taking on this enormous project meant he didn't need me for anything else. I dropped in on editing sessions for other shows when Melissa or one of the other PAs had a problem, or I resolved conflicts on Slack between those same two guys from that same two-guy show, who still had weekly arguments that were officially not about the woman they had in common.

The afternoons were for the Eliza show, which Toby still hadn't named, and for spending a lot of time with Julie, and with Abby and Charlie. I helped fact-check Eliza's biography and everything she had ever said about herself—which had all turned out to be true. Charlie took the lead on the fact-checking of everything I had ever said about myself. He even talked to two of those guys I briefly dated whom I'd mentioned to Eliza, and they agreed that as long as we didn't use their last names, they didn't care if my truthful but elided versions of our breakups were included in the episodes. Yes, it was true that I had talked too much about podcasts. Yes, it was true that we had gone axe-throwing.

I wrote the intro.

I have been looking for the same person for a long time. As long as I can remember. I knew I needed to find him. I knew it was important. And it weighed on me that he might be looking for me, too.

Like a lot of people who want to solve mysteries, I have thought a couple of different times that I had cracked it. I thought I spotted him singing a Nickelback song with his friends in the talent show at Camp Sunfish when I was in seventh grade. That wasn't him. I thought I saw him in my bio class in a Mets jersey and a backward baseball cap when I was sixteen. That *really* wasn't him. And I was sure that I saw him walking next to me on the Brooklyn Bridge in April of 2017, and dancing with me at my sister's wedding, and making me coffee in our apartment while I read a book on our couch. But it turned out that wasn't him, either. So I'm still looking.

There are private detectives who specialize in helping you find someone who slipped away from you in a crowd or left your life decades ago. There are people whose job it is to try to locate the person you've been looking for, even if it's someone whose name you don't know. Someone you've never met, who you can't track down on your own. You don't have a picture of them or a letter from them. You only know they exist because so many other people have managed to find them. The people you envy because they're not looking anymore. But I am still looking. And Eliza Cassidy thinks she can help me stop.

It came out to exactly ninety seconds.

When Toby heard the first draft of the preview episode, he wanted, he said, more of a kicker. Something fun to end on, something that would make people smile and get really excited about the show. He sent Julie on a quest for just the right thing—the kind of assignment you can only pray doesn't turn into a Sisyphean "go find something; no, not that" battle that stretches for days. On a Thursday night at about 9:00, two weeks before the episode was supposed to go out, she asked me to come over to her desk. When I got there, she handed me her headphones.

"I think I finally, *finally* found the kicker," she said. "Toby actually said yes to something, so I hope you like it, too. This was an extra little bit of tape we got at the restaurant right before we left, check it out." She hit her space bar, and the playhead started to move.

`Yeah, it seemed okay. It seemed like your basic date. They talked. He talked, mostly. But, uh, I'm not going to lie. I'm not sure there's a future for a woman like that with a guy who doesn't salt his food, you know?`

I turned slowly to face her. "And that's . . ."

"It's your waiter," she said. "He was really funny, and he's so cute."

I hadn't told her that Will was the dog guy, because it didn't seem to matter, or maybe because I wanted it not to matter. And now I couldn't tell her, because if I complicated this choice after Toby had approved it, she'd have to go looking for an alternative.

So I just nodded. "Sure, that's great." *A woman like that,* he had said. What kind of woman, exactly?

CHAPTER TEN

The Photographer

Eliza wanted me to get new pictures. She was in the process of lining up all my first dates, and while Toby required me to know nothing about them until I met them, she needed my photo and bio in order to get them to agree to show up and be recorded.

She said the pictures needed to be "unassuming" but still make me look "like a wow," which seemed unlikely, but I wasn't the expert. The pictures I had were a couple of years old, and in them, I was wearing my most pensive stare, the one I thought would befit a serious journalist. "These make me want to cry," she had moaned, flipping through them. "You look so sad." I had indeed been a little sad, but that wasn't what she meant. I was pretty sure that to her, "sad" meant something like "unlikely to want a margarita." The photographer she had in mind was in the Czech Republic at the moment, but he'd passed her the name of a friend he promised would do a great job.

She slipped me the address of a photo studio and a time to show up, and she gave me strict instructions: three outfits, black or bright colors, no "clown makeup." ("Thanks for the confidence," I had said, but she didn't react.) She sent me to a salon for a blowout of my shoulder-length hair, which left it stiff and resilient but with the illusion that it might bounce if provoked.

I ran late in part because I was editing an interview in which Miles had needed eight takes to pronounce his subject's name correctly, and by the time I was near the photo studio, I was alternating between swearing and checking my watch, the latter made more difficult by the garment bag I was carrying over my left arm. I first mistook a 6 for an 8 and wound up standing in front of a walk-in medical clinic wondering if my dating photo was going to be an MRI. I eventually found the right number, and pressed a button that read CHERRY TREE STUDIO. The door buzzed.

Hauling both the garment bag and the Beast, I stepped inside and took a dimly lit hallway to the elevator. I looked down at my phone again. "Fourth floor," I muttered, and pushed the button. "I can probably get to the fourth floor without getting lost." I stepped off into a loft space with polished concrete floors and high ceilings.

I had imagined so many things in this studio—bright lights, ugly backdrops, and most of all, myself, attempting unsatisfactorily to smile warmly and being sent home with a note that said, "Perhaps a conceptual drawing would be better." What I was not prepared for was to be bumped for the second time in a month by the enormous head of a black-and-white dog whose nose brushed my waist. "How many of you are there?" I muttered to him as I rubbed his velvet ears. But then I stepped back from him. "Gideon?" I said.

"Buddy!" came a voice from elsewhere in the space, and then Will came around a corner and was walking toward me. When we were facing each other, he raised his eyebrows. "Cecily."

"Will," I said, because it was the only thing I could think of. I watched as he handed a chew to Buddy, who took it from him and decamped to an enormous bed in one corner to begin wetly devouring it. Will turned back to me. He had a smile like a lazy afternoon; it made my shoulders unclench.

"Hi," he said.

"I have so many questions," I said.

He looked at his phone. "My booking just says 'Foster,'" he said.

"That's me."

"I hope so."

"My card just says 'Cherry Tree Studio.' This place is yours?"

He looked around. "Oh, no, are you kidding? I just rent studio space."

"You're a photographer," I said, nodding slowly.

"I hope so," he repeated with a grin.

"Well, this is . . . unexpected." I pointed to the dog. "I thought his name was Gideon."

"It was. It's Buddy now. I changed it."

"You changed it?" I said.

"Well," he said, "after you saved him from the streets and I found out about his rescue, I called a couple more times to make sure he was doing okay. They told me that somebody left him there a few weeks ago, because he had some vet bills that his people couldn't pay, and they were getting evicted on top of that, so they'd had to let him go. The rescue had been working on him, getting him healthy, and they said he was probably ready to rock and roll. They said he was going to be a great dog for somebody. I think it was a hint."

I nodded slowly. "And you adopted him."

"I guess I've always wanted a dog who could push a Honda uphill in an ice storm." He looked fondly over at Buddy, who at the moment was making noises like a wet-vac trying to pick up maple syrup as he went to town on whatever it was Will had given him to chew on.

"In an emergency where he couldn't push the car, you could probably ride on his back."

"Or," he said, "I could sit on a trash can lid and let him pull me." He mimed putting a rope in his teeth. This was hard to reconcile with how cool and serious he'd seemed at Madeline's, but in a good way.

"So," I said. "Here we are."

"Yes," he said. "So, you need pictures. What can you tell me about what they're for?"

"Just personal stuff," I said. "I think my producer talked to you about the thing, the show, when she interviewed you at the restaurant? It's kind of connected to that."

"Ah," he said. "Sure. You're the dating guinea pig."

"Yeah, I guess."

"You want to use the pictures for anything else?"

"Don't know," I said. "Maybe for my work bio, different projects. My FBI file. A T-shirt with my face on it for my mother."

"Ah, sure. My family settles for phone calls, but I get it," he said. He took the garment bag from me and laid it down on a table. He stepped back, and I became extraordinarily aware of my physical body in a way I usually wasn't except at the doctor. He gave me a quick once-over, which was mercifully much less thorough than when the dermatologist checked me for moles, even if I felt almost as exposed. I was in a lightweight black sweater and dark jeans, which Eliza likely would have wanted me to describe as a gossamer onyx pullover and traditional navy laborer's pants. "This will work," he declared.

Having a man with his particular brand of angular attractiveness check me out and say, matter-of-factly, "This will work," is the kind of thing that could have become a recurring nightmare that would wake me up screaming. It was like having your stylist walk around the chair examining your hair from every angle, cutting stray strands, rearranging it, and then saying, "I guess."

I looked around the studio at the lights and the stools, and at the cords crisscrossing the floor where umbrellas on stands competed for space with a lot of equipment I didn't fully recognize. "I should tell you I'm not photogenic at all."

He leaned backward and gave an exaggerated moan, and it

made me laugh. He started futzing with a camera. "Oh, 'I'm not photogenic,' 'I look terrible in pictures,' 'I hate my face.' Every day with this. And I'll tell you what: It's never somebody with a squid for a head or a full set of cat whiskers or something. It's just regular people heckling themselves." He looked back at me. "Besides, you don't have to be photogenic. A good picture is my job, not your job. You're going to be great. The restroom's that way if you want to touch anything up, and then I'll see you back out here."

The restroom in the hall was small, but it had a mirror and a shelf. I took out my brush and tried to neaten my expensive hair without destroying it. I added a bit more lipstick and checked to make sure there was none on my teeth. No bra straps showing? Check. No obvious makeup smudges? Check. Nothing in my nose? Check. I looked at my reflection. It wasn't terrible; Justin used to casually call me "beautiful," like, "hey, beautiful," and although I didn't take him literally (he also called my mother "young lady"), he used to touch my cheek and I could see his eyes skitter around from my forehead to my eyes to my mouth, and I believed it a little then.

But I had been avoiding pictures—not strictly, but when I could—for most of my life. I lined up obediently for family photos when Molly and I were little, wedging in next to her, looking shorter and shorter beside her as she shot up and I didn't. But around sixth grade, I started looking at myself in the mirror every morning and seeing my bad skin, along with what I was certain were my weird nose, my blotchy cheeks, and my dull eyes. I was happier not thinking about it, so when cameras—and then phones—came out, I would offer to take the picture, or I'd say I didn't feel well, or I'd just sit off to the side consumed by something else. Even in Molly's wedding pictures, I had been sure the one-shoulder dress made me look lopsided. Standing next to her friends, I felt stubby and flawed. Molly framed a picture of us from that day and gave it to me, but I couldn't bear to hang it, because every time I looked at myself standing next to her in the gorgeous halter dress she chose, I felt like the off-brand version of her.

I took several deep breaths. *It was for work,* I told myself. *It was for work, it was for a job, it was for a story. They're barely even pictures of me. They're just part of the story.* I stepped out, back into the loft. "Okay," I said. "I'm ready, I guess."

"That's the spirit," he said. He had pulled a stool in front of a gray background that rolled down from a bar. "Have a seat." He stepped back and looked through the lens of a camera on a tripod. "Great, this looks great." He came back over to me. "Turn a little to your right. That's your left. Your right—no, your whole—"

I leaned over with my elbows on my knees. "I knew I was going to be bad at this."

"Hm. Would you rather I move you around a little? I really think you can do it if you just relax. But if you want to go puppet-style, I can do that."

"You can just do it," I said. "It will be faster."

He stepped toward me and put his hand on one side of my knees to rotate me to the right. "I'm going to turn you a little bit this way." He held one finger up. "Then turn your head so you're looking here." He put his finger under my chin and nudged it up. "This is what I'm looking for. As far as the angle."

I was caught off-guard by the feeling of his hand barely brushing my skin, and I said, exactly: "Oop." Now I was focused on not blushing, which would probably make me blush, which would make me look like I had an uneven sunburn.

He kindly pretended I hadn't made a weird noise out of nowhere. "You're going to look right at me," he said. "People angle down because they think it's flattering, the eyes-up selfie thing, but just, straight at me is right." He stepped back behind the camera, and then I started to hear clicks.

"I wasn't ready," I said.

"I'm just doing a lighting test. Don't worry." He looked at the back of the camera. "Okay, good. Now. Without really smiling, like *cheeeeese,* think about the best meal you ever ate."

"What if it was cheese?"

He looked over the top of the camera at me. "Was it cheese?"

"No." I thought about a tapas place in D.C. I'd gone to with Molly. They had kept bringing and bringing beautiful food as we nodded eagerly at each other with every first bite.

"Okay, doing great," he said. "Chin up a little more again. More toward me. Okay, let's try some smiling ones."

I made my best effort at the very difficult task of smiling naturally on command. "Tell me if I look like the Joker," I said through my tight lips.

"I promise you don't look like the Joker," he said. "I would tell you if you did. For my own safety." He looked at me over the camera. "You look great. You're doing great." I sat on the stool and he clicked and clicked, and he told me "Turn toward me," and "Half as much smile," and most of all, several times, he said, "Chin up a little." It was something my mom used to say to cheer me up—"chin up, honey"—and it sounded funny, but good, coming from him.

He moved over to one side. He moved to the other side. He told me to try not looking into the camera, and my first thought was to slide my eyes up and look at the ceiling as if it were about to fall on us, which made him laugh. "Okay, no smile." "Big smile." "Look over at Buddy." "Look back at me." Once, he said, "Do this," and he exhaled a floppy-lipped trill like a siren. I imitated him. "You're doing awesome," he said.

He had me shrug my shoulders up to my ears and then drop them. He had me close my eyes and then pop them open. He told me to make the funniest face I could think of. He told me to look as serious and pretentious as possible. Finally, he clapped his hands. "Okay, I'm happy with that. You want to go try the next thing you brought to wear?"

I stood. “Sure,” I said. As I picked my way past him, avoiding cords and stands and lights, I said, “I’ll be right back.”

“You are perfectly photogenic, by the way,” he said as I passed. “My view’s better than yours.” I hurried off to change so he wouldn’t see me turn bright red.

When I was in my deep green sweater, he took me over to one of the big windows. “Okay,” he said. “I want to do some over here. There’s lots of natural light but it’s not too harsh and sunny, so this should be good.” It was a padded bench that was pushed against the wall perpendicular to it. I sat. “Make sure the sun isn’t actually in your eyes,” he said.

“How many times have you done this?” I said as he changed his lens and set up a reflector.

“Headshots? A lot.”

“How long have you been doing it?”

“Informally, a long time. Here in D.C., a couple of years.”

“What did you do before that?”

“That is a long story,” he said. “Okay, don’t think about the camera, just think about the window. We’re going for something more casual here, a little less official-looking. Little bit of a smile.”

He moved around a little with the camera in his hand, higher then lower, a little closer, then a little farther away. There wasn’t all that much to do but look directly at him. Most of what I could see of him was his curly hair, which had a pleasingly unkempt quality even though I, as it happened, knew exactly when he had last had it cut. I could see his black shoes, and wrapped around his camera were good hands, nicely kept hands.

He had me look out the window, then back at him. I looked past him, over his shoulder. I looked above him. I looked off to the side quizzically, even though it made me feel like I was posing for a severe black-and-white picture to go with a story announcing that I had solved a murder. I got antsy and got up to shake myself all over, so he also shook himself all over, and then I sat back down. Buddy walked over, so he took a picture of me and Buddy, my mouth open like I was shocked at his size.

When we finished the window pictures, he just stood there fussing with the camera. "Am I getting changed?" I finally asked.

"Yes," he said. "Yes." He froze, focused on his hands.

"Is everything okay?"

He looked up at me. "Sometimes I just like a moment. You know?"

I wanted to be able to say yes. I wanted to tell him I was trying to figure out how to have that feeling, or maybe relearn how to have it. But I said, "It's not easy."

"No," he said. "It's not."

The last outfit I had brought was a cream-colored shirt and a brown canvas moto jacket. He led me up a cramped stairwell and out a door that opened onto the roof of the building. Surrounded by aluminum railings and littered in only one corner with beer cans, it had views in all directions. I whistled softly.

"Has its moments, right? The city?"

"It does," I said. "I get wrapped up in everything, you know?"

"Yeah. I'm temporary here, so I soak it up when I can."

"Why temporary?"

"Oh, I came here for a relationship that didn't work out. I'm just here until my lease is up, and then, whatever, who knows. In the meantime, at least there are a lot of nice people." He looked down at the camera and then back up at me. "You know, people who help strangers by having peanut butter at exactly the right moment."

"People who chase dogs for ten blocks that aren't even theirs." We were looking at each other now, and the city blurred behind him, and I felt a little warmer.

He nodded. And then he put one hand on the back of his neck. "I'm talking way too much."

Not for me he wasn't. I had once wound up sitting in a corner with a relative stranger at a friend's New Year's Eve party and ended up explaining to her why I considered *Midnight Run* a romantic comedy. She got up to get a cocktail and I never saw her again. Justin had called me The Opinionator. "Not at all," I said. "Just the right amount."

He smiled, and I felt it. *Zing*. It had been an awfully long time since my last *zing*. And then he said, "Okay. Okay, we're not done. Back to work."

He had me lean against the railing on one elbow with the city sprawled behind me, and when he picked up the camera, suddenly I was self-conscious again. "Okay, these are going to be the most relaxed ones we do," he said. "Just look wherever you like for now." I fixated on a church spire in the distance. "Okay, you look a little tense, blow a raspberry." I did. He kept shooting.

I heard a siren and looked down over the railing. "Aha! There it is," he said, and the camera kept going.

"Wait, I was distracted," I said.

"Exactly," he said. "Some people are most themselves when they're very interested in something else," he said. "Look over my right shoulder and tell me what you're looking at, then take three breaths and do it again. I'll tell you when to stop."

"I'm looking at an office building that's probably half-empty but once had a bunch of, I don't know, tobacco lobbyists in it," I said. *One, two, three.* "I see a bunch of police cars at an intersection, so there's probably an accident. People speed like crazy on that street." *One, two, three.* "I can see some of the streets that are overrun when the cherry blossoms are out." *One, two, three.* He had stopped telling me to relax my shoulders, to relax my face. He had maybe stopped needing to tell me.

We switched to me looking over his left shoulder, we tried a couple of other spots against the railing, and then he began to pack up. "You did great," he said. "I think you'll end up with some really nice ones you can use for your work or, you know, whatever you need." He looked at me and smiled. "So tell me more about this show you're making."

"Ah, right," I said. "That."

"I've never even heard of a dating coach."

"Well, it's a work thing. It's about self-help, I have this woman working with me, she's setting me up on all these blind dates, she's like a one-woman dating app. I mean, normally, this is not what I do. Normally, I'm a producer."

"What do you work on?"

"I've worked on a lot of things. I did *The Perspective* with Miles Banfield." He did not react. "I sometimes step in on a couple of others, *Dear Wendy* and this show *President Hottie.*"

He squinted. "What is *President Hottie*?"

"Oh, I'm so glad you asked. You know *Halls of Power*? The show with all the political people having sex and getting murdered?"

"I may have seen it once or twice. Or binged it at my sister's house when I was getting over the flu."

"Okay. It's a recap show of that. So they run down every episode and sometimes they interview the cast and stuff."

"That sounds fun."

"It is." I paused. *One, two, three.* "I used to work on *Scanner Stories.*"

Now he turned to look at me. "Oh, sure."

Greedily, I wanted him to tell me he liked it, and then I wanted to tell him I halfway *invented* it. I wanted to have it back, without the breakup, without the relationship, just the show I had spent so much time reporting, then even more time laying out as waveforms on a screen that I could snip and mix. I wanted it back with me, back in the story of my work, back in the list of things I told people when they asked me what I had done with my life. "Ah," I said. "You know that one."

He twitched his head to get a bit of hair off his forehead as he stood up with his stuff in his arms. "Yeah, I'm not really a podcast person, but that's Justin Dash's thing, right?"

My lungs emptied. My stomach seized. I tried to keep my face from collapsing, my features sliding down my neck like one of those cakes they make on *The Great British Bake-Off* when it's 100 degrees outside. "Yes," I said. "Justin Dash's thing."

He turned around. "What?"

"Nothing."

"I feel like I just said something wrong."

"Not at all."

"Okay, good. Good." He crossed his arms. "So do you think it's going to work?"

I blinked several times in a row. "What?"

"The dating thing, the coach. It didn't really seem like you were having that much fun." He was trying gamely not to laugh. Perhaps I was overthinking it, but this line of questioning seemed to leave something unspoken.

"I mean, that wasn't exactly a real date," I said. "It was sort of a trial run."

"Not a real date?" Will said in exaggerated surprise. "But you seem like such a good match."

"That's not funny," I said. "I asked him what his favorite book was, and do you know what he said?"

"I'm going to say . . . *Infinite Jest.* Did he say *Infinite Jest*?"

"I almost wish," I moaned. "He said *Keto for Closers.*"

"Mm-hmm." Will folded his arms and squinted at me. "But I shouldn't ask you out."

So much for unspoken. "Oh. I mean, probably not? Because I'm doing this thing?"

"Okay. I do like you, though."

My mouth was dry, my hands seemed to be sweating, my knees went wobbly, and it felt like I blinked about fifteen times. "Yeah. I . . . me too, same. I mean, I like you, not me. I'm not ever sure if I like me."

"You should." He laughed, and I really liked it, and it felt *so* messy. "We could be friends," he said. "Is that a conflict of interest or anything?"

I shook my head. "No. I think we're allowed to be friends."

. . .

I didn't get back to the office until late afternoon, which meant I didn't get home until almost 8:00, which meant it was 9:30 by the time I finally lowered myself into a tub full of bubbles with a glass of wine on the little table next to me. This was my favorite place to listen to anything completely unrelated to work—in this case, an audiobook of a novel I'd been trying to finish for a couple of weeks. As I lay back into the water, my phone buzzed on the table. I reached for the towel next to it and dried my hand, then picked it up just enough to see that it was Will.

Great to see you today. Buddy can't
stop talking about you.

I didn't normally answer texts in the tub, for fear of dropping my phone into the water, but I made an exception. He's probably just mad I didn't have any peanut butter.

No, but he did say he'd like some
cheese next time.

I paused and looked at the words "next time." I'll see what I can do. I added a cheese emoji, because I couldn't figure out what else to say to him.

The phone buzzed again in my hand. It was a picture of Buddy, sprawled across the couch. He says he can't wait.

Monday morning, my first meeting at work was scheduled for 9:00, so at 8:30 I was frantically trying to get going. I picked up what was left of my coffee and managed to spill a splash of it down the front of my shirt. I snapped a selfie, thinking I would send it to Molly so she could commiserate with me over my terrible morning. But at the last minute, I pulled up Will's number instead. Here I am looking photogenic again, as the morning gets off to a great start.

Oh no! (I still think you look fine.)

You have to say that because I'm paying you.

I do not. I can't be bought.

Off to change my shirt.

I promise my eyes are closed.

Later that day, I was between two editing sessions on two different shows when I felt my phone vibrate in my pocket. I pulled it out.

It was a link to a video of a Great Dane even bigger than Buddy sitting on a guy who looked smaller than Will. Worried that this is my future, he wrote.

Oh man, you've joined the dog people.

They're the only ones who know where I can find a toy he won't rip up in five minutes.

The next day, I was coming out of an interview with Eliza when I almost knocked over an intern with an armful of coffees. You wouldn't believe how close I just came to accidentally causing a bunch of second-degree burns to a 23-year-old.

You're supposed to keep the coffee
in the cup, you know.

Ha ha.

I'm sure they wouldn't wear it as
well as you.

It's a wonder I don't drop every cup
I ever pour.

I'll buy you a new one.

A few days later, over evening wine at Molly's when the preview episode was days away from dropping and I desperately needed to not be at the office, she asked about the pictures. "What happened to them?" she said. "I feel like you're hiding them." I had explained to her how Will had been at the restaurant, and how he'd been the photographer, and I suspected her curiosity about him was growing.

As it happened, I *had* been hiding the pictures. I'd been hiding them all afternoon, or rather I'd been hiding *from* them, because it was always my assumption that looking at pictures of myself was going to be disappointing. I couldn't stop thinking I would look at them and suddenly realize nothing that day had been the way it felt. "Nothing happened," I said with a shrug. "He sent me proofs today, but I haven't looked at them yet. He said he was sending like forty, and then I could pick seven for him to edit."

"You haven't looked?" she said, swatting me on the arm. "That's crazy, show them to me right now."

"What if they're terrible?"

"They won't be. But you have to send them to Eliza anyway, so at least we can look at them first and make sure you don't hate them."

I got out my laptop. I opened the folder and pulled up the first picture. It was in front of the background in the studio. I looked good. Professional. The light was flattering, I had color in my cheeks, and my smile did not make me look like the Joker. "That one is actually okay," I said.

"It's not 'okay,' it's really nice. Keep going."

It turned out that on top of everything else I was fond of about him, Will was damn good at his job. The pictures were all subtly different, some a little lighter, some a little more serious-looking. The ones by the window were softer, and the green I wore was flattering. As we paged through the pictures, Molly pointed to one of the early ones he took on the roof. "Look how happy you are here," she said. "You're practically glowing."

I leaned toward the screen. "It's probably Photoshop."

"You said he didn't edit these yet," she said. "It's like you think I don't pay attention at all." The last one was a shot of me laughing and looking off into the distance, over his shoulder. As a headshot, it wasn't much. As a picture of me, it made me catch my breath a little. Molly gasped. "Oh, look at that," she said.

"It's nice," I said.

She leaned in toward it, and then she leaned back. She tilted her head to one side, then the other. And then she said something for which I was unprepared: "He really likes you."

"What's that supposed to mean?"

She rested her chin in her hand. "There's just a way people take your picture when they're into you. I can't explain it. He's a good photographer, don't get me wrong, the rest of these are great. But this one . . ." She sighed. "He really likes you."

"Well, that's nice," I said, "but I am going to start going out on twenty blind dates in a couple of weeks, so it's kind of irrelevant." I looked over at her, but she was still staring at the photo.

She said it one more time: "He really likes you."

"Molly," I groaned.

CHAPTER ELEVEN

The Teaser

I worked until at least 11:30 P.M. for three nights in a row before we dropped the teaser episode. Julie and I remixed. We tweaked the script. We took out pieces of tape, did a few more hours of work, and then decided to put them back in. She fiddled with the scoring. We sent questions to Dava, who was our link to legal (I tried never to talk to legal directly), and she told us when we had to clip out things that might identify people we didn't have the right releases from. People in ad sales wrote to us. People in management wrote to us. Our episode file when we finally turned it in was called teaser1_final_final_reallyfinal_superfinal_USE_THIS_ONE.

It had taken them forever to settle on the title while everybody noodled over lists and crossed off options, and after all that noodling, they just called it *Twenty Dates*. Toby had wanted *Twenty First Dates,* but he was talked out of it because *50 First Dates* is an Adam Sandler movie. The show art, the little square graphic that would represent the podcast unless and until someone picked something else, was a silhouetted couple at a table, and in the foreground, a pad and a pen, like someone was spying on them and taking notes.

The preview, including my date with Andrew, was scheduled to publish at 5:00 A.M. on Wednesday. I set my alarm and pulled myself out of bed at 4:45. I made a huge pot of coffee. At 5:00, I started refreshing all the show feeds it was supposed to drop in. At 5:04, I saw it in the first one. By 5:10, it was in all of them. I shared it on the modest social media accounts I had; scheduled posts from Palmetto's accounts shared it more widely, and would keep it up all day. I knew that the episode was twenty-seven minutes long, pretty close to what we'd been shooting for. By 5:40 in the morning, I was already sitting on my couch, on my second cup of coffee, bouncing my knee up and down.

Julie texted. I know you're awake. It's going to be good. It is good. We did good. A thumbs-up was all I could manage in response.

I had spent all of the gaps in the previous day, whenever I wasn't actively working or worrying, rationally convincing myself to be patient. After all, this was hardly my first launch. I knew perfectly well that only a sliver of the audience would be up at this hour, and only a fraction of that sliver would prioritize their podcast feeds, and only a fraction of that fraction of that sliver would listen, and only a fraction of that fraction of that fraction of that sliver would offer any feedback, no matter what they thought. There was no news. There would be no news for a while. It meant nothing.

So naturally, exactly twenty-eight minutes after the preview episode of the first podcast I had ever hosted became public, I started to panic over the fact that I hadn't heard anything yet about what people thought. I had been, time and time again, the person Julie was right now—the person calmly capable of applying logic and experience. But my little ego goblin had so much more at stake now, as did my responsibility goblin, which suspected in the marrow of its goblin bones that the future of Palmetto (and Julie, and all my co-workers, and all of audio and all of media) depended on the reception this episode received. *No news?* Where were the reactions? It had been twenty-nine . . . twenty-nine and a half . . . thirty minutes!

Other than a handful of other messages from people in my life who knew this was happening—Molly, my mother, my father, my old boss from the station, and of course Eliza—the very first thing I heard about what anyone thought of the episode arrived at 6:13, by which time I had tried to distract myself with two slices of toast, an episode of *30 Rock,* and a series of the vexing word games I subjected myself to every day.

One of the Palmetto accounts received a reply from an account that belonged to a woman (I suppose) who called herself "BeckeтyWeckety." Her avatar was a photo of her hugging a small dog to her cheek. She wrote: "Listened at the gym. This was fun! Oof that guy was a stiff, though. I agree with the waiter. Is the waiter single? Forget the coaching, she can just date him LOL."

"LOL"? "LOL," BeckeтyWeckety?

BeckeтyWeckety was not alone. There were a handful of places we most often got reactions to Palmetto shows, and to my overwhelming relief, which bordered on the pathological, people generally liked it, give or take a few cranks. They thought Eliza was more interesting than they expected, although they weren't sure she knew what she was doing. They appreciated my skepticism. They were rooting for me to succeed.

And more than a handful of them *also* thought I should go out with the waiter. In one thread, they began to call him "Hot Waiter" even though they had never seen him. They said his voice was sexy, which I hadn't been thinking about previously but *now* I was thinking about it. Before lunch, it was already possible to declare yourself "Team Hot Waiter" and have plenty of company.

One person wrote this: "This is why this kind of dating coach bullshit is such a scam. She walked into a restaurant and met a guy who's better than the guy she got set up with. Bullshit!" This comment got a large number of approving thumbs-up reactions.

Eliza had a thick skin, but I didn't intend to bring these responses up with her.

Fortunately for her and her team, there was another *entire world* of reactions. It wasn't just Palmetto podcast people, the ones we were used to hearing from, who were listening. Because Eliza had promoted it on her channels, we also got reactions to the episode from the Eliza Cassidy people, the ones who subscribed to her on every platform and hung on her every word. They said things like, "You are beautiful and so kind to help her!" "She didn't even try on that date! She's lucky to have you!" "I know you will find her the right one!" "Can't wait to watch her journey!"

I paced for much of the morning, then I finally grabbed a link to one of the comments that complimented Will for being so charming and sent it to him with a cry-laughing emoji that I hoped would convey exactly the right level of noncommittal "Wouldn't it be funny if we *did* go out at some point? Just hilarious!" energy.

He sent me back two exclamation points. And that was it. I deserved it. Ask a cryptic question, get a cryptic answer.

Toby wanted to see me as soon as I got in.

In his office, Toby was walking on a treadmill that he'd added to his standing desk. I knocked. "Hey."

"Congratulations!" he said, and he hopped off and came over to me. He gave me a hug, which might have been weird except that he gave very clappy hugs, clap-clap on your back and it was over. "It seems like everything is going really well. The preview went off without a hitch."

"Yeah, I'm really pleased," I said. "I can't wait to get back to work."

"So I did want to talk to you about that."

No. No no no no. They were not going to cancel it when it previewed and people liked it. Wait, they couldn't cancel it! They just promoted it! It was at this moment that I realized I needed to drink a lot less coffee on stressful mornings, but I sat in the uncomfortable green chair. All I said was "sure," because I was confident I could say it cheerfully.

"Obviously, Eliza is feeling a little bit of pressure from the people who thought the first date she picked for you was a dud. Marcela called me. I think she's a little bit anxious about how it's going to come out, whether people are going to make fun of Eliza, that kind of thing. This is sort of a new audience for them."

"I mean, sure. I thought they wanted a new audience."

"Oh, of course, of course. They do. I just want to be careful about our approach going forward. I don't want it to look like you're not happy with what she's doing or you're disappointed or what have you. It's important that she get a chance to do what she does."

"Toby, I'm doing my part here. I have twenty dates I start going on in like a week and a half."

"Right. Just, make sure as you're working on these episodes that they're not too snarky about the project."

"Did you think this one was snarky?"

"No, not at all. It's just something to keep in mind. You know, I'm talking to Marcela, I'm talking to our folks in partnerships, I had a call from Danny Wynn."

Danny Wynn was in marketing at Fitness West. "Wait, what did Danny Wynn want?"

"Hey, relax. Relax. It was a regular check-in. They're thinking about the fact that their name is attached to it, they have a relationship with Eliza—"

"They do?"

"They do now, yeah. She's going to do some additional stuff for them. But this is not a big deal, don't worry about it."

"Then why did you mention it to me?"

"I thought you wanted to be kept up to date."

"So what did Danny actually say?"

"We were just aligning priorities."

"Toby, I'm going to crawl across your desk and pour your smoothie into your eyeballs if you do not get to the point and tell me what is really going on."

He glanced over at the smoothie, unappetizingly gray-green in a chunky tall glass. Then he looked back at me. "They're just making sure everybody's on the same page. Everybody wants this to be a big win for us all."

"Well, I haven't heard any of this from Eliza, so I'm not sure it's really something she's worried about."

"As you know, if I'm hearing it from Marcela, it's probably coming from Eliza. Sometimes talent finds it a little easier to go through agents with something like this, right?"

"I don't know. I guess I'm not talent."

"You know what I mean."

"Do I?"

"Keep doing what she's telling you to do," he said. "Stay on track."

He didn't say it, but I heard it: *Whatever the internet says, you are not going to date the waiter.*

I had seen Eliza so many times on so many screens of different sizes, perched on her pretty sofa, talking about so many things, that it was otherworldly to realize that she was talking about me the next time I picked up my phone.

> Good morning! Well, it's a big day, I've been telling you about this amazing podcast called *Twenty Dates*, and now we can finally share a little taste of it with you. And it's pretty delicious, if I do say so myself. I'm coaching this woman, she's so fantastic, her name is Cecily. She's doing Platinum Goddess, you can find a link to that plan in the

description. She's been out on one date already, she did great. That wasn't her match, but that's not the goal on a first date, that one is just for working out the kinks. Andrew, who was so sweet to be my guinea pig, isn't really the kind of guy I'd pick for her in the long term, so I told them both it was just practice. Doesn't even count.

Also! Also also! You guys. Ladies. I have heard your voices, and we have to talk about the waiter. He is adorable, I agree, and his little cameo at the end is really cute. I'm actually glad that happened, because it's a good chance to talk about exactly what coaching is for. I hear a lot of this from people when they're getting serious about searching for a partner. They start to do the work of really finding somebody appropriate, and then they get distracted by somebody totally wrong for them. They go "oh, how cute," and before you know it, they're quitting the whole process they were about to start, and they're chasing whatever random person showed up. They're like the dog that sees the squirrel, right? And that is not how you make a smart choice! You want to do it in an intentional way.

Doing it in an intentional way is exactly what Cecily is trying to do. It's what I teach. It's exactly what Smart Partnering—that's my concept—is all about. In her case, she has a long history of just ending up with whoever is interested. Her last serious relationship was with the guy who happened to be assigned to the desk next to her, which is the wrong way to pick a partner. The odds are just incredibly long that the nearest person to you is the best one you could pick. And that's what she found out. When you just go with whoever shows up, you're acting like you don't have the right to be picky. And you do, and she does. Everybody does.

So no, my loves, I'm afraid she's not going to call off the hunt and date the waiter. It would be like marrying your mailman because he walks by every day, and sometimes he brings you a birthday card. Just stay tuned, because if you thought one line from one waiter was fun, wait until she starts meeting the actual men I have lined up for her. You're going to see how different it is when you apply some thought to who you're choosing for yourself. You're absolutely going to love it. And you're going to love her as much as I do. Love you all, talk soon.

CHAPTER TWELVE

The Twenty Dates

A week or so later, Eliza and I met again at Sophie's for coffee and some updates. When we sat down and the capsule mic was shining its little orange light, she told me that she had the dates almost all lined up. "I charmed them with your new pictures, which are fab," she said. "They are selling you just great. You look ten years younger."

"I'm supposed to look younger?" I said.

"Twenty-six," she said. I honestly hadn't expected her to spit out a number like a graphing calculator. "From now until you're forty, the aim is twenty-six. From forty to fifty, you'll be going for thirty-five. Fifty to sixty, go for forty. After that, all you want is for people to say you look great for your age."

"What in the hell," I muttered, letting my eyes fall on the orange light on the mic. It was a ridiculous thing to say, and it was very good tape.

"Look, I didn't make the rules," she said.

"You did, you just gave them to me."

"I didn't make them, I explained them. I am telling you how it is for women."

"And I'm sure it's different for men."

"Of course! Nobody knows how old men are. You can show an eighteen-year-old a picture of Tom Cruise now and they'll think he's thirty. People say a guy looks forty from when he's twenty to when he's, like, seventy. The public understanding of how old men are is deranged. Until they're ninety, they can convince people they're middle-aged if they have the right wife."

"This is the most depressing thing I've ever heard."

"Well, you can be depressed by it, or you can make it work for you by having the best possible pictures and taking excellent care of your skin. By the way, I was just at a meeting, and they gave me a bunch of samples of this stuff that's supposed to be great for wrinkles. You want it?"

"I don't have wrinkles," I said.

She squinted at me, then reached into her bag, extracted a small pump bottle, and handed it to me. "Better safe than sorry."

Over the next four weeks, Eliza was, as promised, sending me on twenty dates. All over the city. Dinners, lunches, brunches, a visit to the Smithsonian, and a show at the Kennedy Center. I would rotate four approved outfits, which I would clean or have cleaned obsessively. The team would keep working on production because our episodes were about to start coming out. But for me, there would be practically no time for anything else in those four weeks but dating and talking about dating. I wasn't sure if it was supposed to sound like boot camp, but it did. "At the end," Eliza said, "we'll find out who you want a second date with, and who wants a second date with you, and we'll go from there."

But first, I had to go on twenty dates.

Josh

Josh had an IT job out in the spy/military part of Virginia that he couldn't tell me anything about except that he worked in a room where you couldn't take your cellphone, and he showed me his Phi Beta Kappa key. He was a little shy, and he owned an iguana ironically named Dynamo, because it almost never moved. I thought that was funny.

Paulo

A straight-up beautiful man with soft pink lips who worked at the Portuguese embassy. We went to a French place for dinner, and he wore a suit so gorgeous that I stared, transfixed, at the edge of the cuff while he was talking about his job. I think he did something legal. At any rate, I went on this date when I had just read a story in *The New Yorker* about the Paris sewers, and I talked about it for much too long. I would have kissed him, just so I could caress the suit, but he shook my hand firmly and said, "Delighted, Cecily, really," and he was gone.

Michael the Poker Player (aka Michael #1)

He was a professional poker player. We had upscale burgers for lunch, and even though I didn't have a long history of being attracted to bald men with big rings, I kind of liked him. I had only played poker a handful of times, and I made him walk me through a few hands on an app on my phone. He kissed me before we said goodbye, and it was pretty good. It was a week later that Eliza told me he was unavailable because he had relocated to Costa Rica for tax reasons.

Eric

We had Lao food. He owned three car washes and had a couple of very funny stories about customers who didn't understand how to correctly take their cars through for service. We didn't have a lot to talk about, but on the plus side, those were some of the best noodles I have ever eaten in my life. After I got home, he texted me a link to a podcast he liked about personal finance.

Ron

Eliza wanted me to try—just try—going out with someone older than I was. Ron had about twenty years on me, and he was a lobbyist for the anesthesiologists. A nice man. No chemistry. Good Thai food. I learned a lot about insurance billing and made a note that he might be a good source for a story someday. I mean, insurance billing is crazy.

Shane

Brunch at one of the ritzy hotels downtown. Very good-looking, square jaw, cleft chin, and a tattoo of a hammer on the inside of his forearm, which he told me was a tribute to his father's construction business. He was getting into house-flipping. I'd just torn into a tremendous Belgian waffle when he dragged the conversation around to knives. At first, I worried that this meant he was a murderer, but after about five minutes, I realized he was deep into an MLM and wanted to sell me a knife block and a sharpening kit. I declined. He kissed me. He smelled great; I wished he were interesting.

Damian

Given Eliza's admiration of people whom she considered driven, I found it hard to believe she set me up with a guy in a small-time ska band. A ska band! But it turned out he only did music on weekends, and during the week he sold cars in Silver Spring. In the middle of dinner, there was a small fire in the kitchen of the restaurant, and we had to evacuate. We stood on the sidewalk and talked about ska for about ten minutes (which is to say he did), and then he looked at his watch and said he should probably just get home.

Michael the Doctor (aka Michael #2)

A family doctor who worked in Chevy Chase, Michael looked gentle and wholesome, like a guy who would be targeted by a scammer in a Netflix documentary. We had lunch at a vegan place Julie suggested, where I had braised jackfruit. He'd been single for a long time because he worked so much, but he said he was trying to slow down, and he'd left a hectic practice to gain some control over his schedule. He complimented the alligator pin close to my collar—I never wore necklaces, because they could interfere with the mic. When we were leaving, we kissed, and while I cannot say I felt it in my toes, I did feel myself sigh into it a bit.

Maxim

Oh, Maxim! Maxim was an adjunct professor teaching world history to college first-years. He had dark wavy hair and olive skin, and when he fastened his eyes on me, I wanted to eat him up like a cookie. We were flirting madly over Indian food at Rasika, and I was pondering the possibilities of licking his neck like a Popsicle, when he started to explain some of his more firmly held political views, which amounted to nostalgia for the social hierarchies of the 1950s. Shortly thereafter, I thanked him for dinner and bolted. I texted Eliza, knowing she'd have gotten the skinny from Julie. Are you serious? She wrote back, I didn't know!

Anton

Anton was Russian. He had come to the United States for college years and years ago and ended up working in cable news as a researcher. Over very good plates of pasta, he told me he thought audio was a fad and I should get into virtual reality. I wished him well, but I rushed over to Julie almost as soon as I was finished chewing.

After I gave her my mic back, I just said, "So?" Our first real episode had dropped that day—one of twelve, the one where Eliza went into detail about her background and we mapped out the world of relationship advice. We'd gotten the episode out right on schedule, and Julie had had a late-afternoon meeting with everybody involved, a debriefing that I hadn't been able to grill her about yet. She gave me a thumbs-up. "Everybody is really happy. Everything is good. We're on our way."

Dylan

If Ron was my chance to date someone older, Dylan was my chance to date someone younger. He was twenty-six, and he never stopped talking—he was working on three different fledgling businesses, because he couldn't decide if he wanted to do real estate, open a vape shop, or restore vintage cars. It should have been annoying, but it was intoxicating, because I didn't have to do anything but eat. He had listened to almost all the podcasts I had ever worked on, and he had opinions about every one. By the end of a Tex-Mex lunch, I was exhausted. I liked him a lot, but not to date. In ten years, though, after a couple of character-building setbacks, he was probably going to be a great guy.

Zach

Zach looked a lot like Justin. A *lot.* I tried hard to get over it. If we'd had more in common (he was an extreme-sports guy who hated being inside for any longer than he had to), I might have been more successful.

John

John was a trial lawyer, and divorced. Well, no—John was separated, but he'd been separated for four years, so he considered himself divorced, even though the legal scrapping continued (no kids, just money, cars, and two basset hounds named Frolic and Detour). In the end, it wasn't the status of his marriage that prevented us from connecting over Caribbean food. It was the fact that by the end of dinner, I knew everything about his wife. Which is to say I knew everything he thought about her, which is to say I knew how much he resented her.

Rafael
Rafael was a print journalist who covered Congress. He had a beautiful smile and an air of intensity that seemed well suited to his work. We met up at a cool brunch spot where everyone appeared to be actively in pursuit of getting really drunk (the problem with cool brunch spots), and we talked about interviewing styles for half an hour. He had a cat, played tennis, and was planning a solo vacation to Paris in a couple of weeks. He was handsome and charming, and we had a lot in common. When we were getting ready to go, he said, "Well, I don't think this is a match, but maybe we can get together as friends?"

Brandon
He was a partner at a small advertising agency in Arlington, and he had shoulder-length blond hair and smooth skin that I suspected was costly to maintain. We had fancy barbecue and dark beer at a place Toby had recommended, and he told me about a campaign he'd recently worked on for a nonprofit working to provide clean water around the world. It seemed like very worthwhile work. He also told me he was training for a triathlon, and he flinched when I said, "Oh my God, *why* would you do that?" I recovered, and we had a nice unassuming smooch as I was getting into the car. On the way home, I couldn't stop thinking about how I should probably be working out regularly.

Alexandre
French. Hot. Kissed him after Greek food and a gin and tonic. Couldn't remember anything except his lips by the time I got home. No regrets.

Michael the Architect (aka Michael #3)
We went to a symphony performance at the Kennedy Center, because he had a subscription, and he fell asleep. This didn't offend

me at all—for some people, that's part of the process—but later, when I gently teased him about it (at least I thought it was gentle), he insisted he hadn't been asleep at all, just "taking it in" with his eyes closed. I chose not to tell him he was "taking it in" while snoring.

Drew

Drew was a professional soccer player. When Eliza arranged the date, he was working on a plan to open a beer garden in town. When the date finally occurred, he had signed with a new team and was about to move to Cincinnati. We had Italian food and a lot of wine, and because we lived near each other, we made out in the back of the cab all the way back to my apartment. Ah, what could have been.

Tyler

Tyler was a research ecologist at the National Zoo, which was one of the coolest job titles I had ever heard. We met at the American History Museum and walked around for a few hours while I grilled him about the zoo. I didn't have any idea how many questions I *had* about the zoo until I met Tyler. He was funny and friendly, and it felt like spending the afternoon with a favorite cousin. Late in the afternoon, he told me sheepishly that he was only about a month removed from breaking up with his long-term girlfriend, and he had mixed feelings about dating. I gave him a hug, and we said we'd keep in touch, and maybe he'd show me around the zoo sometime.

Rob

Rob was a six-foot-six personal trainer, and let me be clear: I am as shallow as anyone, and as we enjoyed Brazilian food, I stared appreciatively at his arms, his shoulders, his neck, and everything else he stuffed into his black T-shirt. He had a great laugh, and he was clearly crazy about his family, which he was about to head to

Oakland to visit. When we were finished eating and getting ready to go, we stood on the sidewalk together, and I looked up at him, feeling a genuine strain in my neck, but in kind of a good way. He looked down at me hungrily and said, "I could get you in shape in three months."

"So, what did you think?" Eliza asked, as we sat across from each other in one of the Palmetto studios. She'd listened to the dates, but we'd mostly avoided having me give specific feedback on these guys. "How many of the twenty are we eliminating? How many do you want to go out with again? I want to hear everything."

"Well," I said, "I liked the doctor. The family doctor. Michael."

"He's the cutest!" she said. "I haven't met him, but we talked on the phone, and he seemed like such a great person. That's an amazing start. Who else?"

I hesitated. "Else?"

"Yes. Who else? Who else do you want to see again?"

"Can't we start with that one? If he wants to?" My eyes widened. "Does he not want to?"

"He does want to," she said with a smile and a waggle of her eyebrows. "I'm just hoping you didn't eliminate nineteen out of twenty people on your first shot, and that you have other good news to tell me."

"I mean, some of them eliminated me," I said. "You did send me out with a guy who's already married."

"A technicality."

"Another one thinks it's not natural for women to have jobs."

"Well, that's not exactly what he said."

"One guy fled the country."

"Okay, he didn't *flee* the country."

"A man with a hammer tattoo tried to sell me knives."

"He's an entrepreneur! There were a lot of good prospects. I happen to know you made out with one of them."

"He just moved to Ohio."

"To Cincinnati! He's not going to *stay* there."

"What does that mean?"

She sighed dramatically. "So," she said, folding her hands in front of her on the table, "out of all those guys, you only want to see Michael again. All those great guys—"

"All those *guys*," I corrected.

"All those guys, you have one second date you're interested in." She nodded. "Fine. We can work with that. I'll set it up."

"I need a little time," I said. "I've spent so much time going on dates in the last four weeks that I have barely done any other work, so I'm way behind, not to mention completely small-talked out. This coming week is Thanksgiving, and after that, you have to give me a real week to just process. They're sitting on a mountain of tape from these dates that will turn into six episodes, so there's no hurry."

"Okay. But this is going to be so good!" she said, clapping her hands. "I mean, people think they like us now, but when they actually hear you on these good dates—not the dummy date but the *good* dates—I am telling you, everybody is going to love them. Marcela is losing it, she's so excited. She says I'll end up with another book deal *and* she thinks I can do dating classes through one of those platforms where people study cooking and Photoshop and stuff, *and* she wants to talk about condoms."

"About . . ."

"Condoms, branded condoms. One of the big companies is talking to her about a partnership. That way, if you're not having sex, I can help you. If you're having sex, I can still help you. She's a genius." Eliza got up from her chair and came over and hugged me without my even getting up, and then she was heading out the door. "Happy Thanksgiving! We're on our way!"

CHAPTER THIRTEEN

The Party

We'd worked hard enough, gotten far enough ahead in the producing schedule, that with all my dates over, Toby let the entire team slow down for Thanksgiving week. It was a good thing, since I didn't think I could bear to talk about myself any more right away. I had a small dinner with Molly and Pete; Julie went to see her parents; Abby and Charlie disappeared and didn't even tell us what they were doing—a sensible self-preservation tactic for producers hoping to have actual time off. And while I should have spent that week not thinking about work, I spent it burrowing into the reactions we were getting—including to the first episode where I actually went out on dates (with Josh, Paolo, and Michael #1), which dropped the morning after Thanksgiving. I had promised Julie I would not do this, that I would relax, but she had known I was lying.

The show was fun. The show was misogynist. The show was entertaining. The show was revelatory. The guys Eliza picked were great, or boring, or too good for me, or not good enough. Eliza was sharp and funny, or she was completely fake. I was too negative, or I was the best, or I was a snob, or I was gullible, or my voice was annoying, or they had looked me up online and I was ugly, or they had looked me up online and I was cute, or they had a crush on me, or they wanted to set me up with their brother, their boss, or their best friend.

The men I dated had their own factions from the start. It was as if my dating life had become a sports stadium, with each guy hearing the roar of his own cheering section or the booing of his detractors. Michael #1 had hardcore fans immediately; we had not said anything about Costa Rica, but I had a feeling some of them might have been willing to follow him there. What's not to like about sunshine, cocktails, and tax evasion?

By the time we all got back on the clock at the beginning of December, I wondered whether it was killing Eliza having so many people have so many opinions about her, but of course, she was much more used to it than I was, and she took it in stride. Instead, she was focused on the joint holiday–*Twenty Dates* party she was throwing at her house. "I'm so glad you called," she said. "You're coming to the party Saturday, right? I think practically everybody from your work is coming. You can meet all my friends. And Marcela. And you can hang out with Cody! My sister and her husband are coming, too."

I'd never met any of her family. I was certainly curious. "I'll be there."

"Fabulous. You'll love it, I'm having this tremendous caterer do it, the best in the city. Passed apps to die for. It will be worth it for the food alone. And there's going to be a band, and dancing, it will be great."

When I thought about a party at Eliza's, all I could envision was endless selfies and servers walking around with trays of smoothies with little umbrellas in them, and I felt like I would be preposterously out of place. In this case, though, it qualified as a work event, and at least I would be surrounded by people I knew. "I'll be there, don't worry, I'll be there."

. . .

The party was on Saturday night, and that afternoon I went through my closet until I found a hunter green sweater, and I paired it with one of my many pairs of black pants. I tried once more to replicate the look Eliza had given me during the makeup lesson we did.

Julie had a Honda CRV, or more precisely her parents did, and she picked me up so we could drive out to Bethesda. Up and down Eliza's street, cars were already parked on both sides, and when we got out, music thudded in the distance. As we got close to the house, we could see people, so many people, milling around inside, and along the path to the front door there were arrangements of poinsettias. "Very nice," Julie said. "She can definitely entertain."

Despite the meticulous, contemporary spareness of Eliza's house, the party was emphatically maximalist. In order to allow for drinks that were not exclusively clear liquids, furniture and rugs had been moved and replaced with furnishings I'd never seen, ones in bright colors that I suspected were rentals. Lights had been added, and there was one bar set up in the kitchen and one in the basement where the home theater was. A four-man band in skinny ties played throwback hits on a small platform in the emptied great room. Indoor trees winked with fairy lights, and a catering table with covered chafing dishes took up most of the dining room. We wedged our way inside the front door, and someone took our coats and disappeared with them, and I looked around to see a collection of Palmetto people, people who seemed like they might belong to Eliza or her business, and people I couldn't place at all.

"Should we get a drink?" Julie ventured, peering cautiously toward the kitchen.

"We might as well," I said. We wound our way through the front hall, and when we passed the poster of the wedding photo,

Julie silently pointed at it and raised her eyebrows, and I nodded. Just as we got near the bar, I heard my name.

"Cecily!" Eliza was in a bright pink print jumpsuit and a perfectly complementary pink blazer, and she had a bright red drink in her hand. "I'm so happy to see you! Hi, Julie, thank you for making sure she actually showed up!" Julie laughed at this, which I found moderately traitorous.

"Thank you for inviting me," I said. "This is beautiful. I mean it. I don't know how you do all this."

"I let people help me," she said pointedly. "Now have a drink. I'm having a Negroni. There's boozy cider in a pot in the kitchen, which smells unbelievable, or the bartenders will make you whatever you want. I'm so happy to see you!" She hugged me from the side, around my shoulders, without spilling her drink. Just then, a woman with her blond hair pulled back in a ponytail came up and put her hand on Eliza's elbow. Eliza leaned over and kissed her cheek. "Carla, hi! Carla, this is Cecily, she's the host of the show. Cecily, Carla was my high school bestie. She lives in Annapolis and she came all the way here just for me."

Carla crooked a corner of her mouth. "I mean, I came for the booze, but yes, love, I came for you, too."

I don't know why I expected Eliza not to have friends, or not to have regular friends, or not to have old friends. Somehow, I always envisioned her moving from place to place followed by a gaggle of admirers, perfect people who were perfectly aligned with all the advice she regularly gave them.

But as it turned out, when Julie and I fetched drinks and started to walk around, most of the people we talked to had relatively normal jobs. There were people Cody knew from work, people Eliza knew from the neighborhood, people they both knew from their long history together. Only a few of the guests looked impeccable in the particular way that Eliza always did—one of them was a woman named Jia who introduced herself to me as a juicing entrepreneur. But she had also been a devoted listener of *Otter*

Tail, and unlike most people, who could only go on about the crime and who did it, she asked me about some of the thorniest ethical tangles of true crime. It made her uncomfortable, Jia said, listening to something she thought was so riveting that was about something so incredibly sad. *Me too, Jia,* I thought but did not say.

We listened to the band and had drinks, and I even danced a little. Eliza came down and bumped her hip against mine in rhythm on the dance floor, and she said in my ear, "I'm so glad you're here." She squeezed my shoulder.

It was hard not to look around this place—her home, her husband, her friends, her happiness—and feel like she had something figured out. I had thought maybe she had a shiny life but not a happy life, but it was clear that she had a happy life, too.

I was standing in a corner of the living room watching Julie dance with one of Eliza's other college friends when I felt someone standing next to me. I turned to see Cody leaning on the wall exactly as I was. "Cody, hey," I said. "It's good to see you, thank you so much for all this."

"Good to see you, too," he said, holding a beer bottle in one hand. He clinked it against my whiskey glass. "And congratulations on the show. I heard the first one, I really like it."

"Well, thank you, that's very nice of you," I said. For reasons I couldn't quite explain, the fact that he hadn't heard more than one episode felt like a sublime act of confidence in their relationship. After all, he'd probably had to decide, at some point, that he couldn't possibly digest all of her content. I turned to him. "How is all this for you anyway? All this . . . this?" I waved my arm at my own friends, at my own bosses, at his wife and her pals laughing and popping meatless sliders in their mouths.

He shook his head. "I just hang on tight," he said. "She runs the carnival rides." This could have seemed resentful, but it didn't—it seemed admiring. No, *adoring.* "She just flipping loves people, you know?"

"I can't get over how much energy she has," I said.

"It's no joke," he agreed. And then he turned back to me. "Is she driving you nuts? Little bit?"

I was so surprised by this question that what came out of my mouth was a long "uhhhhhhhh," and the minute he heard it, he started to laugh. "I mean, no," I said, "she's been fine, it's just a lot of big changes for me. I think she's disappointed in me, probably, since I'm not doing everything she wants in quite the right way."

He took a drink from his beer. "I'm going to tell you a secret: She's never disappointed in anybody," he said. "She just wants to help. It's her whole thing. She can't not do it."

"It has to be a lot," I said. "All the . . . carnival rides."

"I knew who she was when we got together," he said. "Maybe I didn't know we'd end up on YouTube, but she was always going to be big. You know, *big*."

"Big like a celebrity?"

"Big like a bulldozer," he said. "She never stops moving. The business has been really bumpy the last couple of years, and she's just rolled on. I don't know if she told you, but we just sold the apartment in New York, and that was really hard for her, but she got used to it. She'll have ten new projects going by New Year's, probably, and she won't even slow down."

"I'm sure she won't." Eliza hadn't mentioned selling the apartment. She hadn't mentioned anything other than new ideas, new collaborations, new products, new opportunities. I almost couldn't picture her accepting *any* development that wasn't to her liking.

Just then, a blond woman in a black wrap dress came up and kissed Cody on the cheek unselfconsciously. "Hey, babe," she said. "How are things over in this corner?"

"They're good," he said. "Emmy, this is the host of the show, Cecily. Cecily, this is Eliza's sister, Emmy."

Emmy fussed over me exactly as much as I'd expect from someone who was related to Eliza, but she had a calmer vibe, a more restful aura, and I knew she was a few years older. Cody excused himself, and the two of us stood there watching the party. "So," Emmy finally said, "how's the dating stuff working for you so far?"

"Well," I said, "I have been on twenty dates, and there were a good number of solid picks. I would recommend her for anybody who needs first dates at high volume."

Emmy nodded slowly. "That's very fair." It was funny how much Emmy immediately seemed to me like someone I would be friends with, and Eliza seemed like the little sister of someone I would be friends with.

"She keeps telling me it's important to be intentional."

Emmy rattled ice in her glass. I had a feeling she was a little bit tipsy. "Ah, I'll bet. She comes by that honestly."

"What do you mean?"

Emmy rolled her eyes. "She never tells anybody this story. She should tell it. When Eliza was nineteen, she got engaged to our next-door neighbor."

"Really."

She nodded. "They grew up together, our moms were best friends, our dads played golf, all that. They get to high school, she and Liam start dating. Literally, she's a cheerleader and he's the quarterback of the football team. You could have plonked them down on the heterosexuality float at the Macy's Thanksgiving Day Parade. They go to college, and they get engaged, and because they're not going to get married until they graduate, she spends—I am not exaggerating—three years on wedding planning. There are spreadsheets. There are albums. There are fabric samples. She shows me five kinds of confetti."

"Jesus."

"Exactly. So they're almost done with school, they start looking for a wedding venue, and this is when she finds out that for the last two years, he has been screwing her roommate and best friend basically every time she wasn't in the room."

"Oh, shit. In the room?"

"On her bed."

"Why her bed?"

"Can't imagine, but that's where they were when she caught them. She walked right in. Just a couple of bare asses rolling around under her Florence and The Machine poster."

"Whoa."

"Exactly. Complete meltdown. She makes it to graduation, comes home, she's just moping around the house. Total mess. The quarterback gets engaged to the roommate."

"No."

"Yes. And El feels like she absolutely has to find somebody. Cannot wait, right? She's never been single as a fully formed person, ever. And at that time, you know, dating apps are taking off, but she's really suspicious, she has a couple of bad experiences, she decides that's a no. So she determines she's going to do it logically. Like the wedding planning. She starts making spreadsheets. She gets referrals. Everybody she knows. Everybody they know. I'm married myself by this point, by the way, and all my husband's single friends get written down. Everybody she meets gets entered into this system."

"This part certainly checks out."

"Right? So she comes up with this list of potential people to go out with, and she starts asking for introductions, and going on dates, and crossing people off—you know those bulletin boards like on a conspiracy show? Where there are all the red strings, and it's either very logical or very wacky and you can't really say which? It was like that. And she followed this whole thing faithfully until she met somebody who told her about Cody, and she did research on him, she looked him up, they went out, and they fell in love. And they're very happy, and he's a great dude. So for her, that's how you become happy." She took a drink. "It's safe to say we're pretty different."

"How did you meet your husband?" I asked.

"I tripped over his foot on my way to an IHOP bathroom."

"Well," I said, "everybody has their own journey."

I stood with Emmy, and we watched Eliza on the dance floor, throwing her arms around one of her friends, effortlessly balancing her cocktail in her hand. Emmy stepped away to greet a friend. And then I did a double-take, because over by the door, a very familiar tall and narrow frame was handing over a coat. "Wait," I said. "What the . . ."

Julie was suddenly next to me. "Hey, look, it's your waiter!" she said. "We felt like it would be fun to invite him, since he's such a big hit with the audience, so we tracked him down at Madeline's. Should we go say hi?"

"Oh. Oh . . . Julie." He looked so good. I hadn't seen him in a while, and he was better than I remembered. This was not what I needed, even though it was a little bit what I wanted. "Look, just so you understand, in case it comes up, I kind of know him," I said.

"What do you mean?"

"I—okay, remember when I told you about the dog, the guy I helped catch that escaped dog?"

"The huge one? That escaped dog?"

"That's the only escaped dog."

She nodded slowly. "And the guy who looked like a handsome man's brother."

"Yes. He also took my new pictures."

"You went to your *waiter* to get your pictures taken?"

"No, I didn't *go* to him. I mean, I did, but I didn't know," I said. "I didn't know he was the same guy as the waiter when I went to get the pictures, and I didn't know he was the same guy as the dog guy when I went to the restaurant. He keeps showing up. Or I guess if you're him, I keep showing up."

"This is complicated," she said, almost admiringly. "Why didn't you tell me?"

"I haven't thought about anything but tape and scripts for the last month. Plus, I was afraid if I brought it up, it would seem like I was making a big deal out of it. And then he was the kicker on the preview episode, and *everybody* made a big deal out of it, and I just . . . didn't."

I wasn't sure this was a very convincing explanation, but we were out of time to chat about it, because suddenly, there he was. "Cecily," he said. "It's good to see you."

Oh, why did he have to look delicious in completely different ways? Every damn time I saw him? He was wearing a navy blue flannel shirt, and there was a little blue thread hanging from a button near his collar, and it was all I could do not to reach out and touch it with my fingers. Instead, I tried not to gulp and just said, "Hi, it's good to see you, too. This is Julie, you met at the restaurant. Julie, you remember Will."

"Sure," she said. "You gave me a great quote, and now the internet loves you."

He grinned at her. "I don't know how that works."

She shrugged. "Me neither, really."

"Oh my God, hi!" Eliza came bounding up beside me. "You're Hot Waiter!"

"Eliza," I said, "this is Will." I put a little extra emphasis on it.

She leaned up and kissed his cheek. "I'm so glad you could come, thank you so much. By the way, I love Madeline's, it's one of my favorite restaurants, and I always tell people they have amazing service." One of her friends overheard and walked up next to her, nodding enthusiastically.

"Thank you," he said, looking at her with a mild head tilt. "I'm glad you enjoy it."

"Did you think that was crazy when everybody on the internet thought you were so cute?" Eliza's friend asked.

"A little bit, yeah," he said.

I slipped into some kind of a fugue state as I watched people come by and make conversation with him exclusively about the restaurant and the internet. I thought maybe I should say something about his photography, say how talented I thought he was, but I wasn't sure he wanted that, and Eliza would wonder why I didn't tell her, and so forth. Maybe he wanted to keep all this as contained as possible. He didn't look miserable, but he did look surprised to be the focus of so much attention.

I was just beginning to think the crowd around us was going to thin enough that we could talk when Toby came strolling up and slapped me on the back in that way he had, that way that always made me involuntarily think of the word "hiya." "How are we doing?" he asked. I introduced him to Will. "Oh, of course. The waiter. Congratulations on your adoring fans," he said.

"I think they're Cecily's fans," Will said. "I was in the right place at the right time."

Toby pulled Will into a conversation about natural wine that I was quite sure Will wasn't interested in, and Eliza and I drifted away in the direction of a small low table with little bowls of nuts and M&M's and trail mix. I popped two M&M's in my mouth. "It's funny," I said, figuring it was better to just tell her, too, in case she found out, "but he and I actually know each other a little bit."

"Right, you said at the restaurant you were neighbors."

"We are, kind of, but we also kind of keep running into each other." I explained about Buddy, and the rescue we effectuated. "And believe it or not, you remember when I got the new pictures taken? He was the photographer."

"So he's an artist," she said with such perfectly crisp neutrality that I couldn't tell whether the rest of the sentence inside her head was "with a big beating creative heart" or "who probably doesn't even do sponcon."

"Yes. He's really talented, actually."

I must have trailed off a little too warmly, or I looked at him a little too hungrily, because Eliza narrowed her eyes at me. "Do you like him? Are you guys . . . I mean, do you like him?"

"I'm just telling you we know each other. And I don't know, maybe if none of these dates pan out—"

"Of course," she said, rolling her eyes a bit.

"What?" There was a way in which I suspected a person like Eliza would feel safe being a terrible snob, and a way that she wouldn't. She was not the kind of person to be caught on TikTok ranting about how someone working in retail took too long to ring her up. She was not someone who would post a red-faced complaint about being unable to get a coveted piece from a new lingerie line on the day it came out. Her whole thing was *positive*. She was *nice*. And even though her livelihood revolved around as many people as possible knowing who she was, it would have been devastating to her image ever to be heard to ask, "Don't you know who I am?"

"I mean, I'm not surprised you like him," she said. "Who doesn't admire a guy who saves a dog?"

"It's not that. He's a good guy. We talked when he did the pictures, he asked me questions about what I do, it was just friendly."

She reached over and grabbed my hand. "Honey, he's not interested in what you do."

I sat back. "Excuse me?"

"You met him, he likes you, and you haven't slept with him. That means that's the situation he's working on right now. So whatever time he spent sitting there fondling your microphones or whatever, that doesn't mean he's really excited to hear about, I don't know, subwoofers."

"What exactly do you think my job is?"

"Listen, I get this. You're starting to open yourself up. All this work we're doing is making you feel more ready, and that's amazing, I'm super proud of you. But like I told the entire internet, the whole point of this is to be intentional about it. 'Whatever' doesn't work, remember? The definition of insanity is expecting to do the same thing over and over again, as they say."

"They don't say that," I muttered. I pulled my hand back a bit.

"My point is that you are a beautiful and successful woman. I don't want you to settle. Somebody saving a dog and the internet thinking he's cute, those are not reasons to go out with somebody."

"So the fact that I like him means I'm not supposed to go out with him."

"No," she said, "just, the fact that you like him doesn't *necessarily* mean you should go out with him." Now she laid her hand over my wrist. "Tell me the truth—do you think somebody who hasn't had success can appreciate the kind of work that you've put in with your career? You told me you wanted somebody who was not going to resent your work. Do you think somebody who isn't driven can understand why you're so driven?"

I frowned. "How do you know he's not driven?"

"To do what?" she asked. "Bring bread to the table?" The way I looked at her, she seemed to instantly realize this was too far. "I'm sorry. I'm not trying to be horrible. I want you to find somebody who's passionate like you, that's all."

"He's just been really . . . kind to me," I said, knowing it sounded watery and unconvincing, and when I saw the pitying expression on her face, I regretted saying it, despite the fact that it was true.

"Kind? Cecily, everybody is supposed to be kind to you. It's not enough. I want you to fall in love and stay in love. And that starts with not jumping on the first guy you meet who saves a dog in front of you."

"I didn't jump on him," I said. "Nothing is happening. Believe me, any interest in an actual relationship would not be mutual anyway, okay?" It was true. While he'd inquired about asking me out, he'd also gone out of his way to tell me he wasn't staying in town. He was short-term only. Even if I *had* been having serious intentions in that direction, which I was not prepared to say I was, he didn't share them.

She sighed and took both my hands. "Do me a favor. Go out

with Michael again. He is a dreamboat, and he really likes you, and he has an actual career, which I know you care about, whether you admit it or not. And if he's not it, we'll keep trying. You said you were going to give it a chance."

"I didn't say I wasn't going to go out with Michael."

"Okay, then. We agree."

CHAPTER FOURTEEN

The Storm

My favorite thing about D.C. is that skyscrapers are illegal. Our skyline is low and blocky by order of Congress, thanks to what is known as—and people often do not believe this the first time they hear it—the Height of Buildings Act, the current version of which dates to 1910. Lest you think Congress has perhaps forgotten about the Height of Buildings Act and wouldn't care anymore, note that in 1973, when the D.C. city government was finally granted some degree of local control, Congress made a special note that while the city council could control some things, there would be no messing with the Height of Buildings Act. A building has been granted an exemption now and then—a hospital, a church, the National Press Club, the Masonic Lodge.

It's this low skyline that makes D.C. a special place to observe the weather. If you can get up even moderately high, you can watch angry-looking clouds advancing, or grab magazine-quality photos of a devastatingly pretty sunset. A story circulated among my friends that once at the big NPR building on North Capitol, everybody went out on their fourth-floor terrace, watched the sunset, and then applauded. I'd also heard that they announced the presence of rainbows over the PA system. Neither of those stories seemed likely to be true, even there, but they *could* have been true.

None of this excuses the weather itself, which can be icy and bitter in the winter and is sweltering in the summer, even if the idea that the place was built on a literal swamp is an urban legend—another falsehood that feels like a simple truth. Throughout July and August, the city, trapped in a kind of slo-mo misery, just sweats. It's as if we're all sealed inside a junior high locker room together, inhaling one another's bodily secretions and sponging salt slicks off our skin when we make the mistake of venturing outside long enough to walk more than a block. Thunderstorms and warnings thereof seem to disrupt as many early evenings as not, with Nats games under constant threat and spectacular photos of lightning strikes over that heavily regulated skyline. This does not break until perhaps sometime in September, when things begin to get more humane. And the rest of the year, it pours down rain a little less—usually.

All of this is to explain why, when I took a walk in the middle of the workday two weeks before Christmas, I was not as attentive to the possibility of heavy rain as I might have been at some other time. I just grabbed the Beast and my coat and took off out the front doors. I should have noticed there weren't a lot of other fools out there strolling around. Apparently, they had checked the weather.

I wasn't far from the office when I felt the first drop. Because it was only about forty-five degrees and there was a stiff wind, it got very uncomfortable very quickly as it started to rain harder. My first thought was that there was a sandwich place maybe another three blocks down, and if I kept going, I could snag some hot chocolate or some coffee, and at least I'd be warm.

The rain got louder, wetter, started to slap fat drops on my bare head. And then, as if I had accidentally walked under a busted gutter, it started to pour. I was not going to make it to the sandwich place. I was not going to make it to the end of the block. I reached into the Beast and took out a magazine, which I opened and held, tent-style, above my head. But I was saved! Farther down on the block, there was a branch of my bank. Its sign was much more welcoming, and more welcome, than it had been the last time I needed to discuss my account.

This time, there was no need to have anything to do with a person. I just needed to get inside the glass doors, into the little ATM enclosure. Holding the magazine to my forehead with one hand, I pulled the door open with the other and stepped inside. I squeezed a trickle of water out of my hair and swore.

I heard laughing. Of course I did. Then I turned and saw Will. Of course I did.

"Hey there." He was leaning on the glass wall, eating a salad-plate-sized chocolate chip cookie out of a wax paper bag. He was drier than I was, having dragged himself in here before it got so bad. He wore a black jacket over a gray Henley, and it was unfair in so many ways: I knew I was at my most bedraggled, I could see a wet flop of hair dangling by my eye. Did he have to look damp and appetizing? Did he *have* to?

"Well, hi," I said, putting down my bag and digging in it to get out my comb. "I guess this makes sense. Why would I think that if I got stuck in the rain and looked like hell, I wouldn't run into you?" I dug out the comb and ran it through my hair once, twice, then I dropped it back into the bag. "Hi. Sorry. I'm just soaking wet."

"You look great. You want a piece of cookie?" He held it out to me, and I reached over and broke off a piece I hoped was small enough to be polite, even though honestly, a piece of cookie was exactly what I wanted. Well, no, an entire cookie was exactly what I wanted, but a piece of cookie was close enough.

"Thank you," I said. Naturally it was delicious, which I signaled by making an unseemly noise as I chewed it. I should have tried to be dignified, but these were desperate times and unusual circumstances.

"Good, right?" he said. "It's from Reggie's."

"Ah, I've never been."

He pulled out his phone, looked at it, then slid down until he was sitting on the floor. "My weather app says this isn't letting up for about twenty minutes, so I'm just hanging here." He swept his arm, indicating the wall perpendicular to his. "You're welcome to stay."

I wasn't sure I could gracefully execute the slide down the wall he had just modeled, so I chose a spot beside him, and I just lowered myself down to the grubby, disgusting floor of the bank, noting for later that I would have to wash these clothes in hot water and perform a cleansing ritual over them.

"It was good to see you at the party," I finally said.

"That was fun," he said.

"Was it really?"

He took another bite of his cookie. "I mean, I think everybody there thought I was a freak because I don't work in radio or the internet, but I liked most of your friends."

"I felt like Eliza was maybe a little rude to you."

"Oh, because she kept yelling 'the waiter'? Whatever. It's true. How's it going with her anyway?"

"It's going well, I think. How's the picture business?"

"I'm taking headshots of a mid-level bureaucrat tomorrow."

"I'm sure they'll be better than any mid-level bureaucrat needs. How's Buddy?"

"He's good. We're working on levels of recall."

"Like, whether he can remember his past lives?"

He laughed. "No, like whether he can come to me when I say his name."

"How's that going?"

"You know, I think his attitude right now is that if he doesn't have any other plans, he's fine to do what I say."

It was so strange having a normal conversation with him while the rain battered the windows and surrounded us with white noise. We sat there for a long time, not saying much. And then I said, "Can you really do backflips?" He looked at me and wrinkled his brow. "When we met. You said that was how you messed up your ankle."

"Oh. Right. Yes. My mother taught me. The backflips part, not the ankle part."

"Ah, an acrobat."

"Well, she was in gymnastics for a long time when she was a kid. So she taught my brother and sister and me some stuff out in the backyard. I think it was a way to get us to burn off all the Doritos we were eating. Wear us out as fast as she could."

"Can you still do one?"

"I have no idea," he said. "Probably."

I looked at him. He didn't look away. I raised my eyebrow. He raised his in return. And then he stood slowly, heaving himself up noisily with the reluctant groans of a creaky-jointed grandpa. He looked down at me. "Are you sure you want to see this? It might be so impressive you can't tear yourself away from this bank when the rain stops."

"I do want to see it. But don't hurt yourself."

He made a noisy *pfft* and frowned at me. "Now I have to do it." He stood in the middle of the vestibule with his arms dangling at his sides. "Okay," he said several times in a row. "Count me in."

"You want 3-2-1 or 1-2-3?"

"3-2-1. Cape Canaveral–style."

"Three, two, one," I said.

He bent down with his arms out behind him, then swung them forward. The next thing I saw was the wide arc of his gray Chuck

Taylors as they flew over his head. He landed on his feet with a thump with his knees bent, then he popped up like he was on springs. "Aha!" he said. "Still got it." I applauded, because I couldn't help it. "I'll have to tell my mom that happened. She'll be very proud. She'll wish I'd been wearing a helmet and pads, and that there were mats on the floor. And that I had a spotter. And a medic. Still proud, though."

"You know," I said, "it would have been very awkward if I had stumbled in here and ended up trying to stay dry with a total stranger. I'm lucky it was you."

"Well, I'm glad it was you," he said, sliding down to sit next to me, facing the street.

The rain got louder. It poured down the windows in unbroken sheets. I could barely make out the form of a person scuttling along the sidewalk, his coat over his head, speeding up until he bumped into a mailbox. Will and I both made sympathetic little "oof" noises when he did, and then we laughed. I looked over at him in time to see him rubbing his knee, like maybe he regretted that backflip. "Okay," he said, "tell me your most embarrassing moment ever."

"Oh, I'm not telling you that," I said.

"Come on," he said. "I did a backflip for you. It's pouring rain, we're killing time, and I'm all out of cookie. Let's go, cough it up, most embarrassing moment."

"Okay," I said. Arguably, my actual most embarrassing moment was when my boyfriend of several years dumped me while I was making him dinner, but that wasn't what he meant. "So, my friend Stacy, we worked together at the radio station where I was before this job."

"This was here?"

"This was in New York. Boyfriend and I worked together there, he got a job down here, we moved, I got hired at Palmetto, he dumped me, he went back to New York to start his company."

"Ah, I didn't realize you moved yourself here for somebody

else. Or, with somebody else. I did that too." He didn't offer to say more. He just waved his hand. "Go ahead."

"Anyway, maybe two years ago, she got married. And when she had her bridal shower, her sister invited me, but I couldn't come; I'm sure I had to work. So obviously I wanted to send her a present, and I knew, because we'd worked together, that she was obsessed with this very special, very high-end speaker. She used to say she thought the sexiest thing in the world was listening to music."

"A thing a radio person would say."

"It is. Anyway, she was a very good friend, and I knew somebody at the company that made this speaker who let me in on their employee discount. So I bought it for her, and I sent it to her sister, to give it to her at the shower."

"And the sister stole it."

"No. So they have the shower, and she calls me, and she says, oh, you know, I just wanted to really thank you for the gift, it's great. I say, oh, I know you really wanted that, you can hook it up to your Bluetooth, I hope it's as sexy as you want it to be, whatever. And she seems a little bit subdued about it, and I really thought she was going to like it, so I was bummed out. I thought maybe she thought it was too much. So I asked her. I said, hey, you didn't think it was too much, right? Because you know I really love you, and I was happy to get it for you. She says, no, no, it was just right, thank you."

"You got her the six-inch speaker and somebody else got her the thirteen-inch speaker or something."

"No. I asked her if she thought it was okay with Nathan, the guy she was marrying—was he going to mind her using it? She says no, she says she already told him it was going to help her fall asleep. I'm not somebody who listens to music at night, but I said, sure, whatever, I hoped it was going to be romantic. But something seemed off, so I was trying to figure out what the problem might be."

"It was a bad speaker after all."

"Stop and let me tell it," I said. "Anyway. I kept going through problems, you know, I asked her if she thought it was going to be too loud for Nate. She says, no, it's not too loud. And somewhere around this point, I start to get just a tiny bit concerned about what's going on. Like, something is definitely not right. So I said, you know, if you'd rather have something besides an audio gadget, I can do that. Obviously, I don't want to give you something that makes you think about work."

"Right, sure."

"And she says, 'Why would a vibrator make me think about work?' "

His mouth fell open. And just then, the doors of the bank opened and a woman came from inside, looked down at us quizzically, opened her umbrella, and disappeared out into the weather. "Oops," he said. "She probably didn't hear you."

"She has an umbrella, she's fine," I said. "Anyway, yeah, the sister accidentally switched the card with this thing her cousin gave her that was called the Satisfier or something like that. I read about it later and I found out that people talk about how loud it is, and she thought that's why I was asking if it was too loud."

"And that's why she said it would help her fall asleep."

"Bingo. Now you go. Most embarrassing moment."

"Ah, okay. So I'm in college, and I'm living in this off-campus house in this cute neighborhood, and I'm out one night with all my buddies, the guys I would do basically everything with."

"Let me guess," I said. "Smitty. Frankie. The Nose."

"Yes, in college I lived with mob guys from 1955." He crumpled up the cookie bag and stuffed it into his backpack. "Okay. My friend Doug is a runner—goes out every day in his varsity wrestling shirt from high school and these bright red shorts, and he runs all around the neighborhood. I'd see him run past our house all the time. And we're hanging out talking, and he says, 'You know, I hate running over by your place, it's the worst part of my route.' I ask him why, and he says, 'Because of the dog.' I knew what he meant, because I lived next to this lady who had a German shepherd named Boo-Boo. And he says, 'Every time I run by your house, that dog comes running out, up the driveway, barking his head off, scares the hell out of me.' And I say, you know, the dog is harmless, his name's Boo-Boo, he's not going to bother you, he's just saying hello."

"Sounds right. Justice for Boo-Boo."

"Right? And a couple of days later, Doug comes running down the street. I can see him from a couple of blocks up, so I have time. And I know that, as it happens, on this particular day, the neighbor has Boo-Boo inside, because I saw her bring him in maybe ten minutes ago. I don't want Doug to be disappointed, so I run down to the front door, open it up, and I haul ass out to the end of the driveway, and I am barking my ass off. 'A-WOO-WOO-WOO-WOOF!,' I'm growling, I'm snarling, 'WOO-WOO-WOO-WOOF!'"

This, of course, was when a man opened the doors of the vestibule, put away his umbrella, and went into the bank. He seemed to be trying to ignore us. "This is uncanny," I said.

"It really is. We're all alone except for when the person in the story is barking or masturbating."

"Anyway," I said, "you barked at Doug. I assume somebody heard you."

"Yeah, somebody heard me, all right. The guy who was running down the street, who was not actually Doug, but an entirely different guy in a gray shirt and red shorts."

"No."

"Yes. Not him."

"What did you do?"

"Well, the guy sort of looks at me, he slows down. Safe to say he's surprised. So I look at him and I say, 'Oh, I'm sorry. I thought you were someone else.' I'm not sure that helped."

"Wow."

"I think you'd have to admit your vibrator has been defeated."

"Hey, it wasn't my vibrator."

"Details." He smiled, and he looked past me through the glass. "Man, we are sure *stuck*."

"Because of the rain," I said.

He nodded slowly, still looking out at the flat gray day, still with the tiniest, most inscrutable smile. "Sure."

We sat there for several more minutes until the rain finally got quieter, then even quieter. We kept looking at each other, and it kept feeling more and more like this bank vestibule was the center of the world, the only place where there was any gravity, and I'd be sucked out into space if I opened the door.

But just as I had this thought, Will stood up, and he put his hand on the door. The downpour had slowed to a drizzle. The air outside was frosty and damp, and we stood on the sidewalk for another moment as the rain freckled his shirt. "So I guess I'll see you . . . the next time I run into you?" I said.

He thought for a minute. "Actually, can I ask you a favor? I have an engagement shoot scheduled on Sunday afternoon, over near my apartment. I'm a little nervous about leaving Buddy by himself—he chewed on my PS5 controller the other day. You're one of the only people he knows besides my neighbor, who's going to be out of town. Would you be interested in dog-sitting? He'll mostly just sleep. And when I'm done, I'll buy some food, I'll bring it home, and we'll eat. Super casual, I promise."

"Wow, we're making a plan?" I said. "I thought I was only allowed to see you at random."

He nodded slowly. "Well," he said. "There was the party."

"Oh, I wasn't in on the planning. I didn't know you would be there."

He stepped close to me. I could still see where the rain had made wet dots on his shirt, sprinkled on his chest where the jacket had been open. He looked down at the sidewalk, and then up at me through his lashes. "I knew you would be there."

I couldn't talk. I opened my mouth, but I closed it again. And then, out of the corner of my eye, I spotted a row of three enamel pins near the collar of his jacket that said HIKE A GLACIER; LAS VEGAS; and HALF DOME, YOSEMITE NATIONAL PARK. They might as well have reached out and poked me. He wasn't from here. He was traveling from wherever to wherever. *Get your goddamn bearings, Foster,* my brain said to itself. "I can dog-sit," I said. I wasn't sure whether this constituted getting my bearings. "I'll see you then."

CHAPTER FIFTEEN

The Lesson

At about noon on Sunday, I headed for the address Will had given me. He lived in a building not too different from mine, about a fifteen-minute walk away. I knocked on the door, and when he opened it, Will was holding on to Buddy by his collar. "Hi."

"Well, hi," I said. I reached down to rub the top of Buddy's fuzzy head. "Nice to see you again, troublemaker."

"Thank you again for doing this," Will said as he shut the door and let Buddy go. "I have to go capture this epic love story, and somehow I don't think the bride-to-be would enjoy a hundred-and-sixty-pound dog trying to get his nose under her petticoats for an hour and a half."

"You would never do that, would you," I said, resting my hand on Buddy's head. I looked at Will. "He would never do that, that's defamation."

Buddy trotted off toward the small living room and immediately jumped up on the couch.

"Is he allowed to be up there?" I asked.

"I've already given up," Will said. I turned to look as Buddy flopped down on the sofa, which he occupied almost completely. His head rested on one arm, and his stretched back legs almost reached the other. I nodded and turned back to Will. "He certainly seems to feel at home with you."

"I have a feeling he can make himself at home just about anywhere." He dragged a plastic bin out of the hall closet and pulled off the lid. "All right," he said. He began to remove items from it and lay them on the floor. "I have chicken things. I have cheese things. I have this rubber thing with a hole in it that he might or might not want to chew on. I have this rope that he uses to pull me around the apartment. And I have these." He held up a bag of long, crusty chews that looked like expired foot-long Slim Jims. "These are bully sticks. Do you know what those are?"

"I don't," I said.

"They're dicks," he said. "They are bull dicks. They are the literal dicks of bulls."

I looked at the bag. I looked at him. "*Those* are."

He looked at the bag. He looked back at me. "Believe it or not, that's like a third of the original size."

"That is a legit amazing animal fact."

"Buddy loves them. But I have to warn you, however bad you think a stretched and dried bull penis would smell when a dog slowly rehydrates it with his mouth, it's much worse in reality, so just . . . if you go with these, maybe open a window. But anyway, all that is there if you need it." He put everything back in the bin and put the bin back in the closet. Then he got on his hands and knees and crawled under the dining table, only to emerge with a stuffed elephant. "This is Caesar." He squeezed the toy. It gave a squeak, and Buddy briefly lifted his head from the sofa before dropping it again and returning to what seemed to be an immediately restorative sleep.

"Is he allowed to watch TV?"

Will grinned in the direction of a large backpack on the floor as he zipped it up, then lifted it up onto his shoulder. "After he finishes his homework. I just walked him, so he should be good for a while, but if you need his leash, it's hanging on the hook by the door."

"Got it."

"Next time you see me, I'll have food," he said. "You want Thai, Mexican, Korean, or Indian?"

"Let's say Mexican," I said, and he gave a nod and turned and headed for the door. "You didn't even ask me if I'm a vegan or anything," I added as he opened it.

He turned back to me and narrowed his eyes. "You had the Bolognese." He had an exceptionally good mouth. I just had to stop noticing these things.

"Busted," I said, and we both smiled, and he gave me a wave and walked off down the hall. I shut the door and turned back to Buddy, who just then stretched his endless legs so they were even more fully extended across the entirety of the living room couch. "Please, don't get up," I told him. "I'll just sit somewhere else."

Human nature comes for all of us in our moments of solitude, so obviously the first thing I did was snoop. I didn't go into the bathroom and open the medicine cabinet, and I didn't open anything that was closed, so in fairness to myself, I exercised more restraint than a lot of people would have. It was a small place, but the little hallway that led to the bedroom and bathroom was loaded—naturally—with hanging picture frames. This family, standing together next to a river wearing life jackets, had to be his. I wasn't sure which of the boys with wide smiles he was, but there was a girl, too, and parents who both looked like the kind of strapping people who go rafting a lot.

There was a teenager I didn't think was Will, wearing a Dodgers jersey in the stands at a game. On the wall opposite what I figured were family photos, there were bigger prints, more what I would expect to find in a photographer's house. One showed a bike racer, captured against a blurred background, wearing bright blue. Another was of a guy climbing a mountain, and it occurred to me in passing that if Will took it, he must have climbed up there, too.

What there wasn't much of was furniture. There was the gray couch Buddy had been sleeping on, with its upholstery worn down to bare in a few places. There were a couple of tables that looked like they might have started their lives as flat-pack items fifteen years ago. It all looked scavenged. Fortunately, however bare the sofa cushions, they were surprisingly comfortable, which I learned when I came back to find Buddy had moved to his giant bed on the floor. "Oh, thank you," I said, settling onto the warm sofa. "Nice of you to share."

For about an hour, I read a novel and Buddy napped and periodically snored a loose, cartoonish snore, clearly in a state of floppy-lipped bliss. But when I came to the end of a chapter, I took out my laptop and opened an episode of *Dear Wendy* I had been working on as a favor to the show's editor, who was out of town for two weeks. The idea behind the show was that Wendy, an advice columnist, would listen to a question, and then she would interview some experts to get their input, and then she would deliver her verdict.

This episode, like a disproportionate number of advice-column questions, revolved around a wedding. There was an estranged brother, a best friend, a years-old resentment over a disrupted birthday party at which someone was overserved—it was messy and appalling and, in that sense, pretty standard. The producer who had done the first pass at the episode was still new and needed some help nailing the basics, although she had solid instincts for what was good and what was boring, which was more than half the battle.

I got quite absorbed in fiddling with some tape Wendy got from a wedding planner who argued that no one is entitled to be invited to any wedding, and I was still on the couch with my headphones on when I heard the key in the lock. I hopped up and paused to look in the hall mirror to make sure I was at least a little presentable and didn't have an egregious case of headphone hair. I ran my hands through it just as he opened the door.

When he came inside, I felt it in my knees, something vaguely lovely that I was hesitant to interrogate beyond simply being happy to see him. His camera bag was across his back, and he lifted both hands to show me two big plastic take-out sacks. "I have come to feed you," he said.

"All *right,*" I said, maybe a little too hungrily, so to speak, as I stepped out of his way.

"How did Buddy do?" At just that moment, the dog dragged himself off the bed and came over to greet Will, who wrapped his hand under Buddy's chin without the slightest bend at the waist.

"Just like you said, he mostly slept. How was the engagement?"

"The pictures should be great. I think the couple is doomed," he said. "She went off to touch up her makeup at one point, and he told me he's looking forward to being married because it will force them to fight less."

"Wow, yikes."

"Exactly. Okay, let me put all this down." He went into the very small galley kitchen, where he pulled down some plates and got some mismatched flatware out of a drawer. "I got some tacos, I got some enchiladas, I got some tamales, and I got some sopapillas in case you have a sweet tooth, I didn't know. I also got some chicharrones, which are my actual favorites."

"Ooh, I think I want them."

"They are fried. They are pork. You definitely want them."

"Sold."

He fished a dried pig's ear out of his backpack and gave it to Buddy to gnaw on—I was apparently not the only one given to producing items from the bottom of a bag unexpectedly—and we sat on the couch, with my open laptop nudged out of the way on the coffee table. The food was stupendous and decadent, and we ate a *lot.* I stuffed my face while he talked about the challenges of new clients; he stuffed his while I talked about radio. "Tell me about Madeline's," I said as I scooped rice onto my plate. "I've never been a server, I feel like it's an enormous hole in my understanding of the world."

"Well," he said, "I would have to take a lot of pictures to pay for even this tiny apartment in this city by myself." He downed a piece of pork—they were as good as they sounded—and went on. "None of this is my ultimate plan. I'm between . . . something. Somethings. I don't know." He looked around. "Practically everything in here is thrifted, you know, so I feel okay leaving it? Everything I really need can fit in my Kia just in case."

"In case what?"

"In case whatever," he said.

I considered him as I finished a bite. "You told me it was a long story what you were doing before you got here and started doing portraits."

"Mm," he said noncommittally.

I sat back and studied him. "Look, I interview people for a living," I said. "I'm going to get there eventually. We'll start easy. Where did you grow up?"

"California."

"Northern or southern?"

"L.A."

"I assume you were a movie star," I said. "I think that's all they have there, right? Just like D.C. only has politicians?"

He made a face I found very hard to interpret. "I mean, *I* wasn't," he said.

I frowned at him. "But?"

"Well, my father was a cinematographer," he said. "And my mother was a stuntwoman."

I put down a forkful of tamale. "What?"

"Yep."

"If I had anything that interesting in reserve, I'd tell everyone constantly. Like . . . jumping motorcycles over canyons or what?"

"When she was younger, it was mostly fights. But eventually, she did a little bit of everything. She did some driving. She fell out of a lot of windows."

"Now it makes sense," I said.

"What does?"

"The fact that you wanted to lasso the dog."

He laughed. "She did ride horses a few times."

"What would I have seen her in?"

"Many, many things, honestly. Most recently *Real Estate Men*. You've probably seen that."

"Does that even have stunts?" *Real Estate Men* was a very beloved but very dopey comedy about a couple of agents who accidentally get tangled up with some mob guys.

"Remember when the guy is showing the house, and he's trying to explain to the buyers how safe the neighborhood is, and then the lady out in the street gets hit by a car, and she flies up in the air?"

"That's your mother?"

"That's my mother. Gwynnie Cabot. Thirty-two films, ninety-four television shows, seven back surgeries, and one ear she can't really hear out of anymore. She's the happiest person I know." He got up and went over to take a photo album off the shelf. He flipped through it and then handed it to me, pointing at a picture of a woman wearing a pair of padded coveralls and a helmet, standing in front of a muscle car.

"And your dad's in that business too."

"Yes. But he's not famous. He's a working DP, a director of photography. He did a lot of police procedurals and TV movies and stuff. They're kind of opposites, honestly. He doesn't ever want any attention, and she will walk around on fire if you put a camera on her. If you talk to movie people, they don't necessarily know him, but they all know her."

I reached over and touched his elbow without really *entirely* meaning to do it but probably not exactly *not* meaning to do it. "I can't believe this. You are officially much more interesting than I am."

"I doubt it," he said.

"I don't have a lot of secrets," I said. "I think you pretty much know everything weird about me at this point."

"Well," he said, "I'm not sure. I've been meaning to ask you: I said something wrong when we were talking about the shows you work on, right? At your photo shoot? We were having a good time, it was good, and then it was weird."

"Oh," I said. "After we talked about *Scanner Stories.*"

"Yeah, actually," he said. "I think that's right."

I took a big breath and let it out slowly. "So," I said, "Justin Dash is my ex. We were together for a few years, and we made the first two seasons of that show together. He hosted it, but we made it. And when we broke up—or when he broke up with me—he kind of . . . kept the show."

"Oh."

"Yeah. And I . . . I just walked away from it, because I didn't want to fight about it. Or think about it, or whatever. And now, it's just, you know, his thing, like you said."

I watched him replay it in his head. I saw it hit. "Oh no, because I said—"

"It's not your fault—that's what everybody thinks, and now it's true. I'm not part of it anymore. I haven't been part of it for years. I got very drunk the night I realized he'd made as many episodes without me as we made together."

"I feel like . . . garbage."

I laughed and reached out and touched the couch between us, like I was putting my hand on his leg when I wasn't. "You don't have to feel like garbage. It just makes me flinch, which is frustrating, believe me, because I would love to just not think about it anymore."

He tilted his head and looked at me. "All right, but I still feel a little bit like garbage. Just a small can. For what it's worth, I still can't walk past the place where my ex works without wanting to kick myself in the shins."

"Where does she work?"

"She's a lobbyist."

"For who?"

"Dentists."

I would love to be a person with a heart so expansive that I'd take no pleasure in the fact that his ex lobbied for dentists and not the environment or human rights. But I am what I am, and I was sort of witheringly gratified that it was regular lobbying.

"Wow, so you could have ended up in the pocket of Big Teeth."

"Big paying for your teeth, honestly. I couldn't get over how boring it was, but boy, was she getting ready to make money." His eyes fell on my laptop. "Is that for work?"

"Yes."

"What are you doing?"

"I'm editing."

"Show me."

"You don't want me to show you this."

"Yes, I do." I squinted at him, but he just pointed at the screen.

I couldn't eat another bite anyway, so I set the plates aside and pulled the laptop over so we could sit side by side and he could lean over to look. "Okay, this is a podcast episode, let's say. What does this look like?"

"Waveforms. I assume that's all sound."

"Yes."

"What are all the rows?"

"This one is the narrator's voice," I said, pointing at the top row. "So it's, you know, 'In a town in Wyoming, there's a cage in a basement, and in that basement, there's a dragon.' " I moved my finger down. "Then this one is the actualities."

He closed one eye. "I don't know what that is."

"They're like sound bites. They're people talking. 'Well, I'll tell ya, the first time I saw the dragon, I was pretty surprised.' Or maybe, 'I'm Professor Oldcreatures from the University of Arizona, and there are only about twenty dragons left in the American west.'" Moved it down again. "This one is music, because this piece is scored."

"Oh, sure. Do you pick the music?"

"No. They have somebody good at that. If I did it, you'd just get a lot of sad piano, because that's my safety zone." I moved my finger once more. "This row is ambiance. And you put them all together." I pressed the space bar, and a vertical line swept from left to right across the screen. "It's just multiple tracks, just like with music."

He leaned closer. "What are all the little dots?"

"Those are all cuts."

He turned to me and seemed to suddenly notice that we were about six inches apart. I certainly did. "There are like a hundred of them," he finally said.

"Yes."

"I had no idea," he said.

"Well, no, you're not supposed to." I clicked to stretch out the tape so he could see the adjustments all throughout the voice tracks.

"What are you cutting?"

"Could be a lot of things. Could just be mouth noises. Mouths are a menace."

He turned to me, and I felt him looking at my lips. "Mouths?" he asked.

I reminded myself to breathe. "They're a curse to human beings," I said. And then I said, "Admittedly, not always."

He laughed. "No."

"Anyway, it's mostly things that nobody is ever going to notice. Here, hang on." I got up and fetched two pairs of headphones and a splitter from my bag. I put on a pair and handed one to him.

He goggled at the big, sturdy Sonys. "Old-school listening, huh?"

"I hate earbuds," I said. "They're never clean, I hate the sound, and I can't stand looking at anything that was just inside my ear. Anyway." I hit the space bar again, and we heard a woman's voice say: *Honestly um I think the truth is that um you don't invite people to a wedding because they deserve it um you invite them because you want to spend that day with them.* "Okay, what did you notice?"

"Lots of 'ums,'" he said. "You'd cut them out?"

"Judgment call," I said. I replayed the beginning of the clip over and over in our ears: *Honestly I think um I think um I think um think um think um.* "This first one can go. But I'd leave the other ones. You want people to still sound like themselves. But you don't want the people listening to be thinking about how much she's saying 'um' instead of hearing what she says."

"I could never notice all this in the first place."

"Well, maybe, but on the other hand, I don't know how to use a camera more complicated than my iPhone. And truthfully, I think you could. I'll tell you what," I said, grabbing a file and popping it into an email. "I'm going to send you a file I use for training. It's me talking. You have to see if you can figure out what I use it to train people on."

"Oh, no. I am going to fall on my face so hard."

"I bet you can do it. Just listen carefully, and I bet you'll hear it. And if you don't, I'll tell you next time I see you." He smiled and I shrugged.

He pointed at the bottom row. "You said this is ambiance. Is that like street noise?"

"Sometimes. Not usually." I played him the ambi track. It was just quiet, with a soft *whoosh* in the background, which I raised the volume to emphasize.

"I don't get it."

"Nothing happening, right?" I moved a few things around and hit play again. "You can hear that, right? When it cuts between two pieces of tape?" He nodded. "That's the sound of nothing happening in two different rooms." He nodded again. We both leaned forward even more. And we stayed that way until I could smell his soap. I played it for him again. Fuzzy silence, then silent silence. Noise, then much less noise.

"What makes them sound different?" he asked.

I tried not to turn toward him to stare at the side of his face, at the hollow of his throat, at those dark eyes. "Lots of things," I said. "The equipment. Big room versus small room. Sitting next to a window versus next to a pile of laundry. Those quiets will all sound different. So that's why we make people record maybe thirty seconds of what the silence in the room sounds like. It's useful. We call it room tone."

"I've shot a couple of weddings where the videographer got room tone, and I had no idea what it was for."

"Now you know." I closed the laptop. "And that is probably as much as you want to hear about that." We took the headphones off.

"So you do all this for other shows on top of the show you're actually making," he said.

"Yeah. I sort of fit everything in around the edges. When I'm not going out on twenty blind dates."

"You really went out on twenty blind dates."

"I really did."

"And? Did you like them?"

"Some I liked. Some I didn't. Some didn't like me. One left the country, although I don't think it was because of me. One was still married."

"Married?"

"Separated. Separated and angry. But anyway, I have a second date with a family doctor very soon."

"Doctor sounds good," he said. "I guess that's something."

"It is. He seems fine. Who knows?" I found myself eager to stop telling Will about Michael #2, and I wasn't sure who that was for. I grabbed for the first change of subject I could think of.

"Hey, you pulled me way off track. You were telling me your life story. We were up to your mother falling out of windows."

"Ah, right," he said. "Okay. Well, until I was in college, I wanted to do stunts. I was taking martial arts, playing a lot of sports, I trained with her a little."

"Your mom taught you stunts?"

"Yeah. Remember the backflips? She taught me a lot, after she wrapped me up in so much padding I could barely move my arms. I would just hit the ground and roll. I wanted to be exactly like her. That was the plan when I was younger."

"But . . ." I prodded.

"But my brother was better at it than I was, and when I was in college, he was already working, and he was really good. But there was an accident with a motorcycle he was on, and he was in the hospital for a long time. It took him months and months to get better, and he's okay now, but he scared the hell out of everybody. Especially my parents."

The other kid in the family photo. The kid at the Dodgers game. "Oh wow, that must have been horrible."

"Pretty bad, yeah," he said. "After that, I think my parents lost their taste for having me jump off buildings. It was like one kid who might end up in the hospital all the time was all they could stand. They wouldn't have told me not to do it, but about a year after that accident, my mom told me that she had a dream I was on fire. And she didn't tell me to try to get me to quit or anything, she was just telling me. And I felt like maybe the time had passed to get into that. Like I said, he was a lot better than I was anyway. He still is. He's doing a Netflix thing right now where he's jumping off some giant bridge, I think onto a speedboat? I can't remember what it's called."

"I admit I saw the family photos—your sister, too."

"That's Maggie. She's a normal person, she's a teacher. She's married, she has kids. And she lives just up in Baltimore." He took a breath. "Anyway, I went to college, and then I just bounced around. I worked in construction for a while, a little retail, some summer camps and parks and outside stuff. Took pictures in my free time. Then maybe five years ago, I started dating Meredith, and eventually she moved here for work. And that's how I got to D.C."

"Do you miss California?"

"I miss the weather."

"That's very reasonable."

"Got here, tried a couple things. I thought I might want to be a sports doctor, I think just because I knew people my whole life whose joints were all torn up, where all they wanted was to feel better. So I went back to school for that, but it didn't pan out. Honestly, I couldn't pass the first couple of premed classes. So that was it for that. And all I really liked was going out and taking pictures. I did a lot of sports stuff at first, but I wasn't making money. So I started working with a buddy of mine who did portraits. I apprenticed with him for a while, and then I started this little business, which I can't live on. And that's why I wait tables."

"You're good at both."

"Thank you," he said, briefly smiling down at the floor. "Anyway, I'm here until the lease is up, and then, no idea. Somewhere. Something. I'm trying to figure out my life. That's kind of what broke me and Meredith up in the first place."

"Uh-oh."

"Yeah. She felt like the photography was never going to get off the ground, and she'd been telling people I was going to be a doctor, and she didn't like telling them I wasn't going to be. She felt like her friends were baffled that she was with this loser, and she finally said, 'I did not move across the country to live with a waiter in a one-bedroom apartment, and I am not going to pay anybody else's way.' That's a direct quote."

"Yikes."

"It was probably for the best. That's what you're supposed to say, right? The funny thing is that I'm probably happier than I've been anywhere else, even though I haven't really settled down here. I spend a lot of my time on something I like. I work the shifts that make the most sense, and it all seems to be fitting together. I didn't even mean to come here, exactly, but I've been here three years, and it's the longest I've ever lived anywhere except at home."

"It sounds like you stay busy."

He looked over at me. "I mean, I have some free time for friends."

I nodded. "That's good," I said. "I could probably use some friends who don't already know what mix-minus is." He frowned. "Maybe I'll tell you next time," I said.

Just then, Buddy noisily rose from the floor and came over to sniff Will's fingers, then mine. "I think this nut is ready for a walk," he said.

"Yes," I said. "I should probably get home." I gathered up my stuff, and he walked me to the door.

"Thank you again for doing this," he said as he swung it open.

"You're welcome. Thanks for dinner."

"I'll see you soon?"

"Next time Buddy gets lost," I said. "If not before. Meanwhile, wish me luck with my second date with a guy who is, I will say, a better prospect than the supplement guy."

"Good luck," he said. "I hope it works out. I'll be listening for sure."

Walking back toward my apartment with the sound of his voice in my ears and the smell of him quickly cementing itself into a memory that, true or false, made my chest hurt, I have no idea how I could have possibly believed the thing I told myself, which was: *I guess that's that.*

CHAPTER SIXTEEN

The Second Date

There was no reason for it to feel awkward that my second date with Michael #2 was scheduled only days after Will and I ate Mexican food in his living room. We were not dating. He was not staying. What's more, I had told him exactly what was going on, and he had told me he would listen. To this very date! It just *felt* awkward.

Eliza was disappointed, I knew, that only one out of twenty of the guys she sent me out with had been a second-date-level match, and it had surprised me, too. I wasn't even good at sending back an overcooked steak at a restaurant; this project had brought out something picky in my personality. I wished that she, who was constantly telling me not to settle, could understand that there was perhaps an upside in my rejecting nineteen out of twenty of her picks, but it didn't seem to be going that way.

It didn't help that our listeners were still plowing week by week through all those first dates, and halfway through, a lot of them didn't agree with me, either—they were hoping I'd follow up with several of those guys, and they felt sure I would. In my defense, Michael #2 was definitely one of their favorites. In a poll someone posted, out of the guys they'd heard so far, they liked him, and they liked Josh (who owned Dynamo the iguana), and they liked Eric, the Lao food guy, and they liked a couple of the guys who had already rejected me (a development we'd dropped from their date episodes to preserve them as candidates for discussion until it was time to reveal their voluntary departures).

But "Hot Waiter" still showed strong in every survey they took. It was a joke by now, an in-crowd wink from listener to listener, or a general rebuke of Eliza's method. Still, it was impressive how they'd clung to—how they'd created—this mythology around Hot Waiter that was, in fact, much less impressive than Hot Waiter himself. Imagine if they knew his mother was a stunt performer. They would die of squealing injuries.

I had promised myself I would tell the truth, and the truth was that Michael was the only one of the men Eliza brought me whom I had liked and who had liked me back. I had the sneaking feeling that the twenty guys represented elements of Eliza's own taste in men as much as any careful observation she had made about mine. They were all different, but they all seemed to call back to something from her own life. Some of them had Cody's shyness, some had a classic quarterback handsomeness, and some of them seemed like Eliza herself, with the hustle and the businesslike handshakes. Some of them . . . I'll just say I wouldn't have been surprised to see them land paid collabs to print their initials on the asses of their pants.

Michael #2 had a little less pepper in his paprikash, as Billy Crystal might say. He'd graduated from medical school younger than most of his classmates, and he'd started out in a high-pressure position, but he seemed at least theoretically interested in exploring some level of work-life balance. That sounded good to me, since work-life balance was something I thought would be lovely to get into someday, when I was less busy. He also had an aversion to discussing his credentials that I found charming. He hadn't told me until about halfway through our first date that he'd gone to Harvard. Ron, the older lobbyist I had gone out with between Michaels #1 and #2, didn't wait that long to tell me that his *brother* went to Harvard.

Eliza felt strongly that if the first date was a lunch, the second should be a nice dinner, because as she put it, "lunch doesn't present possibilities." She was further convinced that better restaurants led to better dates, and she wanted to see what a high-end experience would do to my impression of a guy. (I was not sure whether to be offended by this, since it seemed to suggest I could be bought with fancy appetizers, which I was something like ninety-two percent sure was not true.) So she managed to get us in for dinner at a Peruvian spot that was generally understood to be impossible to get into, where they did a prix fixe menu that Toby freed up some extra Fitness West money to bankroll, tip included. Some of the guys had been insistent on pitching in for previous meals, but there are things I would never let even a doctor pay for as a second date unless I was pretty sure it was on the way to marriage, and maybe not even then.

It was the nicest place I'd ever eaten. Ever. It had the best service, the most impressive hush of prestige, and wine pairings even I, as a person who sometimes drank tequila and Coke Zero at home, could appreciate. The food, including a piece of fish so divine it seemed to sigh itself apart into bites when you touched it with a fork, almost made me want to cry, because I knew it was the only time I would ever have it in my life.

We spent a *lot* of time just goggling at how good the food was. Michael #2 kept shaking his head and saying, "Wow," and it made me laugh, because it was all I could think of, too. We wedged other conversation in around the edges of the calamari, the abalone, the abundant wine. He was trying to learn Spanish so he could serve patients better, and it turned out we had the same frustrations with the more popular apps for language learning.

He told me one had tried to teach him how to say, "This chicken murdered my grandfather," when he wasn't too far into his studies, and he almost quit as a result.

It was nice.

When it was over, we went outside and stood in our coats in the cool evening, and he said it had been very good to see me again, and I agreed. My joints felt loosened by the wine, and this time, when he kissed me good night, I put my hands at his waist, and he pushed a bit of my hair behind my ear. He walked off to get the Metro—or, really, he walked off to do a little interview with Abby, and then to get the Metro—and I hung back to talk to Julie, who had been allowed to sit nearby, but who did not get dinner out of the deal. "That food looked really good," she said as she started our debrief. I looked down at the microphone I was speaking into. I talked about the food. I talked about how amazing I felt, what a great night it was, and then again, I talked about the food. The fish. The little dish of potatoes. The gelato, and the bonbons they sent us out the door with, which were now in my purse. I talked about the wine, all the wine, how perfectly it went with everything and how delicious it was. And then Julie said, "So you like him," and I said, "Who?"

In my defense, I was a little bit drunk, and because we had just been talking about the food, it was quite a swerve to move immediately to talking about the date, at least given my condition. But Julie looked at me like I had four heads coming out of my neck, and I said, "Oh! Yes! Michael! Of course I like him, yes. I like him a lot. He's really a kind, fun, attractive man."

"So it sounds like this is the best date you've had in this project."

"It absolutely is. He's good. She did well with this one."

When Julie turned off the recorder, I said, "If you put that in the show, I will never live it down. Please erase every sign of it from the earth."

"I'm not going to put it in the show," she scoffed. "I'm going to make a copy for myself, though, and you can't stop me. And every year on your birthday, I'm going to call and play it for you."

I waved my hand at her when she offered to get me a car (Toby would pay after 10:00), and I took off toward home. I could walk half an hour in flats, and maybe I'd sneak a bonbon out of my bag now and then.

It wasn't until I was about halfway home that it really sunk into my bones that because of Eliza, I had just had a successful second date at a very la-di-da restaurant with a lovely doctor who had a stable life, good manners, and a plan to get himself from where he was to retirement. The orderliness of it, right? He didn't seem like he'd be threatened by my job. He didn't seem like he'd take me on dates that were centered on weapons. He didn't seem like he'd steal my work or suck the blood out of my career. He seemed to like me.

The thing she did—the thing she said she could do, the thing I was positive she could not do—it was hard to avoid the conclusion that she had done it. I put my shoulders back, adjusted my small bag against my hip (the Beast did not come on dates), and took a deep breath as a successful dater in a world of terrible conversations and hopeless miscues. I had never thought of myself as a person who specifically wanted to marry a doctor, but I started to wonder if it would mean I never had to pay to get a mole looked at again.

CHAPTER SEVENTEEN

The Breakthrough

I needed to clear my head after this exceptionally good dinner, just gather my thoughts and steel myself for the road ahead. So the next night, when my to-do list was light, I decided it was a night to do nothing. It was pouring rain outside. The show was a success. People liked it. They liked having opinions about it. In fact, Paulo the embassy man may not have been impressed with me, but he had been written up on the website of one of our local magazines because everybody thought he was such a catch. They didn't even know yet that he'd bowed out and was still fully available. Imagine when they heard!

Some dedicated members of Team Hot Waiter had managed to track down Will at the restaurant. They posted his picture, which did not *reduce* the number of people who referred to him as Hot Waiter.

Things were even pretty good at Palmetto. Julie was beginning, she told me, to receive compliments from Miles. Actual compliments, and not his usual "I'm glad this went better than last time"/"I think you've almost got the hang of it" rotation of back-handedness and other psychological warfare.

And so: time to do nothing. I got into my stretchiest, least judgmental shorts and my most comfortable and most well-worn T-shirt, and I stretched out on the couch with a glass of wine to watch *Halls of Power,* the recap of which I was scheduled to edit the next week, so I figured I might as well get my bearings. They had recently brought back a congressional aide who had supposedly died in a yacht explosion but turned up in Costa Rica. He now was seeking revenge on the president via a poisoned mango smoothie. All very on-brand.

I hit pause when there was a knock at the door. Since there had been no buzz, it was most likely my neighbor, who occasionally ended up with my mail or asked if I could water a couple of plants while she was away. But when I put my glass down and went to the door, it was Will. He was wearing a jacket, but he was soaked to the skin. His curls dripped rain on the floor outside my apartment door. Somebody must have let him in downstairs on their way in or out—if I had seen him in this state, I probably would have, too. "No breathing," he said.

"What?"

"The thing you sent me. You weren't breathing."

So often, people say "my jaw dropped," and they don't mean it. It's too bad, because if you are surprised enough under exactly the right circumstances, and if you are frozen in place, your jaw will actually drop. And when I realized he was talking about the file I had emailed him while we were talking about audio production, that's exactly what happened to me. He had sat down somewhere and opened that file. He had listened to it, probably a lot of times.

And at some point—I could almost imagine him listening while eating Mexican food in his apartment with Buddy snoozing on the sofa—he had heard it. He had heard that the way the tape had been edited, all the breaths were taken out. While some people preferred it that way, I had always believed, rather stubbornly, that it sounded unnatural, and that the ear would subtly, somehow, register that something was wrong. His ear had worked like mine.

"No breathing," I repeated.

The last thing I remember clearly is that it was me who pulled him in. I forget which of us shut the door behind him, or whether I pulled him to the side of the hallway where the closet was or he pushed me up against it. But there we were. That great mouth, that gorgeous mouth, was kissing me, raggedly dragging across my cheek, coming back to start again. "I'm sorry," he said right into my ear, "I'm soaked."

"No, it's nice," I said, feeling my own shirt start to stick to me. "I needed a shower."

I lifted my knee to wrap my leg around his, and he slid his hand under my thigh. I stopped kissing him long enough to mutter, "You got it right, by the way," and he laughed against my lip and said, "Oh, good."

Oof. "Knob in the butt, knob in the butt, knob in the butt," I sputtered, and the way he absolutely *froze* made me cackle. When I caught my breath I said, "I'm saying the doorknob is poking me in the behind and I need to scoot over like six inches."

"Ah, okay, now I get it," he said, and somehow together we cleared the doorknob without disengaging. He went to pull my shirt over my head, but as he took both sides of it, he saw the words on the front—PRODUCERS DO IT WITHOUT CREDIT—and started to laugh. "This is good," he said, and then pulled it up and off me.

"I wasn't really dressed for this," I said.

"Doesn't matter now," he said, starting to tug at the waistband of my very comfy, very old shorts.

I would not have said I was a sex-against-the-wall person; in most of my prior relationships, I freely admit I was primarily a sex-in-the-bed person. This was not particularly by choice or because I refused it under other circumstances, but more because it didn't tend to come up in other circumstances. Apartments are small and cramped, and as much as people like to talk about the kitchen counter, I could not reconcile that with the knowledge that the next day, I would be cutting an onion on that same surface.

The shower, yes, sometimes, but I always ended up with soap in my eyes or the soap dish poking me in the back. Floors so often mean rug burns, and couches are complicated from a cleanliness perspective. Justin used to throw towels over the couch to give it a try, but such an effort to make sure it *wasn't* gross just made me feel like it *was* gross.

But perhaps I had simply run into an entire cookbook's worth of unusually bad pancakes and one had finally flipped my way. Because there I was, with my shorts on the floor, with his hand moving down my side, with my leg around him, with wet clothes sticking to him until he (the pants) and I (the jacket and shirt) peeled them off and left them in a cold little puddle inside my apartment door.

I touched and touched and touched, but I kept going back to put my hands on the back of his head and feel his curls in my fingers, which I suppose I had been wanting to do since I saw him running down the street in front of my place. As my hand drifted down his chest, down his stomach, he stopped and looked at me, and now there was no question that both of us were very much breathing. He said, "I . . ."

"I know," I said, and I pulled him toward me.

I was afraid I might have cracked my elbow when I abruptly got *extremely* happy and whacked it against the wall behind me. Will got a pretty gnarly scratch on his shoulder when my bare foot slipped on the wet floor and I grabbed on to him to avoid landing on my naked ass in my own front hall. (Worst 911 call ever.) A strand of my hair got caught, somehow, under the palm of his hand as he braced himself. I do have noises; the least impressive was "ow."

But he did something with his lips on my belly that I swear I still don't understand. He kissed the inside of my wrist with this strange . . . curiosity? He said, "You're killing me," which is the kind of thing that sounds terribly and wretchedly corny and obvious unless it is said directly into your ear by a hot naked person you like very much, in which case it is like being made Queen of the Universe, the All-Powerful GODDESS of sex, in which case it is very very good.

And then we were done, and we just stood against that wall making out like a couple of hormonal dopes for what seemed like about a year, but was in fact probably just long enough for me to catch my breath. I pointed him down the hall to my bathroom so he could manage the condom logistics (I had never gone off the pill, but nevertheless), and while he was gone, I stepped into my shorts and yanked my shirt over my head, noticing it was still damp from pressing myself against him like a decal on a car window. I looked at my watch and wondered what the exercise stats were going to say later. I half-expected to see a little high-five hand where the heart symbol should have been.

In my galley kitchen, the wine bottle was open on the counter. I got out another glass—oh, the simple pleasure of getting out another glass—and filled it. When I stepped out of the kitchen, Will was in the hall with my burgundy towel wrapped around his waist. "My clothes are soaked," he said.

"You're welcome to stroll around without any clothes on, if you want. The blinds are down."

He may not have blushed, entirely, but it was a blushing kind of smile. "That's very flattering, but I don't think I'd feel comfortable nude-ing all over your furniture."

"I've got you," I said. I went to the very closet against which I had recently been efficiently ravished and took down a plastic tub from the top shelf. In it was everything belonging to Justin that I had found, here and there, mixed in with my things after I moved. I could have given it all back, and I probably should have, but on my list of priorities, returning his stuff was after everything else I could possibly do with my time, including rewatching all twenty-five seasons of *SVU*.

Lying on top of the box was a pair of swag sweatpants Justin had gotten from a conference called Podcast Pow! that we went to together in Tampa. Podcast Pow! was where I learned that although my vision of podcasting involved journalism and the like, large parts of it were being run by men in khaki pants and polos who were obsessed with passive income. Podcast of the Year at their awards ceremony went to a personal finance guy who accepted in a suit made of hundred-dollar bills. It made me feel like I was the only person there who was going to die broke, owning not even one apartment building, but hey: free sweatpants. I threw them over to Will, who unfolded them and looked at the word POW! that was printed in purple along the lower part of the outside of the left leg. "Pow," he said, and he looked at me.

"Try not to think about it," I told him. He put the sweats on, and I took the towel from him and walked toward my bedroom. "Be right back." I hung the towel back on the peg in the bathroom and rummaged in my dresser for the shirt I got when I saw Bruce Springsteen with my dad. It was big on me, so I figured it would be about right on Will. Was I hoping in some part of my dark soul that he would be impressed that I was the kind of person who went to see Springsteen? Obviously. I pulled it from the bottom of a drawer and went back into the living room, stopping along the way to throw his clothes into the small dryer that was one of my most treasured luxuries.

He had dug his phone out of whatever pocket it had been in, and he was just standing there, staring down at it, wearing Podcast Pow! sweatpants and looking much more appealing in them than they merited. "Hey," I said, and he put the phone down on the back of my couch and turned to me. "Your clothes will be dry before too long."

"Thank you," he said. "I was just texting my neighbor, he's going to take Buddy for a walk."

"Ah, right," I said, throwing him the shirt. "Well, then, you want to have a drink?" He nodded, and I went into the kitchen and brought back his glass. I wasn't sure what we were doing. Were we talking? Were we canoodling? I felt surprisingly uncertain for someone who had so recently had my earlobe in his mouth. So I sat on the couch with my back to the arm and my knees pulled up in front of me. He sat on the opposite end, but he leaned forward and put his hand behind my feet to coax my legs out straight. We ended up mirroring each other, drinking wine, with his feet against my hip and his free hand resting on my thigh.

"So you figured out there weren't any breaths," I finally said.

He laughed, which made the wine wobble in his glass. "Eventually, yes. At first, I was trying to figure out something about what you were saying. And then I decided to turn it way way way up, until I was afraid I was going to blow out my eardrums."

"Don't do that," I said. "I have to have my hearing tested every year."

"Yes, ma'am." He took a sip. "Anyway, when I turned it up in a totally responsible way without damaging my hearing, I felt like the words were, I don't know, sort of coming out of nowhere. Everything seemed a little robotic. At first I thought you had clipped a millisecond from the beginning of every sentence, that was my first guess. But that didn't make a lot of sense. And then it came to me. No breathing."

"And as a result, you got laid on a rainy Wednesday."

He shrugged. "What can I say? Not everybody likes flowers."

"Well, you did the right thing coming over immediately. I'm sorry you got soaked, though."

"Totally worth it." He looked at the TV, which was running a screensaver shot of a meadow. "What were you watching?"

"Ah, it was *Halls of Power,* your flu binge," I said. "It's very exciting. They brought a guy back from the dead. Remember the aide who died in the yacht explosion?"

"He's alive?"

I nodded. "It turns out that a few seconds before the yacht exploded, he climbed inside a metal trunk."

"So naturally he was fine."

"Trunk floated around for a while, he opened it and crawled out, and he was picked up by a passing Scandinavian tourist on a WaveRunner."

"You know, that's what I was going to guess."

I filled him in on several different ongoing plotlines as he started to trace circles and swirls on my leg with his thumb. Finally, I put a hand to my stomach. "Are you hungry?" I said. "I have to tell you, I'm sort of starving."

"I could eat," he said, so I got up and went into the kitchen, and he followed. I opened the fridge. "I have leftover Thai, I have some spaghetti that is probably a little too old, I have . . . I need to go grocery shopping, actually."

"We could do takeout, except that it's still pouring rain, and I try not to ask people to go out in this."

"Agreed," I said. I opened an upper cabinet. "Ooh." I pulled down a box that would be instantly familiar to nearly anyone who grew up anything like I did. "You want mac and cheese?"

He nodded solemnly. "I think we have to."

So we ate standing in the kitchen, talking about Buddy and my sister and Will's sister. He made fun of me for putting Frank's RedHot on my mac and cheese, but I made him try it, and after he did, he shook the bottle over his own bowl, muttering about how he usually doesn't even like hot sauce. We put the dishes in the sink, and I took both his hands, and I walked backward through my apartment to my bedroom praying I wasn't going to trip over anything, and I miraculously didn't. We sat on my bed, and we peeled off our shirts for the second time in two hours, and he felt as good dry as he had just out of the rain.

Again, I like a bed. The hall had been a fast dance with no choreography, and it had happened all at once without a break to breathe, and that was very, very good. But this was good, too, pillows and space, with my top sheet tangling around my foot. I like the mix of working hard and hardly working, if you will, and at one particular moment when I was hardly working and I stretched my arms above my head and touched my headboard with my fingertips, that was, for whatever reason, the moment when I thought, *Oh, uh-oh.*

I had promised to give Eliza's plan a real chance, but as he settled his weight on top of me, he said, into my ear, "Pow," and we both laughed, and I didn't know if I could.

I didn't intend to fall asleep after with the lights still on, but we lay there for a while, talking about the penny-sized birthmark on his shoulder and the burn scar on the back of my hand from the time I touched the side of the oven while taking out a pan of frozen French fries. Between stories, we lay there breathing, facing each other on my pillows and tangling our fingers. And then I suddenly opened my eyes and looked directly into his dead-asleep, still very appealing face, his mouth pink and full. His index finger was crooked around mine.

In the morning I made coffee, because coffee is always the right move. The coffee was good, and the small talk was above average, and finally he looked at me and said, "Is your guru going to be mad at you? For this?"

I shook my head. "I don't intend to talk to her about it, so no. I had a second date with the doctor I told you about, so I think she's focused on that."

"Ah, sure." I couldn't quite read the look on his face, but then he smiled. "This was really fun."

"It really was. Definitely the most fun I've ever had teaching anyone about editing audio."

"Yeah." He started to extend a hand toward me like we were going to shake, and then he stopped himself and leaned forward and hugged me, just for a second, and it made me laugh. "Fun," he said again. "This was fun."

"Absolutely, yes."

"I'm going to go," he said. "I should take care of Buddy."

"Roger that," I said. "I'm sure we'll bump into each other soon."

CHAPTER EIGHTEEN

The First Experience of Bad Timing

It was Friday. Less than a week before Christmas. Our sixth episode had gone out that morning, and now, at the halfway point, we'd take two weeks off for the holidays. Not from working, not entirely. But in keeping with the magical math of landing the finale on Valentine's Day, we wouldn't have another new installment out until the second Friday in January, which felt downright decadent. Everybody was set to take some time off, even me. Even Eliza, who was spending the first week of January on Maui.

And it had been two days since Will. I was not going to text him. I wasn't sure if I wanted him to text me. I hadn't told anyone yet, not *anyone*, that this had happened. It would have been unfair to tell Julie, because it would have complicated her job when it didn't need to. Besides, a week before Christmas, her priority was her family and not my sex life. I hadn't told Molly, because I had a feeling she would say something about the general inadvisability of my actions that I wasn't prepared to hear.

But mostly I didn't know what he was thinking. It seemed like we liked each other, but it was all in the context of absolutely nothing ever being able to happen since I was stunt dating and he was leaving. If I texted, was it going to seem like I wasn't okay with that, when I was? If he texted, was I going to feel like he wasn't okay with that, when I needed him to be?

Training people in audio was something I had done a lot, and it had never gotten anywhere near this complicated. And then my phone gave a ding, and it was happening.

Do you want to come over later?

He had broken the seal. I had taken the day to work at home given the overtime I'd been putting in, so I was reading a solid domestic thriller on my couch when I heard the notification, and perhaps that explains why I jumped about a foot.

Did I want to come over later? Admittedly, I very much wanted to come over later. But at the same time, wasn't it only going to get weirder? Was Eliza going to look me in the eye at some point and realize that I had spent time in a pleasant tangle of limbs with someone who was not on her list? Wasn't this the point at which going further would risk making things, for all the modernity of my thinking, a little complicated? Hadn't I, in fact, leapfrogged naked over that point? Once was once, but twice was . . . well, it was twice. It was a bad idea, or at least a tricky idea, and all it would do was introduce all kinds of strange dynamics into a situation that had already led to my going on dates with a tax cheat and a married guy.

Naturally, I wrote back: Sure! What time?

I did not finish my book, but I did complete an entire round of personal grooming. Honestly, when a guy shows up at your door in the rain, he's going to get what he gets. But since he'd invited me over and I'd said yes, it seemed like perhaps it was a good time to haul out the eyebrow tweezers and the nice underwear.

But because Will was himself, the evening turned out to be rather lower-key than I was expecting, in a way that relaxed me right from my shoulders down to my ankles. While he was making me a hot chocolate in the kitchen, I stood in his living room and stared at a framed picture of the steps of the Lincoln Memorial. I leaned closer and saw that near the top of the steps, you could see a woman with her back to the statue who looked to have just spilled her bag. She was bent down collecting books, shoes, file folders.

He appeared with the mug and handed it to me. "My favorite of the memorials, I think."

"This is great. I love the lady down here who's completely uninterested in this giant of history because she dropped her purse. Busy people in a nutshell."

"Yeah. I printed this one because people sometimes expect the memorials to look like a postcard, and sometimes they do, obviously. But sometimes it's just another messy place people drop their stuff. I'm old-fashioned, though. I'll tell you, a lot of people who do photography, they would just zap her out of existence."

"Yeah?"

"Oh, yeah. People do photo editing where they take, I don't know, Machu Picchu or the Empire State Building, one of these places that's full of tourists all the time, and they'll go in there in their editing program and just zap-zap-zap, take out all the people. It looks terrible, but they have ways to do it. Take out the kids in strollers, take out the people grabbing selfies, take out the guy in the baseball hat who's looking at a map, whatever. I always think it's sad. Erase the people? Make it look like an imaginary moment you spent with nobody?"

I nodded. "We have the same thing. Some people want as many of their interviews in studio as they can," I said. "They just want that dead, *dead* silence, right? Because then you can add stuff from there, you can add music and sound and ambi from wherever you want, and you can put everything exactly where you want it."

"Right, right."

"My favorite interview I ever produced was with this guy who raised goats in Wisconsin. They brought back the tape they got at the farm. And you know, obviously you expect a little bit of animal noise in a farm setting, right? It's color, it's great. But they're talking to this farmer, and he's explaining how hard it is to keep a small business going. It's really wrenching; he's had a hard road, this guy. And over and over again, while he's talking, you hear this goat he's got next to him who sounds exactly like a witch laughing in a cartoon. You know what I'm talking about? '*A-a-a-a-a-a.*' "

"Right, sure."

"It sounds like, 'This season, we could barely afford my wife's medication, *a-a-a-a-a-a,* we might have to sell my granny's ring, *a-a-a-a-a-a.*' I've never heard such goaty goats in my entire life." He laughed. "Anyway, the editor I was working with at the time thought the tape was unusable. He was so pissed at the field producers, he said they had screwed it all up. He said they'd have to get the farmer on the phone to get some of these quotes in a way they could use, because the goat was just so distracting that it took away from the seriousness of the point he was making. And I told him he was crazy, I said the goat was the best part of the story. It reminded people that this guy's whole world was these goats. They were with him all the time, he was relying on them to feed his family, and that's what he'd been doing for ages. Long story short, the goat stayed. Everybody loved it, and that's why everyone at work should listen to me."

"I lost a freelance assignment taking publicity pictures of an amusement park because I didn't want to take out a kid picking his nose."

"You were being an artist."

"In that case, I was being stubborn. I was very opinionated, and I gave that a lot of space back then. It's easier that way. I think I'd rather have to train myself to be more flexible than train myself not to just do whatever anybody asks me to do."

"That makes a lot of sense."

"Do you want to eat?"

I did want to eat. I was starving. I had not wanted to say anything. But I'm quite sure the eagerness of my nod said everything my growling stomach wished it could. He went and started taking things out of the fridge, and then he stopped, and he turned to me, and he said, "I'm glad you're here."

I walked over to him and put my arms around his neck and kissed him, like I had done it a lot, like I was used to it. If I were, it probably would have escalated less quickly, and I wouldn't have quite so rapidly had one hand up under his shirt, and he wouldn't have been pulling my butt up against him quite as urgently. He broke off and pulled a few inches back from my face.

"What are you making?" I asked.

"A chicken thing," he said. "It's only going to take about fifteen minutes." He put his hands on my shoulders and pushed back from me a few inches. "I should have made a frozen lasagna, we'd have had like an hour."

I had a way of waking up in the middle of the night. I'd do one of the daily puzzles I liked, and I'd often just bore myself back to sleep thinking about something that didn't matter to me at all—what breakfast cereal I liked best, or where to buy socks.

But when I woke up in the middle of the night in Will's full-sized bed, in his tiny room in his tiny apartment, I kept thinking about the show. I kept thinking about what to do about being with Will—not *with* Will, but with Will—and what to do about Michael #2, and about Julie and Toby and Fitness West.

Eliza had already told me—hell, she'd told the whole internet—that this was a terrible idea, so telling her about it seemed to be out, as an option. And Will didn't need to hear about Michael #2 or consult on the matter of our planned third date. Even acknowledging I had a problem seemed to be making too much of it, since what were the odds that a guy who was just waiting for his lease to be up wanted to hang around the city because he'd hooked up with me twice?

At some point, he moved a little, and then I heard him whisper, "Are you awake?"

"Yes," I whispered back.

"What are you doing?" he said.

"Contemplating."

"Can't sleep?"

"Maybe."

He reached across me to the nightstand on my side, and he picked up a little remote I could barely see in the streetlight that leaked through the blinds. Suddenly, the ceiling lit up with little pinprick stars that stretched down the walls and poured onto the bed. They scattered across the blanket as he resettled himself next to me.

"You have a projector in here?" I whispered.

"No," he said. "It's magic." He kissed my cheek, my ear, my collarbone, then he fell asleep with his head sharing my pillow.

The next morning, I woke up to my favorite sound in the world, better than angels or an orchestra: a coffee grinder. I opened my eyes and I was alone in Will's bed, and the clock on the nightstand said it was 9:45. I rarely slept so late. When I touched my cheek, I knew it was pink from his day or so of scruff. I was wearing only his Fleet Foxes shirt, having left everything of my own in a pile at the foot of the bed.

I pulled on my leggings and went out into the kitchen, where he was putting ground coffee into the drip machine. "I woke you up," he said. "Sorry about that."

I finished a yawn. "Are you kidding? I get out of bed and make my own coffee every single day. Somebody else doing it makes me feel like Princess Grace." I leaned up and kissed him quick, since I hadn't brushed my teeth yet.

"In case you ever need it," he said, opening a cabinet door, "coffee is up here. Filters, sugar, and there's milk in the fridge." He opened the next cabinet over. "Mugs here." He pushed the button on the coffee maker. "I'm sure you're familiar with this classic piece of machinery."

"I am, I am." I leaned against the counter. "Now we just wait."

"It's the longest wait of the day," he said. Then he looked hard at me. "Do you take a cup while it's brewing or wait until it's done?"

I always took a cup while it was brewing. Always. I let it go until my bagel popped up out of the toaster, and then I yanked the pot out and filled one of my many bookstore mugs. But I narrowed my eyes back at him. "What do you do?"

"Wait till it's done," he said. I nodded noncommittally. "*You don't wait till it's done?*"

"How about half done?" I said. "I'm obviously not going to take the first part that comes out, I'm not an animal." I was sometimes an animal, but he didn't need to know that. When it was finally done, we poured big mugs full, and we sat in his living room, and I did the crossword on my phone while Will edited some wedding pictures. Then I grabbed a shower while he took Buddy for a walk. By the time he got back, I was dressed and working on a second cup of coffee.

There was a knock on his door just as he was feeding Buddy, and we frowned simultaneously. "Who's knocking at 10:30 in the morning on a Saturday?" He went to the door, and I watched from the kitchen. When he opened it, a woman with dark, shoulder-length hair stood there with a paper bag in her arms. "Oh," he said. And then he said it differently: "Ohhhhh. Hi."

This wasn't really happening, right? My very innocent, very low-key hookup being interrupted by a woman showing up and obviously catching him off-guard? Not even I could manage to engineer this kind of train wreck.

She looked past him and saw me standing in the kitchen. "Is it possible," she said, "that you forgot about brunch?"

"I forgot about brunch," he said. He turned around and mouthed, *my sister.* And when he said it, I recognized her from a picture on his wall. She looked different without sunglasses.

"How many times have I told you that you need a calendar? I don't know why you can remember exactly whose wedding you're taking pictures of and when, but when I make plans with you, it leaks out of your ears instantly."

"I got distracted," he said, and I could read his smile, even looking at the back of his head.

"Well, I'm here now, and I brought food, so are you going to let me in?"

He stepped to the side. She came in and smiled at me, without putting down the bag. "Hi," she said. "I'm Maggie. I'm Will's sister."

"I'm Cecily. I'm his—friend." She came into the kitchen and set the bag down, and then she shook my hand. "I should go," I said over her shoulder to Will.

"Absolutely not," she said. "I never get to meet any of my brother's *friends.* You have to stay and have food with us. I have some amazing pastries in here, if the line at the bakery is anything to go by. I didn't know what he was going to want, so I have plenty, believe me."

I looked at Will, and I was surprised to see him swallowing a laugh. "You should stay," he said. I widened my eyes. "Stay. Seriously."

Maggie put her hand on my arm. "Cecily? Don't worry about it, the awkward part is over. Now it's just eating."

And so that's how I found myself having pastries and coffee with Will and his sister a few days before Christmas, after what would have been our second date if these were dates, which they were not.

I don't know exactly what I expected Maggie to be like. Maybe like Molly, maybe like Will. She wasn't like either one. She asked me what I did for a living, and I mumbled something about media, and then I started stuffing food in my face so I didn't have to talk.

As we ate, Will and Maggie talked about their dad, who needed knee surgery he was putting off, and about Will's best friend from high school, who had suddenly gotten very into triathlons. There was an ease to the two of them, a lack of urgency in spite of their shared high energy. He wanted to know all about her wife, her kids, whether she thought she would stay in teaching as the pressures grew and the pay shrank, and whether she thought they'd ever talk their own parents into visiting them rather than the other way around. She quizzed him about how his business was going, and he told her about shoots he was doing, marketing he was trying, and some work he was particularly proud of. He produced a big iPad to show her some favorite shots. She asked for a copy of a photo he took at the National Zoo of a yawning bear, saying she'd do a big print of it for her son's room. ("He's in a serious megafauna phase," she said. "Mostly hippos and rhinos, but a bear is fine.")

They'd arranged this get-together because Maggie was headed to her in-laws' house in Texas for Christmas, and she wanted to see Will before she left. They talked all around why he wasn't going to L.A. to see their parents. Or, she prodded, why he hadn't at least invited them to come to D.C. "I don't even know if I want them to," he finally said. "It's not like they're going to feel better about how I'm doing if they see my tiny apartment and the place where I wait tables."

"What are you talking about?" she said. "They would love this place. Dad would go nuts, you know how much he loves seeing your stuff."

"I don't think it's exactly what they've always had in mind for me," he said.

"So what?" She poured herself a fresh cup of coffee. "Grandpa

Fred wanted Mom to be a nurse, and Mom goes to the emergency room so often that one of the doctors came to her birthday party." She turned to me. "I didn't even know there was such a thing, but our mother figured out a way to be the opposite of a nurse."

Will murmured noncommittally, "The lease is up in three months. They can visit wherever I go next."

"I still can't believe she didn't help." Clearly not one for telling only part of a story, Maggie turned back to me. "When Will's ex moved out, she wouldn't pay a penny of the rest of the lease, because she wasn't on it, which only happened because he's the one who went and found the apartment. He's too nice to do anything about it, so he wound up stuck with the whole thing. She's a nightmare."

"Mags? Cecily doesn't need to know this."

"Maybe not, but I need to say it. Besides, I'm sure she has her own nightmares. And I bet her family hates them." She raised an eyebrow. "Right?"

"I'm pretty sure my sister would still punch my ex in the throat if she saw him on the street," I said. "So yes." I looked at Will. "What? I agree with your sister."

Maggie smiled triumphantly. "And how long has it been since you broke up?"

"Four years."

"Four years! I have so much time left to be pissed off."

"Where do you think you'll go?" I asked him, reminding myself not to sound concerned.

"Maybe New York, maybe Boston. Someplace I can figure out my life."

"'Figure out my life,' 'figure out my life,'" his sister muttered. "You've been saying that for ten years, man. Get to figuring."

I ignored her, because it seemed like family stuff. "But those aren't places you've lived before?"

"No. West Coast, mostly. I've lived in Seattle, Portland, Denver, Minneapolis."

"What did you do in all those places?" I asked. Maggie looked over at me, and I looked at her a little sheepishly. "We're not *old* friends." She laughed.

"Different things," he said. "School, after that a couple of jobs before I met Meredith, just short-term stuff."

I was so accustomed to listening to conversations between other people that it always took me a minute to snap out of it when I'd been sitting back for a while, so when Maggie turned and said, "So tell me more about you, Cecily," I blinked like I was waking up from a nap.

"Well," I said, "I edit podcasts. I have a sister, too, she lives in Silver Spring, she's married. My parents are in New Jersey, they're retired. They're kind of . . . all over the place. My mother was in Sedona last time I heard. My dad is probably at, I don't know, basketball camp or something."

"How did you get into podcasts?"

"Internship after college, at a radio station in New York. Moved down here with a boyfriend, as a matter of fact." I looked up from my croissant. "I mean, like I said, we broke up years ago. Now I work at this podcast company, I do lots of different things."

"What are you working on right now?"

It had been weird enough explaining the show to Will. It seemed impossible to explain it to his sister under these circumstances. But he wasn't rescuing me, so I carried on. "Right now, I'm hosting a show where I get sent on a lot of blind dates."

She froze with a piece of a blueberry muffin in her hand. "Is that how this happened? You went on a blind date for a podcast?"

"No," Will said. "We met the old-fashioned way. She fed peanut butter to my dog."

"I see." Maggie ate a bite thoughtfully. "So this is not part of that. This is just . . ."

"It's unrelated," Will said. "Change the subject, please."

She glared at him. "Rude. But fine. When you're not doing this, what else do you work on?"

"I help out sometimes on a recap podcast about *Halls of Power.*"

"Oh my God, I love *Halls of Power,*" she said. "I am obsessed with that show. So is Will."

He looked hard at her. "I wouldn't say I'm obsessed with it. I keep up with it."

"Believe me," I said, "I don't judge. I sometimes work on an advice show, just . . . whatever my boss needs. Here and there."

"Well, that all sounds really, really interesting," she said. "You might be too good for my brother."

"Like I said," Will told her as he pulled the end off a croissant, "we're just friends, so don't tell Mom and Dad anything they're going to ask me about later. We're friends."

I looked back at him and nodded. "Friends." It was the same thing I would have said. It was what we had agreed on. Why did it sound terrible?

"I would never say anything to them," she said. "Never. I think I'm offended."

CHAPTER NINETEEN

The Second Experience of Bad Timing, and Layoffs

We finished eating, and Will said he wanted to walk me out.

"Of course," Maggie said. "Do what you need to do. Take your time. I'm drinking coffee."

He got my coat and walked me out the front door, and we stood on the stoop. "Well," he said, "I'm sorry I forgot about brunch."

I couldn't not laugh. "Not at all. She's great. I'm glad I got to meet her."

"I'm sure she's going to have a million questions," he said. "I'll try to keep her from texting you, but I can't make any promises."

"She's welcome to text me," I said. "I think she and I are friends now."

He rested his arms on my shoulders, and I put my hands on his hips. "I'll see you whenever," he said.

"Whenever," I repeated. And he leaned down and kissed me, and the sun was shining, and I kissed him back and swayed against him.

People say only death and taxes are certain, but that's not true at all. A lost item you just replaced will turn up. The plane that absolutely has to be on time will be late for once. And when you are standing out on the sidewalk, practically climbing up the front of a hot photographer, the worst possible person to see you will choose that moment to be taking a vigorous walk to a yoga class.

And so, I should not have been as surprised as I was when I heard, "WHAT?"

I spun to see Eliza behind me in a peacoat and leggings, coffee in one hand, yoga mat over the other shoulder. I felt Will jump in my arms and we startled apart.

All she did was repeat it. "WHAT?"

Will just said, "What's . . ."

"The *waiter*?" she snapped.

"Stop yelling," I said. "Why are you even in the city on a Saturday? Why aren't you creeping up on people in Bethesda? What are you doing?"

"A friend of mine invited me to her class, if that's okay with you. What are *you* doing?" she hollered.

"Oh my God, be *quiet,*" I said, dragging her toward the building. "You are overreacting."

She took both my hands. "I can't believe this. You promised me you were going to leave the waiter alone. I set up these dates for you, I fed you the best Peruvian food in the city with a doctor you like who likes you like *three days ago,* what are you doing?"

"Nothing happened," I said. "This has nothing to do with you, and nothing to do with that. I went on all your dates. This is not anything, it's nothing, it's not even real."

"Oh, it's nothing? It's nothing that you're doing exactly what we said you wouldn't do and getting involved with exactly the person we agreed was a dead end? It's nothing that I've been working my butt off for you and you're going behind my back?"

"I am not getting involved with him," I said. "I'm not dating him. He barely owns furniture." I heard myself say it, and I spun to see Will looking like I'd slapped him. "Wait," I said to him. "Just wait. Please." I turned back to Eliza. "Stop freaking out." I lowered my tone. "Let me go talk to him for a minute."

She raised her eyebrows. "Too late."

I spun around again and saw his back heading into the building. "Will—" I sputtered.

He turned to me. "It's fine. I'm going to go up," he said. "I'll talk to you later." He raised one hand, and then he was gone.

I bent over, defeated, with my hands on my knees.

Eliza walked over and put her hand on my back, which was supposed to be comforting, but which made me feel worse. "I have been telling you," she said, "that putting no thought into this doesn't work. When are you going to hear me?"

How had everything managed to go so very badly in such a short time? It was tempting to blame Eliza and the boy-next-door who had cheated on her, but it was hard to argue that I hadn't made, for whatever reason, this mess. I stood back up and looked at her. I held up both hands. "I'm sorry. Okay? I'm sorry. I wasn't trying to go behind your back. I wasn't trying to be dishonest. I'm sorry. Go home. I will call you."

She stood there a minute, assessing me. "I care about you, you know," she finally said. "I know we're doing the show and everything. But I really care about you."

"Okay," I said. "Let's just talk later." She hesitated and smiled sympathetically, which made me feel even worse. "Later," I repeated.

As soon as I got home, I texted Will. I'm so sorry, that was embarrassing. I sort of panicked, and I didn't mean that how it sounded at all.

Forget it. Not real anyway, like you said.

When I got to work on Monday, my own mood was foul, because I had tried a couple of times to call Will, and it kept going to voicemail. The office mood, too, had gone from moderately anxious to maximally grim. Somebody told somebody that the HR person had been in and out of Toby's office four times on Friday. Somebody told somebody that a media reporter had emailed to ask whether they knew anything about layoffs at Palmetto. Somebody thought Toby looked particularly miserable as he went into his office that morning, entirely without his usual gregarious overkill. It didn't seem possible that even Toby would lay people off on December 23, but who knew anymore? I wanted to go talk to Julie, but before I could, there was an all-staff email from Toby.

> Team:
>
> As you know, we've been dealing with a lot of uncertainties in the industry and in the economic climate for the last year. The market for advertising has shifted, and competition has never been greater. We continue to see successes in many areas, but—

At this point, my eyes began to skim. Skim, skim, skim, get to the point, Toby, say what you're going to say.

> Unfortunately, this is going to result in the elimination of eight positions.

He had really done it. He had laid off eight people two days before Christmas.

Toby detailed exactly where these positions were coming from, which, in a company that had only about a hundred people, might as well have been a list of names. He was canceling two of our smaller shows, and he was letting go two producers who were essentially floaters, who pitched in now and then where they were needed. It was not me. It was not Julie. But it was not good.

Two minutes after I got this email, Julie Slacked me two exclamation points, and I walked over to her cube. "I know," I said. "I hate it."

"I don't know how I was still surprised," she whispered. "I didn't know that was coming today, even though I've been afraid of it every day."

"I didn't know either," I said. "Are you okay?"

She leaned back in her chair. "I mean, for now, because of our show. But it's scary thinking that the only thing standing between me and being broke is Toby."

"I think Toby knows you're good at your job."

"Right," she said. "But everybody he just canned is good at their job. And we're not done with our season. If he doesn't like how it turns out in the end, what happens then? I'm not with Miles anymore, so I'm basically screwed. He's going to lop me off like a turkey leg at Thanksgiving."

"He's going to like how the show turns out," I said. "He's going to."

Julie nodded. "Speaking of that, I just got an email from Eliza."

She wouldn't have said anything about Will without warning me, would she? "About what?"

"About Michael #2. He left town."

"*Another* one? Don't tell me he's in Cincinnati, too." For the sake of the show, we'd asked the guys not to communicate with me directly, because nobody wanted there to be a bunch of communication the audience didn't get to hear. But I didn't expect Michael #2 to vanish, I really didn't.

"Not permanently. He's visiting family over the holidays, we knew that. And now I guess he's going to a conference in January? He got offered a spot making a speech about asthma or something. It's in Australia, and since it's summer there, he's making a trip of it."

"I can't fault him for that."

"No," she said. "But the point is, we don't have him again until at least the middle of January. So we'll probably only fit in one more date, possibly two if the third one is good. Toby says that's fine with him. Fitness West wants you to maybe take advantage of your membership to start the new year, and you can do some posts or something. How do you feel about swimming laps?"

"Better than I feel about treadmills," I said. "I'll check it out." I frowned. "I'm suspicious of how relaxed Toby is being about the show. We're getting time off. He's not micromanaging the schedule. He's pretty loosey-goosey for a guy who couldn't stop telling me how much he needs a hit. And who was obviously right."

"I hate all this," she said. "Maybe Michael #2 will marry *me* if it doesn't work out with you and I lose this job. Do you think he'd care that I'm a single mom?"

"I don't know why he would," I said. "But you're not going to lose your job." I reached over to touch her arm, and she raised one hand in a half-wave and walked off.

When bad news like a layoff is announced, particularly in a room full of journalists in an open-plan office, it's like watching prairie dogs pop up out of their holes. Every head rises over the edge of the half-wall, with eyes darting all over the place. Back at my desk, I put on my headphones again. I would not pop up. I would work. *Make the show, do the thing, help Julie, help yourself, get it done. Money! Sponsors! The gym! You have saved yourself!* The scenery on the journey was not attractive, but hopefully, I was at least plodding along in the right direction.

Five minutes later, I got an email from Toby.

> Those eight positions would have been twelve w/o the FitWest money coming in. (Melissa was on the long list.) In case you're wondering whether all the work you're putting in is worth it. So thank you, from all your colleagues, even the ones who don't know it. Now I need you to put your head down and stick the landing on this thing. You can do it.

CHAPTER TWENTY

The Confession

I went to Molly's for Christmas, because our parents decided to go cross-country skiing with a couple my father had met in the summer at tennis camp. Maybe I should have been disappointed, but it was a good time to catch up. I usually told Molly about relationship things, and I usually told Molly when I was in the middle of making an enormous mess out of my life. It appeared that now, I might not be speaking to Will *or* Eliza, and Michael #2 might be making a sneaky exit to avoid getting caught up in my ridiculous life, and who could blame him?

I arrived on their doorstep on Christmas Eve holding a bottle of wine and an overnight bag. Molly took both and set the bag down in the front hall, and I threw my arms around her and said into her ear, "I'm so happy to see you."

"Me too," she said. "I'm honestly happy to see anybody who isn't our flooring guy. My most meaningful relationship at the moment is with our flooring guy. His name is Albert. I think he lives with us now. I won't be surprised if we wake up tomorrow morning and he's under the tree."

I laughed as she led me into the kitchen and poured me a glass of wine. "So," I said, "I need some therapy first. Tell me about the cutest animal you've seen today."

"I gave a shot to a bunny," she said. "He felt like the softest bedroom slipper."

"What was his name?"

"Lucifer."

"Lucifer? Lucifer the bunny?"

"Yes. They have another one named Dante."

"How metal." I took a sip of my drink and looked around her kitchen. It was so cozy here. Maybe I could just move into her house and never leave and never talk to anyone again except to order takeout. It would simplify things considerably.

She leaned back against the counter and studied me. "Cecily, what's going on with you?"

"Wow," I said. "A person can't just stand around in her sister's kitchen anymore."

"What's going on?"

"Well," I said, "I slept with the waiter."

Her eyes got wide. "The dog guy?" I nodded. She put her arm around me. "This is a living room conversation," she said.

It was always easier when I didn't have to look her in the eye; this was one of the reasons we sometimes went on walks. But this time, she sat me down on her sofa and looked right at me. I gave her the quick rundown of how I went from dog to restaurant to photographs to teaching him about room tone. I ended at, "I don't know, we sort of . . . did it in the front hall."

"With the door open?"

"Molly!"

"What? I'm trying to picture it! You said you opened the door and had sex, so you're the one who left some things out. I'm not the one who's confusing."

"We closed the door," I said. "Barely."

"I am . . . surprised," she said. "You haven't done a lot of impulsive things like that, at least not ones I know about. So it was just that one time?"

"It was a couple of times."

"Good for you," she said. "I assume."

"It . . . was," I said. "I like him. His sister dropped by for brunch. We ate."

"That's . . . intimate."

"It was an accident."

"She accidentally came over for brunch?"

"No, I was accidentally there."

"Is he nice?"

"He's great. But I think he hates me now."

"I doubt it," she said reflexively.

I told her how Eliza had found us outside his building. "And I told her to stop panicking, and he stormed off, and now I'm pretty sure he's not talking to me."

"What did you say exactly?"

"Well," I said. "That it wasn't anything. And . . . that he doesn't own furniture. I told her it wasn't real."

"Ouch."

"It's true! It was an observation. It's neutral."

"Cecily, come *on*. I mean, 'not real'? Yikes."

"I was just trying to point out that it isn't a permanent thing. He says himself that he doesn't accumulate more stuff than he can fit in his car. He doesn't stay anywhere, he doesn't commit to anything, and he's only here until his lease is up. How am I supposed to talk about it?"

"Okay, but you can understand how it would make him feel weird. You can see how, sitting there having just spent the night with you and introduced you to his sister, it would sound like you're blowing him off."

"Absolutely not. He's the one who told his sister we were just friends."

"I'm not sure that's the same thing as 'not real.'"

"I think he thinks I was judging him, and I wasn't."

"Are you positive?"

"Of course I'm positive. I can't believe you're even asking me this. I think he's great. He's really talented, he's fun, he's good at a couple of different jobs. He's just . . . not the same kind of person I am. He can come and go and try all kinds of things and pick them up and put them down and it doesn't even bother him."

"Ah," she said. "See, I think we're getting down to it. It's not money. I think it would be fine with you if he were totally broke, as long as you knew he was super into something. And you think he's not, and that's what bugs you. You think you, as a tireless obsessive, can only be understood by a tireless obsessive. Like a doctor. Not by a guy who just does whatever."

"I don't know if it's that," I said, even though as soon as she said it, my stomach dropped. My freaking sister, *every time.*

She took a sip from her glass. "All right." Why was it always, always like this, where she could say two words to me and I would write an entire interior paragraph about what I knew she was thinking? *All right, if you say so. You never listen to me anyway, even though my advice is sound and I'm married, so I am clearly the authority, not to mention I am older, and I am taller, and I own a house.*

"Oh my God, the way you say that, I just—"

"Hey, don't get mad at me," she said. "I thought this whole thing was a bad idea to begin with. You were the one who wanted to get out there and let somebody else pick people. I told you I thought it was a waste of a perfectly good dog lover you had met on your own. This was your call."

I didn't say anything. We just sat.

When we were young, I was the one who talked about boyfriends, about getting married. I watched soaps, I had favorite couples, I loved the idea of love, and I had pictures of Leonardo DiCaprio in my locker. Molly was more serious, not even sure she cared about getting married. Just vet school, thank you very much.

So of course, Molly had met Pete when she was twenty-three. At a friend's wedding where she was a bridesmaid in a powder-blue sheath dress, Pete was a groomsman in a rented tux. They were seated next to each other among the couple's cocktail-hour girlfriends and NFL Sunday buddies, although they were neither. They got the same pasta when they went through the buffet line, they got tipsy and ended up deep in conversation while everybody else was on the dance floor, and inevitably, she wound up barefoot at two in the morning, climbing into a taxi next to him with her shoes in her hand. The next day, she texted me, OMG wedding reception hookup, call me. The absolute orderliness of it! She got married at twenty-five, finished school, opened her practice, bought a house, and everything seemed to make sense.

And yet two years after they got married, they'd started having young-couple fights. They'd been separated for three months. I loved Pete like crazy, but all I could do was call her and spend time with her; the separation, like the marriage, was between them in its particulars. She kept telling me she wasn't holding out on me about any one thing that was wrong, it was just that they hadn't lived together before they got married, and everything was harder than they thought. They went to counseling, they went on dates, and one day she told me he was coming home. Since then they had seemed entirely happy in that way you know from the outside isn't the whole truth, but is a kind of truth.

"I feel like you're sitting there thinking terrible things about me," I finally said.

"I'm not," she said. "But if I'm being completely honest, I'm not surprised this is so messy. It goes back to this show, doesn't it? You got into something you didn't believe in, and that's not like you."

"How was I supposed to say no?" I said. "I was terrified, and I was right. My boss let eight people go two days before Christmas. For all I know, if I didn't do something, I'd have been in that group, and so would Julie. And I'd end up alone forever, sitting around listening to whatever Justin is doing, wondering where my career went wrong."

"Justin?" she said. "Where's that coming from?"

"Nowhere," I said. "Just, he's making a new show, he's going up and up and up, and he's engaged, and I'm still doing exactly the job I was doing when we were together, you know? I'm going to be ninety years old and I'm going to be picking my way through narration tracks to take out burps. If I turn forty and I haven't done anything except all this, it's going to be all over."

"That's ridiculous," she said. "People do exciting things after they turn forty all the time. Julia Child was fifty when she published her first book."

"You know why everybody knows that?" I said. "Because it isn't what usually happens." She reached over and put her arm around me, and I leaned against her a bit. "I don't want to be forty and be sucking exhaust from my ex-boyfriend's rising rocket ship."

"Do rocket ships have exhaust?"

"Massive amounts, yes."

"I never liked him," she said. "I couldn't stand his little—his messenger bag with the little buttons, and the ironic hats, and the way he said everything was 'so real,' and I'm sorry, but offering everybody advice about weed is not a personality. I don't care how many shows he makes, I'm still going to think he's a dope. And I think you should think so, too."

They didn't make them any more loyal than Molly. "Thank you," I said.

"Does it help?"

"It helps a little."

CHAPTER TWENTY-ONE

The Resignation

The week between holidays is always quiet anyway, and it was even quieter because the layoffs had everybody so skittish, so I mostly worked at home. By the time I got back to the office after New Year's, I had decided it was fine. Everything was fine. Will was mad, and he didn't want to date me anyway. He'd probably be living in France or Oregon or the farthest corners of Australia in six months. Don't cry over spilled photographers. Time to work.

The last thing I wanted to do was talk about all of this with Eliza, but we were going to have to deal with each other sooner or later, and inevitably, once she was back home from her trip, she called. I'd known she would. As much as I knew Will wasn't going to talk to me, that's how much Eliza *was* going to talk to me, with or without my agreement. When I saw her name on my phone, I answered it with the same dread I always felt in Toby's office. "Hey," I said.

"Wow," she said. "You sound terrible."

"Thank you," I said, trying not to bite my words off too hard. "How was Hawaii?"

"So good," she said. "I didn't want to come back."

"But here we are, right?"

I could hear her trying to figure out how to handle me. "I'm sorry it's been so long since we talked," she said. "I wanted to give you a chance to cool off. But now I'm checking on you." She sounded a bit less like an ad for herself than usual. "Last time I saw you, you weren't very happy, and I'm wondering how you're doing." Her voice was sympathetic, but I had a hard time not thinking there was a measure of gloating in it, too. It wasn't her fault, the mess I'd made, and it wasn't her fault that she'd been there to watch the meltdown . . . melt down, but had she not told me this was a bad idea? Had it not turned out to be a bad idea?

"I'm fine," I said. "I told you it wasn't a big deal, and it wasn't. I told you I wasn't dating him, and I'm not." There was a long pause. "If you need to say 'I told you so' so you don't explode, you can just go ahead and do it now." I struggled to listen as she assured me she wasn't going to say that, she just wanted to talk about Michael #2 and the delayed third date, which would eventually be at an Italian place in Adams Morgan once he was back in the northern hemisphere. At the moment, as she understood it, he was enjoying the hospitality of one of Sydney's finest hotels.

"I'm not going to say I told you so," she said soothingly. "Don't get discouraged, this is still going fine. I'm right here. We're on the same team. We're on track."

"I'm ready," I said.

Eliza and I got off the phone, and Julie almost immediately appeared next to my chair. "Hey, can you take a walk with me?" she said. "I just want to talk to you about something for a minute."

"And we need to leave the building?"

"Yeah," she said. "Walk with me."

"Wow, sounds serious. You're not abandoning me, are you?" I said as I stood up.

The pause was a tiny bit too long. No no no no no no, it was too long, why was it so long? "Just come walk with me," she said.

I felt it in my stomach, a clench, a pinch. I got up and grabbed my coat and followed her, and we walked without speaking to the elevator and rode it down. I was afraid to look at her, because I knew it could only be one thing. When we were out on the sidewalk, we got about half a block before she said it.

"So, yeah," she said.

"You're leaving."

"I got a job at Tappan." I could see her breath, could see these words leave her body and hang in the air, then vanish. Tappan Square Audio was the big shop, the shop that had gotten in before all the other ones, gotten in before the floods of stuff made it so hard to get people to subscribe to anything new. It had been written up under funny little illustrations and pictures of its founders in huge pieces in *The New York Times, The Atlantic, The New Yorker.* It didn't have a reputation for voracious growth-chasing or budget-slashing. It won awards. It paid people well. They even had a union. How could Julie do this to me?

"Oh, God," I said. "Okay." I could hear myself giving prompts inside my own head—*Say that's great, say that's great, say that's great*—and so I said, "That's great," but I knew that I said it like I was being poked in the back with a stick.

"I'm sorry," she said.

"No, no, don't apologize," I said. "It's *great.*" I felt a hint of Eliza, of her babbling hooray-for-everything energy creeping into my own voice. "You're going to have so much fun, tell me what it is."

I heard little bits of what followed. I heard names I knew. I heard a job title that was better than the one she had now, and probably better than anything she could get by going to Toby with this offer in her hand. It was unqualifiedly good news, such good and happy news, and I was trying to handle it the way I should, and all I could feel was frustrated. I kept saying "uh-huh, uh-huh," and then it appeared, unbidden, the thought in the back of my head, with perfect clarity: *Oh, great, now you tell me.*

Maybe if I had known she had been looking for a job, I

wouldn't have made protecting her the demand in return for which I agreed to do a project I didn't really want to do. Maybe if I had known, I wouldn't have stuck with that project after it started to crack my life in half.

She said, "Are you upset?"

"Oh my God, no," I said. "Why would I be upset? Julie, this is amazing for you, it's exactly what you want, it's great for your career, that team is so brilliant. And no more Toby and his divorce and his . . . layoffs."

"And it's New York," she added. "You know I love New York."

I hadn't even been thinking. Like practically everybody else who wasn't Palmetto, Tappan Square had their offices in Brooklyn. She wouldn't just be leaving, she'd be *leaving*. "New York," I repeated. "That's right." I turned to her. "What about Bella?"

"Well," she said, "we talked. She's a little bit scared to be moving, she likes her room, loves her school. But I told her about the Natural History Museum, and I told her about the gigantic parks all over the city and I told her the subway is way better than the Metro and she will ride it everywhere. She's coming around. My parents are, too. They wish I was bringing her out west, obviously, but they're willing to be bicoastal. I think mostly they don't want me to be dependent on Chris, because they know that's going to be a nightmare."

Bella really loved the Metro. It wasn't particularly convenient to their apartment, but Julie would take her just to ride around, out to the end of the line and back. From the time she could babble, she'd been calling it the Mat-wo.

"It sounds all worked out," I said.

"Cecily," she said, "I know that we talked about making more things together. I know that you have these plans, and I was so serious when I said I wanted to make them with you, and I am going to help find you the most amazing person to make your pilot. We're going to find somebody."

"Stop," I said. "You don't owe me anything. You have been perfect. You have to do what's right for you, Jul. It's business." I had made a promise to myself a long time ago that I would *never* become a person who said, "It is what it is," but I felt so bitterly stung that I could almost feel it on the back of my tongue, and I had to swallow so I wouldn't say it. "I can't blame you for saying yes to them. It's exciting that they came looking for you, how great is that?"

"Well," she said, "I applied, actually."

"Oh. You did? When?" It had felt strange to me not to tell her about Will, but here I was learning I didn't know all her stuff, either.

"A few months ago. They were doing some hiring, and I talked to the guy, but then everything was on hold. I didn't want to say anything, because it didn't seem like it was going to come to anything. I didn't hear back forever, and I was sure they forgot all about me, but then he called, and I took a day off and went up there."

"Right."

"Ceci, I'm sorry I didn't tell you. I didn't think anything was going to come of it, and I didn't want to stress you out when we were in the middle of all this. I just figured I would keep it to myself. They didn't make the offer until the end of last week. Until that happened, I was mostly obsessed with not losing *this* job, you know?"

Oh, I did know. "Sure," I said, "sure. I don't blame you for keeping it quiet."

"Nobody knew I was talking to them. Nobody even knew I was looking except Toby."

I turned to her. "Toby knew?"

She nodded. "Not about them specifically, not until today, but it turns out he knew I was looking. I made one too many phone calls, I guess. Everybody knows everybody, and nobody keeps their trap shut."

"So Toby's known you might be leaving for a while."

"That I might be, yeah," she said. "I don't think he ever thought these guys would hire me, though."

My mind was racing through the little power move I had tried in Toby's office, where I thought I got him to save her job, when in fact he knew she probably wasn't staying. He must have thought it was hilarious that this was one of my demands, something that cost him nothing to pretend to give in to. "I really wish I'd known you were looking," I said, and as hard as I tried, my voice had a rough edge, and I heard it as soon as it was out of my mouth. "I don't mean it like that, Jul, I honestly—"

"I know," she said. "But really, I didn't know this was going to turn into anything. Like I said, I didn't want you to have to even think about it unless I thought it was really going to happen. And I'm not trying to put you in a spot, like I said, we're close to the end of *Twenty Dates,* and we're going to find somebody you trust to make your pilot," she said. "It's not like you're going to get sent back to Miles."

"I'm sure I won't," I said, though I wasn't sure at all. I was the utility player, and especially now that we were shorthanded, I was going to be sent wherever the lineup had a hole. I envisioned myself putting in extra hours cutting out Miles's Mountain Dew tooth-sucking, because there was no question that he would accept nothing else for the months that remained on his contract.

"Are you okay?" she asked. "I mean, new jobs are a normal thing, right?"

"Sure, yes, of course." I thought about Toby. And Miles. And Eliza. And Will, walking away from me. And Molly, disappointed in me. And now Julie, leaving. I nodded. "Yes, of course. It's fine, of course."

We were just passing a bench, and Julie stopped and sat down. "Come sit with me." When we were settled, she said, "What are you not telling me?"

"Nothing," I said.

She just stared. And finally, she said, "Ceci."

"Oh, you're going to be mad at me."

"Well, now you *really* have to talk."

I exhaled and then pulled a chest full of icy air into my lungs. "So, when I agreed to do *Twenty Dates,* you'll remember I had a lot of doubts. And one thing that happened was that Toby told me that he was probably going to be looking at layoffs, and he mentioned the end of Miles's show, and I got the impression that if we didn't do it . . ."

There was a long pause. "I would lose my job."

"He didn't say that, in quite those words, but the point is I told him I wouldn't do it, I wouldn't do the project, unless both our jobs were safe. During and after."

"Oh." I couldn't tell right away whether she was impressed, horrified, something else, or maybe a little bit of everything.

"I figured if I suddenly had a little bit of leverage, I might as well make the best of it."

She squirmed a little. "Look, I don't have a problem with Toby getting blackmailed, but I don't know if I'm all that thrilled at the idea that I might have ended up with a job *only* because you blackmailed him."

"It wasn't like that," I said, although it had, I suppose, been a little bit like that. "I didn't blackmail him. I . . . coerced him. I pressured him. I was trying to help."

She looked at me, and her forehead creased. "You know," she said, "you should have talked to me. I would have told you not to do that. I would have told you I was looking. And besides, how many conversations have we had about this kind of thing, all this jumping the line and knowing the right person, how it makes everything less fair? You've gotten screwed by this stuff yourself so many times. I don't want you doing it for me."

She was right. Obviously. "Well, I didn't do it entirely on your account," I said. "I did it for myself, too. I was trying to keep both of us out of all the crap that was going on. It's not like things are great for me, either."

She sat back against the bench. "You know," she said, "you could find another job. Other places would love to hire you if you would just pick your stuff up and go."

"Maybe a couple of years ago," I said. "I think things are different now."

"They're not that different. And this show is doing well. It's going to give you an opening. You could try something else. You have choices."

I cleared my throat. I was not going to cry about this. "Julie, I think I went all-in with Palmetto at some point, you know? This is the bet I made. Nobody offers me jobs anymore."

"That's because they think you're too stubborn to leave."

"Well," I said, "maybe I am. I've waited a long time for Toby to give me something in return for all this work I've put in. And he promised to make this pilot, which is more than he's ever done in the past, so I can't pick up and go now, right before it actually happens."

She reached over and put her hand on my knee. "He's not going to give you what you want," Julie said flatly. "He might make your pilot. But he is not going to give you what you want. This place is never going to give you what you want."

"You don't know that."

"Cecily, the only reason you have to think he's going to let you make this thing is that he said he would. How many times has he gone back on things that he told you?"

"Maybe I think he's going to do it because I deserve it."

She made her eyes comically wide, like a cartoon. "Cecily. Of course you deserve it, but he doesn't think that way. You know he doesn't think that way. Have you *ever* seen him think that way, about *anybody*? Have you ever heard him notice that somebody has turned themselves inside out for him, and change his plans for them?" I hadn't. "You have to think about what you're going to do if that part doesn't happen."

"Well, what do you expect me to do?" I said. "Just . . . what, go figure out a whole new place?"

She nodded, fast, like she'd been waiting to hear me say this. "Yes, exactly. A whole new place. I think that's exactly what you should do."

"I don't want to move to Brooklyn," I muttered.

"You don't have to move to Brooklyn," she said. "So many things are remote now, somebody would make you a deal if you don't want to move. You've been working at home your whole career, you've just been doing it on Saturdays and at three in the morning."

I smiled at her. "I think I'm too stuck."

She squeezed my hand. "You're not. You think you're stuck because you're only looking in one direction. And I am begging you to look around, because you can pick up and be on the way somewhere. You are too talented to act like you live in this building, at your desk. Because you don't."

"I know I don't," I said. It was bright and cold, and I whipped a pair of sunglasses out of my bag and put them on so she couldn't see my eyes. I reached over and squeezed her arm. "I'm being a drag. I'm so excited for you. Tell me where you're going to live."

CHAPTER TWENTY-TWO

The Third Date

"I want to talk to you about sex," Eliza said to me as we sat in the studio talking about my long-awaited third date with Michael #2, scheduled at last for that night, only a little more than three weeks before we were supposed to send out our finale.

"That's the naked thing, right? I think I've heard of it." The microphones were not where I was going to refer to Will even existing. Especially existing naked at my apartment. Or existing fully clothed on the street where she yelled at us. Better just to forget it ever happened. Right?

"In general, what do you think is the right time to have sex with someone?" she asked.

"I don't know, 10:30? Maybe a little earlier if you don't have dessert."

She rolled her eyes back so far she probably stabbed herself with her eyelashes. "Hilarious," she said.

I had slept with Justin on what I supposed could be considered our first real date, but we'd known each other for a year. With other people, it ranged from "first date, because I felt like it" to "after kind of a while, around the time I was starting to wonder if he didn't want to because he was very religious" to, unfortunately, "when I decided he was about to break up with me if I didn't," although that was college. (And then there was always "when he successfully completed an assignment about audio production.") I certainly wouldn't consider any of those necessarily the *right* time.

"I guess it depends?" I said.

"Good answer," she said. This was satisfying, because I rarely felt like I gave her good answers, at least not to the degree where she would announce it. "It depends, although I do have a rule of thumb."

"Of course you do."

"I honestly feel you should wait until at least the fourth date."

"Why the fourth date?" I didn't know much, but I did know that pop-culturally, the conventional wisdom seemed to be that it was the third date. Maybe Eliza was a sex contrarian.

"Well, you might be aware that a lot of women go with the third date." I nodded, rather than yelling "AHA!" "So because of that, I think some guys are just waiting to get to that third date, and they're assuming that will be the one with sex, and then after that, they won't hang around. Unfortunately, I see a lot of post-third-date ghosting."

"That's a terrifying-sounding diagnosis," I said. "Wait, are you saying men *you've* picked do this? Men you've approved do this? That seems impossible when they've been vetted so carefully."

"Look, it happens almost never. It's not a nice thing. But yes, occasionally, obviously, even I have been known to arrange a date with a man who is waiting for the sex part, and then after that, he moves along."

"Please tell me your next book is going to be called *Waiting for the Sex Part.*"

"Can you focus, please? You'll remember we talked about this once before, the fact that sometimes people who *appear* to be interested in getting to know you actually aren't. You can't know," she said. "You can't *know,* but you can give yourself the best information. And I personally believe you get the best information by waiting until at least date number four. If you decline on date number three and they come back for date number four, it clears a certain amount of clutter."

"Human clutter," I clarified. "We're trying to clear human clutter."

"Human clutter!" she said. "Exactly. You clear out the human clutter, and you're left with the, you know, better-quality human furnishings."

"This is getting weird," I said. "You're going in a very 'I turned my date into a lamp' kind of direction. I don't like it. And to be honest, I don't know that the thing with Michael is all that sparky, so I'm not in a hurry."

Her eyes narrowed a little disapprovingly but pityingly, like I'd bungled the pronunciation of the name of a country where she, but not I, had vacationed. "I really think sparks are overrated," she said. "That's a common complaint, 'no sparks.' But if you think about it, what creates sparks is your gut reaction to someone, right? That spark is just your gut instinct and their gut instinct crashing into each other. They react to you, and you react to them. It doesn't necessarily mean anything. So don't get wrapped up in that."

"But sparks are fun. They make you want to see people again." *Up against the wall inside your front door,* I added, but only to myself.

"Yeah, but sometimes it's just because you're sensing that the person is your usual type."

"I don't know if I have a type, really."

"You don't think you could describe, just generally, what kind of guy you like?"

"I'm not sure. I guess I don't have a list, I just like what I like, it's by instinct."

She rolled her eyes. Again. "Oh, okay, you're an I-don't-have-a-type type. Here's the truth: Everybody has a type. I have a type, you have a type, everybody does. And people want to say they don't, because they think it makes them sound phony, when actually, I find it a *little* bit phony when people tell me they don't have any standards, they just take it completely fresh with every person they meet."

"I try not to have lists in my head, I guess," I said.

"Oh my *Gooooooddddd,*" she moaned. "I'm asking you, I am begging you, not to pretend there isn't anything you want in a person just because everything you want makes you feel guilty." I was glad we were in the studio, because I felt that prickle on the back of my neck that I sometimes get when I know the tape is good. "I get it, I get it. You can't say anything you haven't run through twenty different filters to see how it sounds. You say you want a guy with a good job, and you think it makes you sound like a gold-digger. You say you want a guy who turns you on, and you think it makes you sound obsessed with looks, when all it means is that when you're picking someone you are ideally going to end up having sex with for like fifty years, you should pick someone good-looking."

"You just told me not to think about sparks!"

"I told you not to think about sparks, not sex. You're definitely supposed to think about sex. In fact, I'm trying to save you from fifty years of sex with someone you aren't actually all that attracted to but you settle for because you don't think it's polite to have preferences."

"I never said I didn't have preferences. I just don't like listing them like I'm ordering a sandwich off a menu board."

"Exactly," she said triumphantly. I was so lost. "That's exactly right. You're the kind of person who refuses to order off the menu board. So you say 'Make me anything.' And they make you a sandwich and you don't like it. But you don't tell them you don't like it, and you don't learn anything, you just throw the sandwich in the trash, and then you're mad that you're starving at two in the afternoon eating Cheez-Its out of the vending machine because you refused to start a sentence with *I want,* even when somebody asks you to."

It seemed impolite of her to improve upon my simile and beat me to death with it. She didn't say anything more. I thought maybe she would charge back into it, but she didn't. She sat back, just an inch or so, and she looked at me, so I said the first thing I thought of. "I want someone who improves bad days," I said.

"It's not very specific, and it's *very* Cecily to frame your perfect partner through something negative, but it's a start. What does improving a bad day look like?"

"It looks—"

"Start with 'I want.' And you are making a face, don't make that face, they can't see it on the podcast. People of the podcast, Cecily is making a face."

"That's just my face!"

"It is not. Do it. 'I want . . . ' "

"Fine. I want someone to care why the day was bad, and then I want him to want it to be better. I want us both to know what the thing is—the little, seemingly insignificant thing—that will make a hard day just a tiny bit easier."

"What is that for you?"

I let the dead-flat quiet settle around me. "Make me a drink," I said. "A cup of coffee, a really cheap beer, a bourbon and Diet Coke, an iced tea. You set that little mug, or glass, or bottle in front of me, and I feel five percent better, no matter what. So I guess *I want* a drink."

"I think," she said, "that you want someone to know enough about you to know that you want a drink, and to care enough about you that for that moment, he's going to stop what he's doing, make you a drink, bring it to you, and then . . . do what?"

"Sit with me. Have a drink with me."

"Yeah," she said. "Exactly."

"Well, hooray for me," I said.

She smiled. "I'm not going to tell you that you're the easiest person I've ever worked with. But you sat here with me and you gave me one thing you are genuinely looking for, that you want someone to do in a relationship with you, and this is pretty much the first time I've gotten you to do that, so I, for one, feel encouraged. And I think you'll find that Michael is a guy who will make you a drink."

"Oh, good."

"So, you're getting ready to go out with him again. Tell me about that."

"I am," I said.

"*I want,*" she said. "Start with that."

"I want . . ." My voice sounded uncertain.

"Do it!" she ordered, and we both laughed.

"I want to go out with him again. I want to see what it feels like on a third date. I want to give it a try, and I want to find out a little more about him."

"Well, that is fantastic," she said. "He's excited to see you, too. I just want to make sure you're getting my original point. Do you even remember my original point?"

"Do not have sex with Michael. You're afraid that I'm going to be overcome with desire and I'm going to tackle him in the back room of this restaurant, and we're going to do it among the raw chicken and the kale, and it's going to be very unsanitary, and you're against it, that's your point." I turned toward the booth. "You can stop rolling," I said. "I think we've covered this territory." Abby gave me a thumbs-up.

"Oh, that reminds me!" Eliza said.

"How can that remind you of anything?"

"It does, it does. I was supposed to tell you, we had an issue with the reservation at the other place we picked for date number three, so tonight is Madeline's again. We had to improvise, and they can take us on short notice and accommodate the production and everything."

Madeline's? Where Will worked? "Eliza, I'm not sure that works for me."

"Don't worry. I checked, and he's not working tonight. You're not going to run into him. It's at 7:30. Call me after. I have to go. And please, give Michael a chance. You promised me you would, you owe me."

Madeline's. Well, hell.

All there was to do was put on a brave face, go on this date like a professional, and try to think on the walk over there of as many ways as possible to avoid Will if somehow it turned out he was working after all. Disguise? Sudden flu? Spiritual need to be seated in total darkness? Demand for a particular server who *wasn't* Will, if I could remember anyone's name? But the truth was that the odds were on my side to begin with: There were lots of tables, and there were lots of servers, and even if Eliza was wrong, the odds that Will would be our server were substantially lower than fifty percent. In all likelihood, he might be there somewhere, but he would not be our server.

Obviously, Will was our server.

Michael #2 and I had just sat down, exchanged a cheek-kiss, and started in on some red wine he'd ordered without me when I was overcome by the feeling that someone I had slept with was standing over me. I looked up. And really, we had reached the point where neither of us could possibly act surprised. If I had flown to Australia instead of Michael, and I had visited the Sydney Opera House, and I had tripped over a wombat on my way up the steps, Will would be the person who helped me up. If he had gone on an African safari and been eaten by a lion, I would have already been in the belly of that same lion when he got there, looking at him and going, "Well, *this* is unfortunate."

"Good evening, sir, ma'am," he said. I blinked twice.

"Oh. Yes. Hi," I said.

"I'm Will, I'll be taking care of you tonight."

Didn't I wish.

He rattled off a couple of specials, and Michael #2 ordered a salad and something with fish that sounded very virtuous, and he handed his menu back.

"I think I'll do the filet," I said. "And the little burrata thing to start." Will nodded. "Very good, I'll be back with your starters." I watched him go. Crisp white shirt, great hair, good arms, little scar on his ribs, smelled like that soap . . . obviously some of this was from memory.

Michael #2 put on his very appealing smile. "It's so nice to see you again."

"Oh, you too," I said, and it went on like this. Nice to see you, how's your work, how was Australia, how's your mother, how's podcasting, how are your patients, treated any sore throats lately? And then Will appeared and set down the starters—cheese for me and salad for Michael #2, which I tried not to take as a comment on our respective merits. "Thank you," I said. "It looks delicious."

Michael didn't say anything. I flicked my eyes up at Will, whose face was unreadable. His smile was missing. And missed, by me.

"Can I get you anything else?" he asked, and Michael gave a flat smile and shook his head.

I straightened the napkin on my lap. "No, no, thank you, this is great." I tried to smile at him, but I honestly wondered whether I was now looking at his secret identical twin, so complete was the lack of acknowledgment. I *had* been naked with this person, had I not? I was almost sure of it. Had he not winked at me once?

I tried not to let the phrase "human clutter" seep into my brain—Was he human clutter? Was I human clutter?—but by then, it was already there.

When Will was gone, Michael #2 reintroduced his warm grin. "My dad used to say waiters are the people who didn't have the grades to be plumbers."

I bit my upper lip with my bottom teeth, which was my most effective method of forcing words back down my own throat. I knew someone who used to say, "Plumbers are highly trained and probably make more money than ninety percent of their clients," but it was me, so it seemed like the wrong thing to say. *Give him a chance,* Eliza had said. Anybody can have a bad day.

"Well," I said, "I love the food here, so I'm glad things worked out this way." I did love a plate highlighted by cheese.

We got through the first course talking about Michael's niece, who had recently gotten the fourth-highest mark in the state of Maryland on some kind of standardized test that sounded very dystopian, and that I assumed I'd have heard of if I had children. She did sound like a smart kid. I'm sure he was delighted to feel confident she would not wind up as a waiter *or* a plumber.

He remained a mostly very nice man, but by the time he asked me if I wanted dessert, all I wanted was to get out of my uncomfortable shoes and my shape-perfecting bra and get in bed for a week. "I think I'm going to make it an early night," I said, "I'm feeling a little off."

"It's probably the cheese," he said. "I couldn't handle that much cheese, I'll tell you that."

Maybe I would get in bed for two weeks.

He got the check, which he had told Julie he thought was important now that we were transitioning into real dating and not just show dating. And as we got up to leave, I couldn't help peeking. He had tipped a flat ten percent, to the penny.

He smiled and extended his arm toward the door to walk me out, leaving no particularly graceful opportunity for me to reach into my bag and pull out an extra bill or two for Will. I smiled weakly and followed him out through the door he was holding open. He signaled for a cab, because he was the kind of guy who always seemed to be able to magically cause cabs to appear, and when he offered it to me, I shook my head.

"Oh, thank you," I said, "but I can walk from here, I'm not far. This was fun."

He came back toward me, but as he approached, I put out one hand, like I was discouraging a hungry dog. "I'm just going to play it safe since I'm not feeling well, I don't want to get too close. Don't want to make your patients sick."

He nodded. "Good thought, I have an early appointment anyway." He extended his arm and put it on my elbow. "I'll call you?"

"I—sure, sure." There was literally no reason to get into it standing outside the restaurant when I was so close to watching him disappear into a cab. He shut the door behind him, and the cab drove off, and I buried my face in my hands.

"Nice guy."

I turned. Apparently, we'd been so taxing to wait on that our server had needed to take a break.

CHAPTER TWENTY-THREE

The Mess

Will had emerged, I suspected, from a spot between Madeline's and the building next door, where he'd been drinking from what looked like a bottle of orange soda.

"Yeah," I said. "Oh, wait." I reached for my mic, unclipped it, shut it off, and stuffed it into my pocket. I dug in my bag and pulled out my wallet, and I walked over to him and held out a couple of bills, folded over. "He's a terrible tipper."

He just looked at it. "Come on," he said. "Don't give me money."

I was so happy to see him—so happy to be talking to him—that I kept wanting to make it better than his face told me it was. "I feel bad," I said.

He nodded, but he made no move toward the money, so I put it away. "That's the doctor, huh?" he asked.

"Yeah," I said. "Michael."

"Third date?"

"Third date."

He nodded. "So it's working out."

I shrugged. "It's only the third time I've ever met the guy, and this time wasn't as good as the last one."

"That was the Peruvian food," he said. He'd really been listening when Eliza was ranting.

"Yeah. It's a nice place."

"I couldn't have taken you there, that's for sure. Can't compete with that with my two jobs."

I coughed out the kind of chuckle that you offer up when nothing is funny. "Were you trying to?"

"No," he said. "I don't know what the hell I was trying to do."

He was looking at the ground, looking grim, looking angry, and maybe it was the weird date or the weird show or Julie leaving, but the thin thread of patience I'd been carefully maintaining snapped. "You know, you seem upset, but you're the one who won't talk to me," I said. "I called you. I'm sorry I said the thing about your furniture, I'm sorry if it sounded mean, I admit I was caught off-guard when Eliza showed up, but—"

"It wasn't just that," he said. "I heard you."

"You heard me when?"

"I heard you tell her that you weren't interested. I just didn't know until she showed up and you started yelling at each other that that hadn't changed, at all. Even after . . . everything."

"What are you talking about? I never said that to her."

"Yes, you did," he said. It was the first time I'd ever seen him angry. "At the party at her house. You said whatever feelings I had, they weren't mutual. You even said, 'Believe me.' And then everything else kinda happened, and I guess it wasn't really great to hear you say it again."

I briefly thought he had to be making this up, genuinely inventing it to hurt me, or to avoid me, or to get rid of me. "I would never say that, once *or* twice. I didn't think that. I don't think that now. I can't even . . ." And then I thought about the word "mutual," and something about it *did* ring a bell. What had happened? What had I said? I *did* say something. "Oh." I said.

He looked at me. "Remembering it now, maybe?"

"Will," I said, and I felt the muscles in my face soften. "That's not what happened. I told her any interest in an actual relationship would not be mutual, yes, I said that."

"Right." He started toward the door.

"Will you listen? I said it because *you* were not interested in *me*. Because you are gone when your lease is up. Because you were talking about being able to pack up and get in your car and go. I wasn't talking about my feelings," I said. "I was talking about yours."

"Really," he said.

"Yeah, really. God, why didn't you tell me you heard that? I could have explained it. I'm sorry you thought I had said that the whole time we were . . . whatever."

"What would have been different?" he asked.

"What do you mean?"

"You'd still have been here, on this date, with this doctor. Right?"

"Sure, but I explained all this to you," I said. "It's work."

He rubbed his eye with one hand. "You know, I've got to tell you, it feels a little bit like you want to have it both ways. You're going out with these guys, but you're not, but you are. You're making this show, but you think it's stupid, but you're still doing it. You're doing whatever this woman tells you to do, even though you think it's a crock."

"I don't get why you're upset," I said. "I explained the misunderstanding from the party. And as far as Eliza throwing a fit on the street, I tried to tell you I was sorry and you wouldn't answer me."

"I heard why she was mad, Cecily. She was mad because she'd talked to you about me already. She said you promised her. You promised somebody I didn't even know that you wouldn't have anything to do with me, because it's so obviously not worth your time," he said. "And I guess because you're bothered by my thrifted coffee table."

"That's not what I said. We were standing out on the sidewalk, she was freaking out, what did you want me to do?" I said.

"What do you *want* to do?"

I felt my jaw set. "I am so sick of this question. And given how you seem to feel now, I don't understand why you care, what's your—"

"Why do you think?" he said. "Look, it's obviously fine that you're dating these guys, we didn't make any deals, I knew about it, whatever. But through this whole thing, people called me *the waiter.* That's what she said, *the waiter.* She yelled it. 'The *waiter*?' Don't get me wrong, I'm proud of this job, but *she* says it like it's embarrassing, and *you* just sit there, and you sit here while your date stiffs me, and I hate it, Cecily. I really hate it."

"Oh my God, it's not like that," I said. "She's just referring to you by what she knows, she's not saying—"

"Sure she is! Do you think she would say it the same way if I was your lawyer?"

I cleared my throat. "Probably not. But I don't feel that way. I like your life. I like your place, I like your dog." I looked at the ground and then back at him. "I can't help it that she's like that."

He looked like he was freezing in his shirt sleeves, and he put his hands in his pockets, then pulled them back out. "Look," he said. "It doesn't sound like it right this second, but I *really* like you," he said, stepping toward me. "Yeah? Is that okay? You are driving me nuts, but I . . . like you." He put this emphasis on the word "like," this very very *hot* emphasis. "And I think you don't understand that you keep getting asked what you really want to do because other people can tell that part of you does want the doctor. You want a life that goes in a straight line from here to wherever. And when I'm looking at you, I wish I was built that way, but I'm not. I'm not even sure you are, either, deep down. But you are hanging on to it," he said. "You are stubborn as hell and you are trying as hard as you can to walk in that straight line.

And if you want that that much, I don't think there's anything I can do."

"You're . . . you're wrong about me," I said. "I . . . you're wrong."

"I don't think so," he said. "But hey, maybe if I hadn't flunked out of premed, I could get your coach's full support. And yours, too." He looked at his watch. "I have to get back. I hope all this turns out to be what you want."

CHAPTER TWENTY-FOUR

The Errant Email

Eliza didn't use email that much. She texted, she called, she posted on Instagram. But her team sent a lot of email. Marcela, in particular, created long, agonizing threads from which I was mercifully omitted most of the time, since they had to do with Eliza's collabs, subscriber numbers, media coverage, and, of course, gobs of money. Occasionally, someone wanted us to be interviewed together about the show, and sometimes those requests came through Marcela. But usually, I was separated from Eliza's email by way of my lack of interest and her habits.

So it was surprising when, walking to work one morning, standing on the corner and waiting to cross the street, I looked at my phone and found an email from Eliza with the subject line "Re: Progress report." All she wrote was:

Glad we're on track for #12!

Episode 12 was the finale, and we were almost finished with it. It was scheduled to go out to our listeners in nine days. It included a sunnier take on my third date with Michael, and on the future of that relationship, than I actually felt.

Julie was, quite understandably, in the process of unclenching her teeth over the whole project and over Palmetto in particular, and I had made a chaotic mess out of my personal life, so all I wanted was for the show to end as smoothly as possible, so that at least that could be a success. Toby had called me into his office a couple of days after Madeline's and told me, as he had in his note on the day of the layoffs, that he was counting on me to "give it a great close." He talked about Marcela, and Fitness West, and Brick, and the advertisers, and how important it was to everybody that the finale be "satisfying." The current draft of the finale ended with me saying that it was hard to know the future, but I'd keep seeing Michael and see where it led. It also included a fair amount of philosophizing from Eliza, and her praising me about what a good job I'd done.

Trying to follow where this email thread had begun, I started reading down the screen.

Right under this lovely little note she had written, on which I was cc'd, there was an email from Toby almost two weeks old, and it just said, "Ha, exactly." And below that was another note from Eliza that I'd certainly never seen before. The one that "Ha, exactly" had been in response to. It was dated right after my last dinner with Michael.

> LOL yes I am trying my hardest! I am pushing the doctor! Def trying to get to the perfect ending. thx for the backup, T. Last night worked, I think. Seeing them in the same place helped. (Doesn't hurt that the waiter didn't like it lol. I think he's out of her way!) When the season is over, she can do whatever she wants. Until then, she's mine! xoxo E

I was obviously "she," which meant this was not intended for me.

The light changed. People pushed by me. I looked around and spotted a bench next to the sidewalk, and I sank down to read.

I have been working in journalism for a long time. And so, while it took me a minute to piece it together, I eventually figured out what had happened. The key was that Eliza had two phones and four or five email addresses. The addresses were supposedly for different things (business/personal/fans/whatever), but she used them interchangeably a lot of the time, just multiple addresses she would be signed into on her laptop, her tablet, her work phone, or her personal phone. So she was forever forwarding things to herself from one address to another so she could deal with them later when she was on a different device.

Some kind of very innocuous note had gone out to some combination of Palmetto people and people on Eliza's team. It was called "Progress report." This was the one she had intended to respond to and cc me, saying she was glad to hear the finale was on track.

But for a couple of weeks, Eliza had also been part of a long, gossipy thread about the show (and about me) with Marcela, Toby, Brick, and some other people, some with addresses I didn't recognize. I assumed they were from somewhere in her orbit. This thread also had the subject line "Progress report." This was bad luck for her. And so, between all the forwarding and the replying and the fact that she was trying to handle her email on her phone (probably while simultaneously eating a protein bar and taking a phone call), she had ended up hopelessly confused.

I read what she had written again.

I am pushing the doctor. When the season is over, she can do whatever she wants. And the thing about Madeline's. *Last night worked.*

I read the entire thread. I scrolled down, down, down until I found the beginning, and then I scrolled back up, bit by bit, watching a story unfold that I could not, in my most frustrated moments, have imagined. My stomach started out queasy and got to a miserable roil, and then I actually thought I might throw up.

The headline was that Eliza had immediately told all of them about catching me with Will on the day it happened, before Christmas. Toby knew, Marcela knew, freaking Brick the ad guy knew, and the brand manager from Fitness West knew. They didn't all need to know, not really, but she had told them anyway, letting it out with a gush, reminding them not to say anything to me, or Julie, or Abby, or Charlie.

She lamented that I had gotten off-track with this "man-child," as she put it to them, which was perhaps supposed to sound concerned for me. But she spent many more words on the idea that this was a potential business problem, for all the reasons Marcela had laid out to Toby way back when we dropped the preview episode and the fans got their little voice crushes on Will. It would not do for me to meet someone on my own. It would not do for me to end up with someone Eliza had so confidently sat down in front of her ring light and told everyone was wrong for me.

Ever since she told them that I had been "sloppy-kissing the waiter," there had been an ongoing discussion, sometimes quite serious and sometimes just ruthlessly bitchy, about how to make sure the season ended "smoothly" and "successfully" and with "a satisfying narrative," which meant I continued to see Michael #2, and Will was not a distraction, and I ultimately agreed that she had given me the right advice all along.

There was also a lot of Eliza and Marcela griping about the fact that I'd only wanted a second date with one guy out of twenty. *We can make that romantic, though,* Toby had said. *It only takes one, etc. etc.*

Marcela had said, *Honestly, no wonder she can't meet anybody.*

Eliza had quoted this line and added, *Seriously!*

It was Marcela who had come up with the idea of changing the reservation from the Italian place in Adams Morgan to Madeline's. She made noises about how this would be "clarifying" for me, seeing the stark difference between the doctor and the waiter, but Eliza got the real point of it immediately: *It's going to make things clear to the waiter, too. She likes Michael. He won't hang around.*

I read Eliza's words over and over. I read these notes where all these people were making fun of me. Her team, Toby, these guys I barely knew, they were all *talking* about it, yammering about what to do about the fact that I had (okay, fine) fallen for Will all by myself when I was supposed to be following a plan that Eliza wanted to charge people money for. They'd set up that disaster at Madeline's. For all I knew, maybe they'd told Michael #2 to treat Will like that. Maybe somebody had told him, *Whatever you do, make sure you tip like a piece of crap.*

CHAPTER TWENTY-FIVE

The Fury

Sometimes, the only good thing about knowing the truth is that you can do all the things you would have done all along if only you had known the truth.

Part of me wanted to hang on to this level of poisonous rage, just chew it and chew it and keep on enjoying it, like it was a never-fading stick of fiery cinnamon gum. But my head was pounding, and I didn't yet have a next move, and the only way to think was to let a little bit of it come hissing out of me until I could think. I walked the rest of the way to the office. When I got there, I let myself into the building and headed for the elevator. I punched the up button with my knuckle so hard I thought it might crack in half, and I was almost surprised when it just lit up, oblivious to the blow it had taken. After I got off at our floor, I walked straight to Toby's office, where the door was closed and I could see through the glass wall that he was at his standing desk with his back to me. When I was about to reach for the door, I realized I had no plan, and I was dealing with people who had nothing but plans. So all I did was whisper harshly at the door, "You suck," and walk away. As a bonus, I walked by Brick's office, where the door was open, and I whispered, "You too." I heard him say, "Huh?"

When I got to my desk, I told a lie, as a tribute to the many lies that had been told to me. I sent around an email saying I was going home sick. I never went home sick. My sick days had piled up, multiplied, and become an abstract number I looked up from time to time, congratulating myself on never ever being sick at sea, as Gilbert and Sullivan had written once, and Aaron Sorkin had written more than once. Especially once I mastered editing remotely, the need to exhale on other people and the need to work had decoupled. The guilt of being present and infectious was gone, so I would sit on my couch cutting tape and coughing. I'd had pneumonia when I cut the last episode of the first show I ever did at Palmetto, and I held my breath so I could get the feel of a particular silence over the sound of my own lungs crackling.

Besides, in this case, my illness wasn't entirely fictional. My stomach hadn't stopped flopping in my belly since I saw that email, and it turned over every time I pulled out my phone and looked at it again. And I was, to be sure, very sick of my desk, that building, Toby, Eliza, everyone who had been patting me on the head every day while they made plans behind my back.

What I craved, I knew instantly, was Will—his apartment, his smile, his shoulder and jaw and neck, and the sound of his voice and the feel of him. And maybe his bed instead of mine, where I could live inside the irony of being annoyingly happy, in a way insufferable even to myself, when there was meant to be a whole thing, a whole narrative *project,* about the idea that I was miserable without a program, unfixable without help, unsalvageable without intervention. But I had ruined it.

When I got home, I didn't even want the clothes of the day to be hanging on my shoulders. I peeled them off and added them to the laundry, shoving them into the middle of the pile until they were gone. I opened the dresser drawer and picked out new pants, a new thin sweater—I even shoved the Beast in the back of the hall closet, refusing to look at my five pounds of solutions to every possible problem.

I did nothing right away. I fantasized about bursting into Toby's office and throwing my ID at him, trying to get the lanyard clip to land in his eye and leave him a Halloween pirate for the rest of his natural life. I considered erasing all the files from the server—my interviews with Eliza, my dates, everything I had left. But the producers were working on turning the third date into the final episode—a sunny glimpse at the promise of Eliza's method—and that would throw off everything they were doing.

I thought about going to some other publication and offering an exposé of Eliza and her skulduggery at the expense of someone she was supposedly trying to help, but I was not spoiling for an impetuous war with her team of extremely online aspirational-quote devotees quite yet.

I called in sick the next day. And the day after that. I didn't answer when Eliza texted, and called, and messaged me on Instagram. I didn't get out of bed. I spent the weekend watching movies, and for once, I didn't do any work at all. I thought about dragging myself into the office on Monday, but the finale was almost finished, ready to go out the door Friday, so I stayed home and listened to it over and over, suggesting tiny tweaks—the tiniest—just to distract myself.

But when I stayed home again on Tuesday, my sister texted me. Are you okay? I heard you're calling in sick and nobody has talked to you. This had to be Julie. I had told her once that if she ever thought I was in trouble, she had my permission to alert my sister.

I'm just taking a couple of days, I texted Molly. Everything is a complete mess, I screwed it all up, I'm an asshole.

You are not! You have to come to dinner. Come tonight.

I can't. I would have to take a shower and put clothes on.

Yes. That's the point. You come over here or I'm coming over there.

So I hauled myself into the shower, where the water landed on my shoulders and ran down my body, and I scrubbed off the sweat and the stink and the lying and how tired I was, and by the time I pulled on fresh clothes, I felt like at least I could breathe again.

I went to the Metro station late that afternoon, carrying a small plant in one hand. I always took something with me to Molly's, even though I knew she didn't expect it. It had driven Justin crazy. Justin, who never brought anything anywhere, because he knew I would, whether we were going to my family's house or his.

I mentioned this to him once, that he went empty-handed every time, and he said, "We're not the three wise men, I don't think we need to make a big production out of bearing gifts. And anyway, you like doing it, so." Apparently he thought it was my hobby to bring candles or little packets of tea to his mother, a diversion he was allowing me to indulge for my own enrichment. I never told him that, once a year, I went to an art fair in Bethesda and bought enough gifts for everyone we visited that would last a long time: soaps, pots, dishtowels, stationery sets. I kept it all in a fabric box that sat at the top of the coat closet in our apartment, and every time we went to see anybody, stay with anybody, I'd take it down, grab something, write a little note, stick it in a little bright-blue bag from a stash in the desk, and we'd leave.

I always got the sense that Justin didn't want to know how it happened, he just knew I materialized beside him with something in my hand, and it made everyone smile at both of us. Despite his hemp clothes and his flirtations with socialism, his deep traditionalist streak came out in strange ways, and one was that hospitality was a Me Thing, while watching me be hospitable was a Him Thing.

I knew Molly usually changed when she got home at the end of the day, just like I did, trading her work uniform of smart slim pants and a simple top for something slouchier that didn't wrinkle, but she still had her office look on when I got there. "Hi," I said, reaching forward to hug her.

"Tell me everything," she said, and I just collapsed on her shoulder and sobbed, very big, embarrassing sobs, and she said "Oh no, oh no," and she stroked my hair.

"Everything is ruined," I said.

"Everything is not ruined," she said. "I promise you everything is not ruined." She stepped back. "Oh my God, did you bring me a plant?"

"Well . . . yeah." Molly always complained that she loved plants but couldn't keep them alive, and while I would have liked to argue, I didn't. I brought her fresh ones over and over, and she rotated them through the house as long as she could, starting every one on the dining room table and moving it to the living room or the front hall or the powder room, wherever it fit, gamely watering it until the inevitable dried-out leaf appeared, and she knew her time with this one was growing short.

"You did not have to bring me a present."

I shrugged and handed the plant to her, and she lifted her free arm and dabbed at my damp cheek with the end of her sleeve. "Well," I said, "everything else is a disaster, but plants still work."

"Cecily, what's going on?" she asked.

Should I start at the beginning? Should I start with mistakenly trusting a woman who was conning me? Should I start with the guy I really liked, whom I'd given up for no good reason? I exhaled. "Can we just have dinner first? I promise I'll tell you both all about it later."

"Of course. Come in and eat. Food and a glass of wine will make everything feel better. Did you even eat today?"

"I had a bowl of cereal this morning."

She sighed heavily. "Cecily."

"I'll eat, okay?"

Pete was where I so often found him, juggling pots and pans on every burner of their stove, little blue flames dancing while he switched from a wooden spoon to a whisk to a spatula, scraping and stirring, moving a lid onto this and off of that. "Hey," I said, going up and squeezing his shoulder.

Pete looked over, his spoon still stirring a pot of what I was guessing was a risotto. "Hey, kiddo," he said. "I don't want to abandon my rice, but we'll be eating in maybe fifteen minutes."

It was more like twenty, but Molly's table was, as always, the warmest one I knew, even with her house in chaos. Her dishes were simple white ones with subtle textured dots around the rims, and she took the little plant I'd brought and put it in the middle of the table, moving the one I'd brought last time to her windowsill.

Pete brought in a mushroom risotto and a plate of chicken with crisp skin and fresh herbs, plus a salad with lace-edged curls of cheese perched on top and a bowl of charred green beans.

It was, paradoxically, one of the best dinners of my life. It was the company, it was the fact that there was nothing left in my life for me to break, and it was the fact that there was such comfort in this place where I was loved. But Pete also made a fantastic risotto. I suspected I'd never master it.

After we cleared the dishes, we went into the living room with wine. Pete sat on the couch, and Molly sat leaning against him with her feet up. I sat opposite them, envious. "Honey," Molly said to her husband as he rested his hand on her shoulder, "remind me that I have to get somebody in to do the grout in the upstairs bathroom."

"Roger that," he said. "Remind me I'm meeting the kitchen guy Tuesday to get started on Operation Double Oven." Pete looked over at me. "I won. So get ready for two Thanksgiving turkeys."

"Why would we need two Thanksgiving turkeys?" Molly said.

"To use both ovens."

Molly rolled her eyes. "So," she said, holding a glass in one hand and resting the other on her husband's thigh, "tell us what happened."

I took a deep breath. "They conned me," I said.

She froze. "Who did?"

"Everybody did." It was good to let the story unwrap itself from around my neck, to explain to the person who'd been my confidante the longest how the whole show was a front for a piece of influencer content, just another outlet for a YouTube star, just another way to sell worthless lessons. I told them all of it, from the confrontation outside my apartment to Michael #2 who barely tipped, to the misdirected email and the way they'd been messing with me for weeks. Molly periodically said "good grief" or "oh no," and waited until the end of the story and then said it again: "Oh, *no*."

"Yeah, exactly," I said. "Fortunately, Julie is leaving anyway, so whatever happens, I don't have to give a damn."

"She's leaving?" Pete asked.

"She's going to New York for a better job," I said. "Better than the one she has, better than the one they'd give her."

"So what happens now?"

"I don't know," I said. "I feel like the whole thing is ridiculous. But most of it is already out there. The last episode is just about done."

"What about Will?" Pete asked.

"That ship has sailed. By which I mean that I burned it up in the harbor and sank it."

"You don't know that," Molly said. "If there's one thing we know in this house, it's tenacity in love, right?"

"It's probably silly anyway," I said. "It's not like this is the right guy just because we kept running into each other. I got distracted by all these spectacular coincidences, you know? We saved the dog, and he was at the restaurant, and then he was the photographer, and then in the rain."

"Those coincidences are not that spectacular," Molly said. "You're a couple of creative people who are about the same age who live in the same general neighborhood. It's not exactly bumping into each other in Times Square on New Year's Eve."

"Believe me," I said, "if I went to Times Square on New Year's Eve, he'd show up. Especially if I looked like hell." Pete laughed, and then he apologized for laughing. "My point," I added, "is that with him, it's just things that happened. Maybe Eliza's right that I focus on all the wrong things."

Molly thought about this for a minute. "Did you know that *Big Brother* gets people married just as often as *The Bachelor*?"

"What does that have to do with anything? You want me to go on *Big Brother*?"

"Obviously not," she said. "What I'm saying is that if you lock a bunch of roughly compatible people in a house for a couple of months, some of them will start making out with each other, and some of *those* people will have sex with each other, and some of *those* people will decide they genuinely like each other, and some of *those* people will marry each other. And that works just as well as recruiting a bunch of people for a romantic Thunderdome where everybody is specifically hoping they're going to find a mate. Take it from somebody who married the one groomsman who happened not to be dancing to 'Shout.' Logic is overrated," Molly finished, and she took a big drink of her wine. "If you like him, you like him. That's my best advice. And by the way, it's free."

CHAPTER TWENTY-SIX

The Ex

The next morning, I decided I was ready to face the office again, and I was about a block away from Palmetto when I heard it. "Cecily!"

For a minute I thought it was Will, but it made no sense that it would be, and for once, when I didn't expect him, he didn't appear. I turned around. And I saw who it was. "Oh, for the love of . . . what are you doing here?"

"Well, I'm glad to see you, too," Justin said.

"I am so much too tired to talk to you, you have no idea."

Justin was wearing his business uniform, which was a blue wool blazer over a T-shirt, jeans, and boots. He took out a pair of earbuds I was sure were worth at least $500 and tucked them, loose, into his pocket. "It's good to see you," he said, ignoring what I'd just said. "I've been getting a kick out of your show." The smirk made me want to dunk his head in a vat of glue.

"I'm so glad," I said. "What brings you to D.C.?"

"A work thing," he said. He smiled. "It's been a long time since I saw you."

"I guess it has, yeah." I looked at his hand, half expecting him to be wearing a diamond ring, because that's just how scrambled my brain had gotten. "Congratulations on everything, by the way."

Just then, Julie walked up to us and stopped. "Oh," she said.

"Julie. This is Justin Dash. Justin, this is Julie Nazari, she's one of the great producers here at Palmetto. She makes *Twenty Dates* with me."

Justin did this thing when he heard himself introduced; it was funny to realize I'd forgotten all about it. He was cursed by the fact that he was modestly well-known inside a particular part of the world (the part that listened to podcasts), and from time to time, someone recognized his name and said, *Oh yeah, big fan!* or something like that.

But usually, they didn't. I was lucky, because at least until recently, nobody ever recognized my name, so I didn't expect them to. But Justin was chronically afflicted by this tiny flame of hope, and now, in the right settings, all he could do was wait and see. Of course, it didn't help that the kinds of people who recognized his name often hoped to be too cool for him to be able to tell, so they would *pretend* they had no idea who he was. They'd end up in a standoff, looking at each other, one person too cool to give validation to a celebrity and one person dying to be more famous than he was, neither of them getting what they wanted.

Julie knew exactly who he was, for several different reasons. But she gave him nothing that would qualify as a reaction, not even a cold glare. I adored her. After all, Justin *particularly* would expect a producer I worked with to recognize his name and to be impressed. He would assume that surely, I would have told everyone I worked with that I had dated oh-my-God Justin Dash, and that I had even worked with him. To Justin, our association was by far the most interesting thing about me, and he assumed everyone else would think so, too.

Julie's face was as nonreactive as a mannequin. "Oh sure, hi," she said.

"Hey," Justin said back, and he shook Julie's hand, because what else could he do?

"Nice to meet you, I have a lot of work to get to." Julie stepped back and gave a little wave, and then disappeared into the building. I took a breath. There's something about a really good producer that makes you feel, just briefly, like everything truly will be all right. I couldn't believe we weren't going to be working together anymore.

"How've you been?" Justin finally said.

"I've been great," I lied effortlessly, as only this encounter could motivate me to do. "Work's good, family's good. You? Besides Clarissa?"

"Great," he said. "Lots of irons in the fire. I'm consulting, working on more *Scanners*." He smiled at me and made a little gesture, almost like a bow. "You know how much work that is, of course."

That smug little bastard. "I sure do." I suddenly turned and looked over my shoulder at our building, then I looked harder at him. "What's your work thing?" I asked. There were only a handful of places he could be in D.C. to visit if he was, indeed, here for work. What was he doing in this neighborhood?

He smiled. "It's nothing definite yet."

"Uh-huh," I said.

He smiled again, and this time, he added a calming hand gesture, as if steadying a goat. "It's nothing definite yet."

"Cecily?"

I turned. It was Eliza.

Justin turned to her, too. "Hi."

And she turned back to him. "Oh," she said. "Have we met?"

"Wait, you two know each other?" I said to Eliza.

"I think we met at a thing," she said. She pointed back and forth between me and Justin. "*You* know each other?"

"Justin is my ex," I said.

"Not the shitty ex," she said. I didn't budge. "Oh!" She turned to him. "You *are* the shitty ex!"

"I'm not the shitty ex," he said, and it was somewhere around this point that I began to find it very funny.

"Wait," I said, "where did you two meet?"

"We met at Podcast Pow!" he said. Freaking *Podcast Pow!* "We had drinks."

Eliza leaned toward me. "With a lot of people," she said. "We didn't *have drinks*." She breezily waved a hand at him, saying, "I just never put it together that you were *that* guy." She turned her attention back to me. "I haven't been able to get you on the phone. Are you ready to do some work?"

I glared at her. "Not really. I need to talk to you. Justin, I don't even know what you're doing here, but I would really appreciate it if you'd go away. Anywhere you want is fine except in my direct line of sight."

Justin looked back and forth between the two of us. "Okay," he said. "I need a cup of coffee anyway." He raised one hand and walked off. I wanted to say something cutting to him, but I couldn't summon the energy, not if I was going to save enough for everybody else I had to yell at today. Instead, as he walked off toward the coffee shop down the block, I just muttered, "How does this keep happening? Why can I not walk down the street in peace?"

Eliza had her green tea latte in her hand, and with the other one, she reached over and touched my arm. "Hey, I'm glad I ran into you. Michael told me you're not answering him either. What is going on?"

"I'm glad I ran into you, too," I said. "You can give him my regrets. He deserves to go out with somebody who wants to be there, and I deserve to go out with somebody who knows how to tip at a restaurant. And more to the point, I think I need to figure out my next step without you and Toby and Marcela and half the staff of Fitness West scheming behind my back about how to keep me from accidentally becoming happy without your approval."

I hadn't ever seen her look guilty until that very second. As far as I'd known until this moment, Eliza Cassidy simply didn't do regret. She didn't question herself. But as soon as that look had landed on her face, she pushed it away again. "What are you talking about?" she said.

"I know that you told all those people that you saw me with Will that day. I know you've been gossiping about it, and I know you set up that mess at Madeline's. I know you've been whispering in my ear to get me to do what you want this entire time, and you don't actually give a damn if I'm happy."

"That is not true," she said, affecting a wounded expression. "I give a lot of damns." Now she paused. "Toby couldn't keep his mouth shut, huh?"

"Oh, you did this on your own," I said. "You really need to stop forwarding your emails to yourself. Look, all I want to do right now is finish this show and forget it ever existed. Fortunately, I think every interview we need with you, we already have, and if we don't, Julie can come and find you, because I really don't want to talk to you. We're going to finish this project and get it pushed out of here, and then we don't ever have to see each other again."

"Cecily," she said, "don't say that, that's horrible."

"What did you think was going to happen?" I said. "You were making fun of me. You and my boss, you and your manager. How did you think I was going to feel if I found out you were giving me all this advice and you were just being mean about it the whole time?"

"I already told you, I want you to be happy. I don't want you to settle, I don't want you to doubt yourself, I want you to—"

"Stop it," I said. "Stop reading me bullet points. This is my life. It's my life, my real life, are you listening?"

"Do you think you're the only person with a 'real life'?" she asked, putting furious finger-quotes around the last two words. "Do you think I'd have done all this if I didn't genuinely want it to work?" I didn't flinch, and this was where I could have said something about knowing they'd sold their apartment, but I decided not to. "Every time I turn around, everything about my business gets thrown out the window because somebody changes some rule or some way you can or can't make money. Or they hide you from your fans, or they charge your fans to see you. Or they stop letting you do what they told you yesterday you absolutely had to do. Somebody makes a new app, or somebody decides the old app isn't cool anymore, or the old app violates everybody's privacy or it gets sold to a monstrous creep. I hustle because I have to hustle. I put months into this, and I told my partners it was happening, and I don't apologize for trying to make it work out for myself while also trying to get a nice doctor for you. While, let me add, you resisted the entire time."

"I didn't even want to do this," I said. "I didn't want to do self-help. Do you remember sitting there over lattes and talking me into it?"

"Hey, don't blame this on me," she said. "You're the one who said yes."

"I said yes to save my job!" I said. "To save Julie's job. Toby was threatening to lay her off."

"Oh, *bullshit,*" she said, and I realized I almost never heard Eliza swear. "You could have kept your job, you didn't have to say yes to this. And I bet you didn't even talk to your 'friend' before you did this. You didn't ask her what she wanted. It wouldn't have even mattered whether she *wanted* that job or not. Bossy bossy Cecily jumped in to run the whole thing."

"So you think I never cared about my friend or my job, I was just dying to experience the Platinum Goddess Package?"

"You were being aggressive," she said, "and I don't know why it embarrasses you so much. You saw a chance to do something you've always wanted to do, which is host a show. This is the most like-me thing you've ever done, but unlike me, you make excuses for it. You have to be 'Oh, I did it for my friend.' You did it because you wanted a better job. You did it because you wanted to be more famous. You wanted to be a bigger deal."

"It's that hard for you to believe I was at least partly interested in a single mom not getting fired?"

"Did she thank you?"

"What?"

"Was she grateful when you did that? Julie, whose job you saved?"

"I didn't tell her."

She laughed. "Perfect. That's absolutely perfect! You don't have to ask her what she wants, but you get to sit there knowing she owes you. That's why you pull Band-Aids and wet wipes and pens out of that bag you lug around, so everybody owes you. Don't you get that this is all ego? Building your whole life around chances for people to be indebted to you? Your ex owed you, your friend owes you, your boss owes you. You set everybody up to owe you, and then you're mad when nobody pays you back."

"*I'm* all about ego? I'm not the one with the testimonials on my website that talk about how I transformed people's lives."

"Listen to me," Eliza said, leaning close to me, almost spilling her latte. "I will stand right here and tell you, person to person, ambitious bitch to ambitious bitch? That's my job. I get paid for it, and I wouldn't do it if I didn't. I'm not waiting around hoping that I'm going to be so good to these women, help them so much, that they thank me so I feel good about myself. I feel good about myself when they pay me on time."

"Well, that sucks," I said.

"No. It doesn't," she said. "What sucks is wanting to be thanked instead of loved, because you can believe you deserve it. You know why I didn't want you to be with somebody who wasn't successful? It's not because I'm a snob. Date whoever you want, date a waiter, date somebody who hires himself out for medical experiments. But." She stepped closer to me. "You're going to look at him one of these days, and you're going to say, 'This waiter needs my help. This man needs to chase his dreams. And whose job is it to make sure that can happen? My job.' That's why I wanted you to find somebody successful. You need a guy who will never have to owe you, or you will never, ever believe he can love you."

I just looked at her. I aspired to her evident comfort with her position in the world. She never seemed nervous, even as she was stacking pronouncements about someone's life—my life—one on top of another without slowing down. She considered herself qualified for any job she decided to pursue, attractive enough for anyone, appropriately dressed at all times. She never questioned that how she acted was the way people should act. How she reacted was the way people should react. She'd had a book on the bestseller list. People came to her for advice about the most intimate things in their lives. Companies paid her to hold a bottle of their vodka in her hand, or wear their sunglasses, or stay at their hotel. She didn't have a boss who took advantage of her, she didn't have a project that could be yanked out from under her at any time, and the fools she suffered were the ones she chose. She'd never subject herself to Toby the way I did.

I nodded at her, feeling how final it was. "Thank you for the very last advice I'm ever going to take from you. I've had enough," I said. "I've just . . . had enough." I took off toward my apartment, ignoring the texts she started sending almost as soon as I left.

CHAPTER TWENTY-SEVEN

The Apology

I would be the first to admit that I had no business showing up at Will's building that night. I just couldn't figure out what else to do. I could say I didn't text him for some other invented reason, but honestly, I was afraid that if I asked to come over, he would say no. Still, people did not do that anymore, just show up, notwithstanding the fact that he had done it once and we had had extremely nice doorway sex as a result. Maybe he had used up the one free pass that we had for appearing without discussion, particularly given how things were now. Besides, what if he was in there with someone? Someone else, who was not me?

I tried to ignore the voice that said, *There is no one there, because of course he is waiting for you,* because that was an irrational voice, and it was engaged in magical thinking. But I sort of believed it anyway, so I came very close to just knocking, but the idea of this visit had been to return to some kind of rationality, not to set myself up for more embarrassing disasters, and so I didn't do it.

Standing on the sidewalk, I texted him.

Hi.

I was in the neighborhood, and now I am outside your building. Can we talk?

I waited. His light was on, I was sure, although there was always the possibility that I had miscounted windows or floors, and that in fact, he was out on U Street somewhere, pounding booze and making out with very beautiful and very accomplished women at the exact moment I was standing outside on the street like a fool, in my soft clothes and my slip-on shoes that I had put on in my state of exhaustion and surrender. What if he wasn't even here? What if he was visiting his sister? What if he was visiting his parents? What if he was in the middle of wild and passionate sex with one of those people he met on U Street?

I just got back from walking Buddy.
Do you want to come up?

Yes, thank you.

The door buzzed. I jogged up the steps, and when I got to his door, it was open, and he was standing there. "Hey," he said.

"Hi," I said. "Thank you for this. I was . . . not nearby at all."

"I figured." Buddy came up next to him and stood with his head against Will's hip. The dog might have liked me, at least at one time, but his loyalty to Will was total, and I admit I felt his big, wet eyes appraising me with disappointment. Even the dog knew I had blown it. "Do you want to come in?"

"Yeah, thanks." I stepped through his door, looked around at the spare furnishings, and suddenly wanted nothing more than to be ravished on his cheap-ass secondhand sofa. He didn't sit down, so I didn't either. "I just wanted to apologize," I said. "I keep having these terrible conversations, and every time I finish one, I feel worse, and I think it's because I was horrible, even though I didn't mean to be. To you, I mean." He didn't speak. "I'm sorry for the thing I said about the furniture. And I'm sorry that I brought that guy to Madeline's, that wasn't fair, that was—well, whatever happened, I should have made sure it didn't happen. You're probably not wrong that part of me gravitates toward kind of predictable, easy people and then doesn't actually like having them in my life. I feel silly about that. But the—the point is, I'm sorry about everything, and I really feel like garbage."

"You don't need to feel like garbage," he said. "Well. Maybe a small can." He was not exactly smiling, but he maybe let his shoulders drop a couple of centimeters, maybe let his eyes soften enough that I almost involuntarily leaned toward him.

"For what it's worth," I said, "I found out recently that Eliza and Toby and a lot of other people were manipulating me in ways I didn't really know about, trying to make sure I screwed everything up with you so the show would turn out well and I'd end up with Eliza's guy. And I should have understood that was happening, and I should have prevented it, but I didn't, and I think I let her get in my head." I watched Buddy go over and settle himself on his bed on the floor, apparently satisfied that I posed no immediate threat. "Which, I mean, it's still my fault, it's on me, but I wanted you to know."

He nodded, but did not smile. "Okay."

I so wanted him to say something comforting to me. I so wanted to tell him absolutely everything, down to the word, down to the most granular detail of the scheming that had gone on behind my back. I wanted to complain about Michael #2 some more, how he was cheap and ultimately boring and how he was merely the best of an underwhelming crop of men I didn't like that much and men who didn't like me at all. I wanted Will to make me dinner and fix it, and I wanted to fix something for him in return, and I wanted us to just stay in this place together and not quit yet.

"I guess that's all I wanted to tell you," I said.

"I appreciate it," he said.

"Okay."

"And." That's all he said at first, he said "And." I just stood there, waiting out a suspenseful pause any producer would admire. "For what it's worth," he finally continued, "it's not entirely . . . your fault, I mean. I think I do have a thing about what I do for a living. Or maybe what I don't do. And that's not because of you, that's because of . . . well, it's not because of you. I *am* unsettled. I *am* not very prepared for anything serious, and it's not your fault that you noticed."

"I don't think about it that way," I said. "I promise you, I really don't. I think your life is much more on track than you think. I mean, you take pictures of congressmen."

"Well, bureaucrats."

"And hang gliders."

"Really just kites."

"Anyway, I might have thought you weren't obsessive enough, but I didn't think you weren't special enough. I think you're more . . ." I looked around. "I think you're more at home than you think."

"What makes you think that?"

Just then, with what was, for once, perfect timing, Buddy's head popped up behind Will and then dropped back down to his bed. "I don't know," I said. "You adopted a hundred-and-sixty-pound dog with a skull like a tackle box." When I said "dog," Buddy's ears twitched, then stilled.

"So you're using the dog against me," he said, almost smiling, almost, almost.

"I don't mean to use anything against you," I said. And I did smile, because I couldn't not, because I was beginning to realize I always did when we were together. "I just came here to tell you I don't think anything is wrong with you. And I'm sorry that's how it felt." I thought about telling him all about the unfolding disaster at work, the way everything was collapsing, but that wasn't his to carry for me. So I just said, "I think you're just right exactly as you are, and if your life in twenty years looks anything like your life now, I think you'll still be just right. And that's . . . that's all I wanted to say." I moved to leave before I started crying, because that didn't seem like the thing to do at all.

"Wait," he said.

"I have to go," I said. "I didn't—I didn't come here to talk you into anything." I walked over to Buddy, bent down by his bed, and put my hand on top of his enormous, fuzzy head. "Be good, bubba." Then I got out as fast as I could.

CHAPTER TWENTY-EIGHT

I Want

I somehow made it through the next day at the office, listening to the finale over and over, taking final signoffs from legal and partnerships and marketing and publicity, reading comments online speculating about where I was going to end up. "She'll find someone," one person said. "Spoiler alert: She's staying single forever," another countered. I wanted to feel some kind of victory that we were so close, that the show was about to complete its run, and that it was, in fact, a hit by many standards. We had listeners. They liked it. Advertisers were satisfied. We had opinionated people online expressing thoughts both sensible and not so sensible. There were a couple of good reviews from the regrettably small world of audio criticism, and I read them and reread them. I wished I felt as successful as I could demonstrate on paper that we'd been.

The minute I got home, I changed into leggings and a very old T-shirt with an unraveling hem that was soft from being washed a hundred times. I flopped down to lie on the couch with my hand over my eyes. It was February 13. Tomorrow they were dropping the finale, which left me at my third date with Michael #2, happily in the early stages of something good, and made Eliza look very skilled at what she did. Toby had made us cut out anything about the tip, anything about Will. I had sleepwalked through the interviews. Even Julie didn't know what had happened.

I want.

I had not started out wanting, when it came to almost anything. All I wanted was to be capable of things not everyone was capable of. Ten percent better at the regular things, willing to take on the extraordinary things.

I had started working when I was fifteen, helping out at my uncle's office. When I was done with my classes for the day, I would take the bus to the accounting firm of Reynolds & Guff, where I made $6 an hour doing what they called "general office." At the beginning I opened mail, I collated and stapled little handouts for presentations they were doing about changes in the tax laws, and I printed out research. I sometimes answered the phones when the receptionist went on break. Then, when I'd been there for six months, I overhauled their filing system. I printed new folder labels and peeled off the old ones, rolling them between my fingers into tiny balls that I threw in the trash.

I thought then that I might be a lawyer, maybe someone who went around in clackety heels, telling the truth, fixing people's problems, driving a cool car, absolutely unafraid, all the time.

I worked at a summer camp when I was seventeen, supervising art activities and living with ten girls in the Owlet cabin. I walked two different campers through their first periods that summer, listened to several kids explain how their parents' divorces had either hurt them or saved them, and over the course of the summer, taught three hundred eight-year-olds how to do blot art and tissue paper art and beading.

I want, I want.

I worked in a mall store. That job I remember mostly as endlessly folding shirts, even though I also got my first experience on a cash register. I listened to the mid-level inoffensive rock station for about twenty hours a week, discovered my talent for trouble-shooting other people's problems (like how to reload the register tape), and was promoted as high as they could put me, given that I couldn't close on school nights. My friends at that job made fun of me for being named Employee of the Month three times in five months. It irritated me; it wasn't like I could help it.

When I went to college, I worked in the dining hall where I ate, setting up and breaking down lunch three days a week. I was a crew leader, which meant that it was my problem if somebody didn't show up, and it was my gloved hand that always ended up grabbing whatever gross thing got stuck somewhere it wasn't supposed to be. I suppose I might have been better off at the college radio station, but I was years away from the bloom of that interest, and even later, I wouldn't have aspired to spin records at 4:00 in the morning for two hours on Wednesdays. And honestly? We had iPods already. Radio? Really?

I went home for the summer and went back to the mall store, where I got another promotion, because now I could close.

I was an English major, and my first job out of college was answering phones that rarely rang at a dying publishing company. It got very boring and very lonely, and I was six months into that job when I first heard That One Podcast that everyone thinks invented podcasts. I had already started listening to a motley collection of public radio stuff and comedy stuff and things created by internet weirdos, but all of a sudden I didn't have to tell everybody what a podcast was when I said I was listening to one. I perked up like a beagle with a sausage under my nose.

My father's college roommate worked in public radio in New York, and he told me I should apply for an internship. I have a feeling that what clinched it was my recommendation from my mall store boss, because when I got there for the first day of my internship, my boss said, "I have heard you are the greatest retail employee who has ever lived." I also wrote a very good cover letter, let's be serious.

I did all these things because they seemed to be next, and smart, and yes, eventually, without realizing it, I had begun doing something I loved. I had begun to do what I wanted, even if I felt at times like I'd just stumbled into it. I hadn't, of course—the people I knew from high school hadn't gone off to become radio interns or audio producers, they were doing what *they* wanted, in insurance offices and real estate brokerages and car dealerships and in homes full of kids. But wasn't this what I wanted? Wasn't that how I got here?

Maybe Eliza was right. Maybe "I want" was the key to everything.

So I sat there, and I did what she asked. I tried to just want things besides my job. I wanted someone to understand that I was distressed and hurt and I felt *betrayed* because Julie was leaving, but also I felt proud of her and guilty that I hadn't given her the reaction she deserved. I wanted someone who would distract me, who would have his *own* problems, who would rattle around an apartment with me and make dinner and have sex and tell me a joke and watch a movie with me and tell me I did not have to do everything right. I wanted company, and I wanted a hand on the back of my head, tangled in my hair, while someone said I was fine the way I was.

I did not want to protect anyone's job—maybe not even mine. I did not want to sit in Toby's office and beg him, just beg and plead with him, to take me seriously instead of sending me out over and over again like a dishwasher technician, tinkering with other people's dreams until they worked, until they hummed and performed and met standards. I did not want to be alone. I did not want to hurt Julie. I did not want to pretend that going out with Michael #2 felt anything like being with Will. I did not want to have made a show that was a lie. I still, somehow, despite everything, did not want to disappoint Eliza. I did not want to disappoint my sister. I did not want Justin to defeat me. I did not want anyone to feel sorry for me. I wanted to tell the truth.

I want.

I looked at my phone. It was 9:45. I texted Julie. Are you free?

Yes. Just finished a marathon game of Ticket to Ride with my parents and Simon. Bella is in bed.

Can I call you?

Of course.

She picked up on the first ring. "Hey."

"Okay," I said, "I'm going to say something that's going to sound . . . I don't know how it's going to sound. Is there any way you can meet me at Palmetto?"

"You want to meet right now?"

". . . Yes?"

"Okay."

"I do have an explanation."

"Don't need it. I'll see you there in about thirty."

I didn't even get dressed. I just put shoes on, got my phone and my bag and my coat, and walked out the door.

I want.

Julie and I sat in a production room with two giant carafes of coffee. We were the only ones in the building, but because everybody worked all the time when they needed to, our badges worked, and the lights worked, and everything worked. All you had to do to put in overtime at Palmetto was show up, just like I always had. I'd met her at the door, and now we were settled, just the two of us. I started by telling her the entire story: Will. Eliza. Toby. The restaurant. The email. Everything. "So," I said. "In conclusion, this finale is supposed to drop in nine hours."

She raised her eyebrows. "Supposed to?"

"I made a lot of mistakes," I told her. "And I'm not sure I have a career to worry about. And Will doesn't want anything to do with me anyway. But the one thing I still want to do here in this building is tell the truth. About him. I don't care about Eliza, I don't care about Toby, I don't care about Palmetto, but I want to tell the truth, which is what I said I was going to do from the beginning. And not telling the truth is why I feel like crap."

She leaned closer. "What *is* the truth about Will?"

I took a breath. "We had a thing, and I might be in love with him, and I've never taught a guy about room tone before. It was really nice, but I think I totally blew it, and I cannot pretend the end of this story is that I'm dating a doctor who doesn't tip well. I would settle for telling a little bit of the truth. Not the good sex part, they don't need to know that."

She looked around the room, then back at me. "Wow. This is a lot for me to absorb at once."

"And I just want to acknowledge that asking you to mess with the locked episode, and asking you to mess with the feed—it's completely unfair. And you have my word that nobody will ever know you were part of this."

"Wait," she said. "You're asking me to break into the system and make Toby really mad, right before I'm done with this job forever. And we're doing this so that you can declare your true feelings to a guy you couldn't stop running into, who you met while saving a dog, who the audience immediately knew was the guy you should actually end up with. And all of this is going to go down on Valentine's Day." She took a giant slug of her coffee. "Cecily, believe me, *everyone* is going to know I was part of this."

We worked, we wrote, we tracked, we cut, we recut. It made me feel better knowing the new ending we were writing was going to be good for Eliza's business anyway, even though I suspected she might not immediately think so. This wasn't the first story about self-help I had ever done, heard, or read, and there are no exposés in that world, even in the worst cases. You always end up spreading the gospel and it lands all over somebody. You can run a story about a guru and his green juice that's literally called "This Guru's Green Juice Claims It Melts Pounds, But It Actually Dissolves Bone and Leaves You as a Pile of Goo," and you'll get a hundred emails demanding to know where it's sold. You can put data on a whiteboard showing that no, rubbing your toes with cardamom pods does *not* cure plantar warts, and every podiatrist will get new questions from patients about what *kind* of cardamom pods to use. Whatever I ended up saying about Eliza, plenty of women would conclude that it might not have been what *I* needed, but *they* would be different. There was no way for it not to be good for business. Even if I had wanted to torch her, I knew I couldn't. *Tell the truth, tell the truth* was all.

At 1:00 in the morning, Julie called Charlie, who we both sensed had started to hate this project somewhere around my sixth date, and she told him what we were doing. She put him on speakerphone and described the final product we were going for, and she asked if he could dig into the royalty-free music libraries and find something we could use. The best thing about that call was hearing how excited he was to participate in this bizarre quest. The second-best thing was that we heard a woman's voice in the background and briefly felt very bad about interrupting until we realized that *it was Abby*, which meant she could help us too, and which made the two of them the sneakiest and most discreet producers I had ever met, and I had met some brilliantly sneaky ones.

At 4:30 in the morning, we finally stumbled out the front doors onto the sidewalk. We stood facing each other. "I am really going to miss you," I said. I looked up at the building. "You, and everybody, you were why I loved it here." I heard myself talking in the past tense, without ever really deciding to.

"I miss working with you already," Julie said. "You were the only reason I ever came here. And you were the reason I stayed. And I'm glad we got to make something together that was really ours before I left." She laughed. "Toby is going to be so mad."

"He is."

"Is Eliza?"

I looked up at the dark sky, as if the answer were up there. "Eventually, no. I think deep down, some part of her really does want me to be happy. And she told me from the beginning, before this even started, that she wanted me to tell people how I really thought it went, and that's all I'm doing. Her manager will get over it. Besides, she successfully set me up on twenty dates, at least . . . fifteen of which I would count as real. She does know how to get you a high volume of first dates if that's what you want. This isn't going to be bad for business."

"Okay," she said. "I'm going to go home and sleep for about a year. I suggest you do the same." She reached out and hugged me, and I felt her put one hand on the back of my neck. "I love you, Ceci."

"Love you too, Jules. Thank you so much."

She walked off toward home, and the night was chilly, and I wrapped my scarf tighter around my neck and took out my phone to call a car. The driver was a woman, and as soon as I got into the back of the car, I realized she was listening to *Scanner Stories with Justin Dash*. I put my headphones on and listened to music. No talking. Just music.

I jerked out of my semi-snooze when she pulled up in front of my apartment, and I thanked her and got out of the car in a hurry. Up in my own bed, I burrowed under the covers in just a big T-shirt and socks, and I fell asleep hard. And while I was asleep, the finale of *Twenty Dates* went out to the world.

CHAPTER TWENTY-NINE

The Last Episode

[CECILY NARRATION] I'm Cecily Foster, and this is the final episode of *Twenty Dates* from Palmetto Media and Fitness West. Today we're wrapping up a story about my life, my dating coach, twenty guys I went out with, and one other guy I haven't said anything about quite yet. I'll be back after this.

<<ad break>>

Welcome back. Have you ever been really, really wrong about something in front of a lot of people?

<<music under>>

I was wrong about a lot of things when I started working with Eliza Cassidy. I was wrong about her, for one thing. I figured she would give me a makeover and introduce me to a bunch of guys. I didn't expect her to teach me very much. But write this down in case anybody ever asks you how the story ended: Eliza Cassidy is really smart. She's reinvented her business every year for the last six or seven, because that's what her world demands. She told me that when we were first getting to know each other.

[ELIZA CUT: *I never know what the future is going to be. I barely know what the present is. I've had accounts die on five or six platforms. You just keep going, it's the only option.*]

[CECILY NARRATION] She's also very determined. She knows how to ask for things. She doesn't agree to take on a job if she doesn't want to do it. She doesn't listen to people who think she's going to fail, not ever. She will never, ever accept that anybody else can guard a door she needs to walk through to get to where she's going. It would be a big mistake to pretend I didn't learn from her, even if maybe it wasn't the things she intended to teach me. She just didn't find me the right person. I really tried. We both did. And when I listen back to the conversations I had with my producers after these dates, I can hear myself. Trying.

[CECILY CUT] *It was fine. He's a nice guy. . . . I guess I'm not sure what to say.*

[CECILY CUT] *Yeah, I don't know. He's definitely good-looking. Um, seems very into his job.*

[CECILY CUT] *It's possible I'm just in a bad mood. He seems like a good person.*

<<music fade>>

[CECILY NARRATION] But it wouldn't be a finale without a twist ending, so let's cut to the chase. The truth is that I found myself a guy. I didn't just find him once. I kept finding him again and again. And again. I was not trying to, I was just out in the world, being a kind of nosy and curious person, which, to be honest, is a thing I like about myself. Anyway, I met this guy, and it sounds funny now, but I guess I thought it would be more honest to pretend that didn't happen than to admit it did.

I don't want to tell you too much about him, because he didn't ask for this. But you'd all like him, I'm pretty sure. I started to spend some time with him, and I realized that all I wanted to do was spend a lot more time with him.

I wasn't trying to go behind anybody's back. He knew about the show, he knew about all these dates. I couldn't tell what he was thinking. But to make a long story short, I should have taken better care of that whole situation. I should have taken better care of him.

<<music under>>

[CECILY NARRATION] I didn't, so I'm single again. I'm not seeing Michael anymore. See, it's not enough for a guy to have great qualifications. And sometimes the food really does make something seem like a better date than it was. That's just a tip, from me to you. I wish him well.

But I am hopeful. More hopeful than I've been in a very long time. Because if I can be as happy once, with anybody, as I was in little moments with this guy I met all by myself, then I can do it again. And I know now that there's no method. You can throw twenty blind dates at me, and none of them will take. I could spend months and months on apps, looking, and there would be no guarantees then either. I honestly never needed a dating coach, and

I definitely didn't need a makeover. I just needed to know when to stop looking. Because this guy liked me—we liked each other—and even if it didn't work out, that was the best thing that could have happened. The next time I am happy, I will make that the most important thing. The next time I find something I've been looking for, I will stop looking for it.

Thank you so much for listening. *Twenty Dates* was hosted by me, Cecily Foster, and written and produced by me, Julie Nazari, Charlie Harper, and Abby Bohm. Eliza Cassidy is at ElizaCassidy.com, on Instagram at RealElizaCassidy, and on YouTube at ElizaDoesItAll. Special thanks to Toby Dennis, Molly Cozer, Cody Cassidy, everyone at Madeline's, and Buddy the Dog.

CHAPTER THIRTY

The Departure

When I got to Toby's office, he was, as I so often found him, sitting at his desk, shopping online. I knocked on the doorjamb.

"Hey," he said without his usual grin. "Get in here." I sat in that uncomfortable green chair with my flawed ass one last time. "You put up the wrong episode, and my guys are having some problems with the system. I want you to go in and take it down. We'll restore it to what it was supposed to be, and we'll put it out next week."

"Toby." I laughed. "It's way too late for that. They've already heard it. You know you can't do that. Besides, the old episode we cut, the one you signed off on, is . . . you're not going to find it."

"We have backups."

"I know. You made me write all the documentation. You're not going to find it."

"It's unacceptable for you to put something out without getting your sign-offs. You're going to get a warning."

"Don't bother. Everybody on the team signed off. That's everybody I care about."

He shook his head. He didn't seem as angry as I expected. It was like he was affronted, but he didn't really care, like he was going through the motions of being pissed off. Finally, he just said, "What in the hell is going on?"

I showed him the email, the very special email I had inadvertently received, and I watched him read it, read it again, and read it again, apparently in the hopes that if he kept on reading it, it would change in front of his eyes. And then he started to talk. About my responsibilities, and what I owed him, and how much trouble I could get in at any other company, and on and on and on, and I didn't listen. For once in my life, I just couldn't be bothered to pay attention.

Instead, I looked at the tops of his bookshelves, where a handful of niche awards few people outside our industry had ever heard of sat in a neat row. Best New Show. Best Investigative Podcast. Best Relationship Podcast. Best Subscriber Content. I looked at him, and he looked smaller, older. He'd read as pretty cool at one time. He'd turned fifty last year, and it had to burn his bacon that his fleece-vest years were flying by, to be followed before he knew it by his thick-knit cardigan years.

He had, I realized, stopped talking. "Any questions?" he asked.

"Oh, I wasn't listening, sorry. But wait, I do have one question. You want to tell me why I ran into Justin on the street yesterday?"

He made a contemplative and very serious face, like he was about to let me in on a national security issue. "Can I count on your discretion?"

I didn't even know if I wanted to know. I could easily imagine going the rest of my life without ever learning what bomb he was holding in his hand. "I don't know. For how long?"

"For about two hours," he said. "We're making an announcement today. We're being acquired."

There was the bomb going off. "By who?"

"By Caravan. And Justin was here because they're also buying his company. He's being hired as their director of podcasts, and he's running point on this acquisition from the editorial angle." When I didn't say anything, he went on, "They're buying us, Cecily. And that means whatever you want to do with your career, you're going to be taking it up with them, and I really think they'd like to have you on board."

"You mean he would," I said. "You mean Justin would like to have me on board." I laughed and looked around the office. "I thought he was doing a new show with Paul Casper."

"He is. That's a collaboration. Paul will carry the bonus content in one of his feeds, Caravan will carry the main show. It's meant to raise the profile of the division. Which is going to be us, plus a couple of other places they're planning on buying that are smaller than we are."

"And what about you?" I said. "Are you staying or going?"

"I'll be here for six months for the transition," he said. He did not add the part he didn't need to add, which was: *and then I will take the many, many millions of dollars they just gave me and spend it on online shopping while boring my next wife to tears.* This was why he didn't really care that we changed the finale. Toby wasn't thinking about my dumb show, he was thinking about all the money he was about to make.

Caravan had started as a video company. And then it became a content company. And since then, it had become a devouring company. And nobody there was going to care about the people who were gobbled up when it acquired Palmetto. Charlie. Abby. Brick. Kevin. Carl the business guy. You only need so many people. Synergy, which is another word for making human beings unnecessary, is the whole point. "So," I said, "when you promised me that we'd make a pilot of my show if I did this, you knew you couldn't make it happen. Because by then, somebody else would be in charge."

"I didn't know that for sure," he said. "Things like this take months to close. Our partnerships people brought in Eliza, I thought it was a good idea, it's that simple."

"You knew," I said.

"It doesn't matter," he said. "What matters is that you have colleagues here, and they're going to look to you for help with this adjustment."

Bossy bossy bossy Cecily will be in charge of it.

"Toby," I said, "I will not be helping with this adjustment."

"I'm really disappointed to hear that," he said. "I've thought of us as family, and I thought you did, too."

"You know, I don't have a perfect family," I said. "They drive me crazy sometimes. We don't communicate that well. I go a long time without seeing my parents. I'm pretty sure they are at two different wellness retreats on two different continents as we speak. We argue about where to do Christmas and what kind of stuffing to have at Thanksgiving, and sometimes somebody is too critical or wants to borrow money. But if my mother sold my family to a bigger, more profitable family and didn't give me any of the money, I like to think she wouldn't expect me to smooth it over with my sister." I stood up and started to leave.

"You matter to me, Cecily," he said to my back.

I stopped. I turned around. "Fuck you, Toby. I quit."

CHAPTER THIRTY-ONE

The Recovery

I had two big canvas bags in the bottom drawer of my desk, plus the Beast. I hadn't expected to go home toting everything I'd ever brought to my desk to keep me from going crazy while I edited at night, while I slept there so we could meet deadlines, so the last edit could go through, so the last tiny mistakes could be caught.

I sat in my desk chair. I took the pictures of Molly and Pete and the ones of my mom and dad, and the one of me and Julie and Bella at the zoo, and I laid them inside one of the bags. I took two legal pads that were filled with my notes, with only one or two blank pages left. I took my pens and my headphones, my Post-its and my two water bottles. I slid open the big desk drawer. I took out the Advil and the Tylenol, the cold medicine, the nail clippers, the warm socks for when the office was cold and the handheld fan for when it was hot. I packed up the aspirational apple and the night chocolate and two granola bars. I packed up the floss, the toothbrush, the deodorant, and the hair ties, all left over from when I couldn't go home.

I took down a few complimentary notes I'd gotten over time

from people I admired, which I'd tacked to the wall of my cubicle. I packed my spare sweatshirt and a mug that said SOUND IS MY VISION. I took out a fat stack of business cards and threw them into the recycling.

I picked up all of it and headed for the elevator. But as I got close, I realized I could not, in fact, carry it all. I couldn't bear to go and find anybody to tell them what had just happened and ask them to help me with my stuff. Not like this. I was going to have to make two trips home. No glorious exit. Just slinking back in to get my other bag. The moment I had dreamed about was ruined. I would, as I so often had in this building, settle for so much less than I'd envisioned.

I took the elevator down with one of the bags, and I passed through the lobby. I stepped out onto the sidewalk, and when I looked to my left, I thought I was hallucinating. Either I was hallucinating, or the damnedest series of coincidences I had ever experienced or even heard of had come for me one more time.

"Hi," he said, and he smiled.

Maybe I'd brought Will here. Maybe I'd brought him here with my mind. I'd certainly tried hard enough over the last two days. "Hi," I said back, on a long sigh, and I put everything down. "I guess it's inevitable this would all end with bumping into you again."

"You didn't bump into me," he said. "I came to get you."

I was afraid to believe it. "Why?"

"Well, your friend Julie texted me. She thought I might want to hear the big finale. Which I did. And she told me you might have a hard day with your boss. So I figured I'd come by in case you needed me."

"You came here looking for me?"

"Yeah." He pointed to my bag. "I found you just in time, huh? You ready to go?"

"No," I said. "I actually have to go back in there for one more bag."

He shook his head. "I'll get it. Do I need your ID?"

I took my badge from around my neck. "The bag is just sitting right outside the elevator on the third floor. Canvas bag, red straps. And hey, can you do me a favor? Just throw my ID in the trash on your way back out."

This was all so emotional to me, but he was so calm. "Got it. Don't move." He vanished into the building, and I glanced down at my phone, which I'd been ignoring, and which was filling up with messages of every kind from practically everyone I'd ever known. They loved the finale. They couldn't believe what I had done with the finale. They were shocked by the finale. I could think about all of it later.

But as I slipped my phone back into my pocket, I looked up to see Justin, *again,* walking toward me. There was nothing to do anymore except laugh, so I did.

"You look like you're in a good mood," he said. "Did Toby tell you we're going to be working together?"

"I'm afraid you're a couple of important developments behind, Justin," I said. "I just quit."

"What did you do that for? You just finished your show."

"I'm aware of that. Listen, be decent to these people, okay? They don't deserve any of what's about to happen to them."

"They'll be fine," he said confidently. "I'm going to take care of them."

"Uch," I said, already feeling the sweet freedom of unemployment.

Just then the door opened, and Will stepped out. "Okay," he said, "we're all set. My car's around the corner."

Justin looked at me expectantly. Will didn't appear to care. "Will, this is Justin. Justin, Will."

"It's great to meet you," Justin said.

Will just stared at him, then after looking like he was perhaps counting to ten in his head, he said, "Oh. Sure." For some reason, I found this the funniest thing he possibly could have said.

Apparently looking for an opening to talk about himself, Justin said to Will, "So it's a big day for all these guys, right? Are you, like, really, really into podcasts?"

Will thought about this for a second. He reached out and picked up my other bag of desk stuff, leaving only the Beast for me, and he leaned conspiratorially toward Justin. "You know what?" he said. "I'm not. I'm really, *really* into her." He gestured toward me with a tiny flick of his head, and he walked off, and I tried to burn into my memory the way Justin's face wilted. He didn't say another word. He just walked into the building, into his future, into whatever. I didn't have to care.

As we walked to the car, Will said, "Sorry, was that too much?"

"Oh my God," I said. "The only thing I didn't like about it was that you had clothes on. I'm glad Julie told you what was going on."

"Well," he said. "What happened first was that my sister heard the episode. She got very excited, and she called me, and she was upset when I told her that I wasn't, at that moment, naked in your apartment or anything. Because that's where she thought I would be. And I explained to her what was going on, and I told her you came to see me, and a little bit of what we talked about. And she said, 'I love you very much, but you are being a dipshit.' And so I did a lot of thinking while I was walking Buddy all over the city, and it occurred to me that I was being a dipshit. And my sister is always right. And then your friend texted, and then I listened, and that's about the size of it."

"I just quit my job," I said.

"Yeah, I hope so, because I threw your ID into the water feature in the lobby."

"It doesn't really matter, because I'd probably get fired anyway. They sold the company."

"To who?"

"Caravan. And Justin's going to run it, which is why he was there. It's just the kind of hilarious, extravagant disaster I specialize in these days. I don't honestly know whether working for him or getting laid off by him would have been worse, but with Julie gone and Toby pissed at me about the finale, I decided not to hang around to see."

We got to the car, and he unlocked it, and we put all my stuff in the back. When we were settled, he reached over and picked up my hand. He laced his fingers through mine—he *locked* them in mine—until it was like we were making one joint fist. And then we just sat like that, and he put his other hand over mine, and he said, "I told you everything I really need I can fit in the Kia."

"You did," I said. "You did say that."

"Let me take you home, okay?" I nodded.

It turned out that by "home," Will meant his, not mine. As soon as he opened the door of his apartment, I almost tumbled into it, as relieved as if I'd found a king bed at the end of a transcontinental flight in coach. "Ugh," I said, dropping everything I had on his floor.

"Aww." He pulled me to him and I just stood there with my head on his shoulder, feeling him squeeze me almost tight enough that I couldn't breathe. It was what I wanted; it was all I wanted. "Are you okay?" he said into my hair.

"Ugh," I repeated. "I quit. I don't have a job, I don't have anything."

"That's not true," he said. "Look, you have Buddy." The dog came over and sprawled on the carpet by my feet. I was back in his good graces. "That's loyalty."

"I think he's about the only friend I have left," I said. "Present company excepted, obviously."

"Tell me everything."

We sat down, and I did. About Eliza. About Toby and Julie, and all of the screwy conversations I'd been having for the last few days. And when I was done, I said, "I really don't know what I'm going to do. I don't think anywhere else is necessarily going to be better. I just feel . . . I mean, I loved what I did. I never saw myself as somebody who was going to need to walk away from my work to be a happy person."

"Not your work," he said. "Just maybe your job."

I turned to him. "That sounds good. Talk more about that."

"Well, your work is still your work. I've seen you do it, you could sit right here and do it. Just not for these losers."

"But everything is changing, you know? I feel like maybe sound is dying and we're all going to be screwed, and I don't know how to feel about that."

He moved closer to me on the sofa until he was right next to me, and he lifted one arm and put it around my shoulders. I wiggled around until I could settle my head by his collarbone. "Did I ever tell you about my dad's darkroom?" he said. I could feel his voice vibrate against my cheek; it was one of the most instantly sedating things I'd ever felt. The anxiety drained out of me.

"I don't think so."

"When I was a kid, my dad had a darkroom in our house. He had a Nikon he bought used. He'd go around and take pictures of L.A. He loved paint that peeled in patterns, or the way buildings would get a patina after a while. So sometimes he'd let me come in the darkroom when he was doing prints. I used to sit in there, and he made this chair for me that I had to stay in so I wouldn't get into the chemicals or be in the way. He built handles onto the sides of the chair, and I could only stay in there if I held on to the handles the whole time, so he'd know exactly where my hands were."

"That's genius."

"He was very smart. No touching anything, but I could ask as many questions as I wanted, and he'd tell me exactly what he was doing."

"So that's where the photography started for you?"

"It is, yeah. So this was maybe mid-late 1990s. You were just starting to see regular people ditching their film cameras for digital. And he told me, 'Will, it's all dying. Nobody wants to make prints, nobody wants to handle film, nobody develops anymore.' Really upsetting for him, right? He just kept saying that everything was going to be fake now, everything was going to be cold. Not real."

"Do you agree with that?" I put my hand flat against his chest, so his voice could buzz against it, too.

He laid his hand over mine. "Do you know what a polarizing filter is?"

"No. It sounds like something you turn on to make the internet worse."

"A polarizing filter is a little round piece of glass. You screw it on the end of your lens. They do all kinds of things with light and reflections, they change how everything looks in the picture that you're taking."

"So you're telling me the thing on my phone that makes it look like I have bunny ears is not the first filter in the history of photography?"

"It's not, no. Anyway, what I told my dad when I was a little bit older, old enough that he'd listen to me, was that digital photography wasn't any less real than those filters. It was all a vision of how you wanted the picture to look. You just got it to look like that in a different way."

"What did he think?"

"At the time, I don't think he was very impressed. But now, he's very good with a digital camera."

"So I gather you don't want me to fear change."

"I don't, but it's not that exactly," he said. "I just think . . . something's always dying. It's film cameras and darkrooms or eight-track tapes or CDs or tube televisions where people watch three channels. And the business models die all the time. *Halls of Power* is still on, and how many times has TV already died since that show started? TV with ads, TV without ads, TV over the internet, TV for a fee, TV for no fee, and still, that freaking guy survived in that metal trunk until a beach bum on a WaveRunner picked him up."

"That is definitely the most inspirational possible use of that storyline."

"My point is that stories about people coming back from the dead aren't going away. Photography isn't going away. And sound isn't going away. And I don't know what your next thing is going to look like, but you're going to be okay." He squeezed my shoulder.

"I had a way that I wanted things to go," I said. "And I worked very hard to make them go that way, and they're just not going to. And I'm really disappointed."

At exactly that moment, Buddy heaved himself up, limb by giant limb. He sat down in front of the couch and put his chin on my knee, which required him to lean down like a tall person trying to get into a selfie with a short person.

"Did you train him to do that?" I asked.

"Absolutely not. He just knows what you need."

I put my hand on top of Buddy's head. "I guess he always has, right?" Satisfied that he'd done his job, Buddy wandered off.

"So what now?"

"I have no idea. I quit. And . . . that's how far I am."

It took this long for us to lean toward each other, for me to put my hand on the back of his neck and kiss him to say sorry, to say I didn't mean it, to say I should have known better from the beginning, while he said the same. But just as I was really starting to enjoy it, the noise from the kitchen turned into a sloppy, slapping, splashing racket. I tried to ignore it, I really did, but a dog going to town on his water bowl while you're trying to make out on the sofa can really make you self-conscious about the actions of your own tongue. We pulled apart and he swore and I laughed, and he smiled and ran his hand over my hair, from my forehead to my neck, and he said, "Come with me."

We stood up and he looked back at me, and I said, "I know I don't look great. I was pretty discombobulated when I left for work. I didn't even brush my hair."

He turned and started leading me toward his little bedroom. "I'm just going to mess it up anyway," he said. "Happy Valentine's Day."

We both were awake at 3:00 in the morning this time. We just lay there, and he wound a bit of my hair around his finger and unwound it, over and over. "Are you working in the morning?" I asked.

"No, I have to work brunch on Sunday, though."

"Is that bad?"

"It's good money. It's a pain in the butt, though. When I did it last weekend, I think I had twelve people at one table. The drink orders make it seem like more."

"Ah, they got you on the drinks," I said.

"Exactly. I don't mind the omelettes, I don't mind all the crab and the bacon and the cheese on everything. I don't even mind the people who are so hungover they're still drunk. But the drink orders. When people order dinner, they drink some water and some wine. But when they come to brunch, they end up with glasses and tumblers and those giant coffee mugs that are constantly trying to spill all over the place. Up at the coffee bar, the barista paints a fern on the top of a latte and by the time I get to the table, it looks like a skeleton."

I turned toward him in the dark. "Now I have to know, what were they having, the twelve-top? Or is it too much of a blur?"

"Oh, no, I'm up for it." I could hear a smile in his voice, and I just wanted to keep making that happen. "Two of them were having coffee. Coffee, coffee, coffee, nothing else. Loved them, they were my favorites. Keep the cup full, top up the milk once or twice, they're happy."

"That's who I would be."

He tugged, just barely, on my hair. "Of course it is. One was doing lattes with skim milk. One, lattes with oat milk. Cappuccino on the end—the kind of cappuccino guy who's always surprised a cappuccino is a little short drink, you know? Let's see. One Bloody Mary that was followed by several more. A mimosa, an orange juice in a mimosa *glass,* another mimosa."

"The mimosa contagion."

"Listen, 'I'll have that, that sounds good' is real. It's why I try not to start the orders with the person who's going to ask for four substitutions."

"How can you tell who that is?"

"Oh, believe me, I can tell. Okay, I'm on a roll, I'm almost done. The leopard jumpsuit was having cosmos—four in two hours, at least. An iced green tea next to her. And . . . the guy on the end with the sunset margaritas." He put his face into my neck. "I think those are all right, give or take an orange juice and a cranberry juice I probably forgot about."

"I could never keep track of all that in a million years."

"I have a good memory."

"I could never tolerate that many people asking me for things at the same time."

"I have a lot of patience."

"Can I say something to you?" I ran the tips of my fingers down his forearm.

"Sure."

"If you're happy doing both of these jobs, and you're good at both of them, why is there this thing about needing to figure out your life? Maybe this is your life. Maybe you found it, and you didn't notice."

"Are you suggesting I should stop searching for my next great adventure?" he asked.

"I'll tell you what," I said. "You stop, and I'll start."

CHAPTER THIRTY-TWO

The Signing Off

"I am unemployed," I said to Will as he stumbled, half-asleep, into his kitchen the next morning to find me already making coffee.

"Cool," he said. "How do you like it?"

"Well, I'm not sure." I paused, then threw an extra spoonful of ground coffee into the filter before I shut the lid and hit the button.

"How long has it been?"

"Since I had no current job? Six years. Since I had no current job and no upcoming job? Twelve years. Since I had no job to go back to, no school to go back to, and no plans for the future at all? Probably since I was about fourteen, just sitting around and taking quizzes in *Teen People*."

"Listening to, what . . . Amy Winehouse? Alicia Keys? Coooooldplaaaaay?"

"What do you have against Coldplay?"

"I might have had a fight with my ex about them. Not about them, but they have a song that she really liked that rhymed 'lost' with 'lost' about fifteen times. She played it whenever she was unhappy about anything."

"Well, I'm sure I was listening to something very cool at that time. And look how it turned out—I'm here with you, and she's . . . wherever she is."

"She moved to Boston," he said, "and the next thing I knew, she was in love with her longtime best friend."

"Oh, so you got *When Harry Met Sally*-d."

"Well, except for the fact that they're both women, but yes. It was all very modern."

"Please don't tell me you think it's very modern that your ex is bisexual."

"Not at all. I knew that part. I thought it was very modern that I found out about her new relationship by watching a TikTok where she danced around in a T. rex costume."

"What was she doing in a T. rex costume?"

"I don't know. Holding her girlfriend in her tiny tiny arms?"

I could see the edge of his smile poking his cheek out wide. I went over and wrapped my arms around his waist, inhaling in the space between his shoulder blades. "Good morning," I said softly.

"All right, all right, I'm going to make eggs, don't distract me."

"I have to tell you something," I said, not letting go, speaking into the back of his shirt.

"What is it?"

"I really like that Coldplay song."

He laughed again, and it went into my fingertips, which were pressed against his ribs.

"What's on your agenda for today, now that you have no obligations?" he asked as he stirred the eggs.

"I have one left," I said. "But it shouldn't take long."

. . .

"Well, hi!"

I hadn't known whether Eliza would be willing to talk to me. I hadn't heard a peep from her about what happened in the last episode; I sort of hoped Marcela was now at war with Toby. But when I asked her whether I could drop by the house, all she texted back was "Of course!" And then there was a party hat emoji. I didn't know that we were going to have a party hat kind of discussion, but why not go with the flow?

I should have known that this was what would happen when she opened the door. That she would say, *Well, hi!,* because nothing deterred her, and because she probably had a hundred new deals already, her bottled cocktail and her sneaker collab and whatever else her team of agents and reps had negotiated on her behalf as she paced her home office, probably doing lunges at the same time. I was entirely in her rearview mirror.

"Hi," I said. I held up both hands. "No microphones, no nothing."

She grinned. "Of course, come in!" When I stepped inside, I saw that she'd made a massive change to the aesthetic of her living room by adding three bright blue throw pillows to the white sofa. She saw me staring. "Do you like the pop of blue?" she said. "I'm experimenting with it. My friend who does interior design is obsessed with throw pillows."

"I do like it," I said.

"Well, come sit in the nook," she said, gesturing into the depths of her house.

"I can't stay, actually, I have to go meet my sister for dinner. I just wanted to come by because I didn't want to leave things the way they were the last time we talked."

"Well, I'm glad," she said.

"I wanted to tell you that I'm sorry I didn't take more responsibility for how things went toward the end," I said. "You weren't wrong that it was my decision to make the thing, and that I should have been more honest with everybody. I hope you don't feel upset about the finale."

"You know what?" she said. "The beautiful thing is that nobody cares. Everybody got to hear me set you up with all those great guys, they know I did my best for you, and now, whatever happens . . ." She shrugged. "It happens. I'm still on track, I have a zillion dating clients hitting me up, and I think I'm going on Seth Meyers next week."

"Wow," I said. "Well, that's great. You're happy, and I'm even happy. I know it wasn't your choice, but I'm seeing Will, and it's going well."

"Yeah?" she asked.

"Yeah. It seems really good. It's a happy thing. Obviously it's new, but right now, very . . . yeah, very happy."

She held up both hands. "If you say so."

I crossed my arms and looked around her entryway, over to the poster of her wedding and her magazine covers. There just wasn't any point in defending the coffee ritual in my kitchen, pastries with his sister, talking about photography. She didn't have to like it. And so I took a big breath and went on. "I also came over here to thank you."

"For what?"

"Well, I'm sure you know I quit," I said. "I didn't hesitate, I didn't feel guilty, and when Toby told me that I was going to hurt a lot of other people and that I was being selfish, it actually didn't work on me. And that's new. And as soon as I started thinking about new jobs, I realized I'd never get myself walked into a situation like that again. I'd never let somebody own my work just because I liked them, or loved them. If somebody tried to steal my idea, I honestly don't think I'd ever sit there and take it again. And I think I owe some of that to you."

"So you liked my advice?" She brightened a little.

"To be completely honest, I don't like your advice. I learned all that from just who you are. I might not know what goes into a bottled cocktail, but I know that if you didn't like the idea they brought you, you would tell them no, and you wouldn't feel bad, and you wouldn't have regrets. You'd tell them to go to hell. You'd have one of your reps say it, maybe, but it would come from you. I got a lot from watching how you are in the world. I do admire that."

She didn't say anything at first. She nodded, and then she looked me up and down. She smiled. "You know, I'm still such a fan of you. I still think I could help you meet somebody," she said.

"Eliza! I met somebody. Do you understand? I met somebody."

"But is this really the right person, or are you just—"

I put my hand on her arm. "Please stop. We don't have to do this anymore."

I watched her face, and I believed briefly that I could trace so much of her story there: how she started off making little videos for fun, and then one took off, and then another one, and she had *tenacity*, and she got on the phone, and she picked and chose and strategized, and she studied her website and agonized over the colors, and there was a book deal, and another book deal, and all she'd ever done was what was next. And just like me, she could feel it slipping away from her, the chance to make money and do as she chose and make something she'd be proud of. She was at the mercy of algorithms that could change at any time, and she wanted so badly to have something that would be her own, and here she was.

Finally, she shook her head a little. "I want you to be happy, I really do. I care."

I nodded. "And I really do wish you luck," I said. "I think you're very talented. And I'm sorry I didn't turn out to be a very good Platinum Goddess."

"Well," she said, "there's room for plenty of goddesses in the world, right?"

I nodded. "Take care of yourself, okay?"

"You too." She seemed to have nothing to say, for once. Turnabout was perhaps fair play.

I walked out of her house and down her driveway, to Will, who was waiting in the car.

EPILOGUE

The Future

It was snowing. I hadn't had a regular day job in almost a year. I had a boyfriend, and he had a dog—really, we had a dog. And so we took Buddy to the dog park around the corner from my apartment.

Buddy *loved* the dog park. Little dogs took to him the way a cartoon mouse might befriend a cartoon lion with hearts for eyes. They would jump at his jowls, pawing and mouthing while he played back with such carefully controlled vigor that he wrapped strings of slobber around his own snout. He really only needed one of us to take him. Sometimes I did it while Will was on a job, or Will did it while I was working—by then, I had a decent side-line in consulting and editing—or just camped out on the couch of my own apartment watching something he didn't care about. But today, we decided we'd all three go together.

We put a red-and-black plaid jacket on him, not because he really needed it, but because while he always got his share of stares and compliments, when he had a lively print on, it happened even more. "That's a horse" was a very common opinion, but I remained convinced, as I had been on the day I met Will and

Buddy both, that what he actually looked like was a cow. There were a lot of people out today, so looking his best could only benefit the good boy Buddy now was, having spent a fair number of weeks going to classes with Will. He had solidified into a reliably well-behaved, always gentle, mostly obedient, and ruggedly handsome dog.

For all these reasons, when we were a block from the dog park, it came very naturally to me to say, "Man, I love this dog."

"I love *you,*" Will said.

I was acutely aware of turning red, and I felt it happening faster and faster as snowflakes fell on my cheeks. "Well," I said. "I mean, I love you too."

"You still blush every time," he said. "It is the greatest."

"I can't help it," I said. "I still get shook."

"It's understandable. I think the snow, the walk, the quiet, the dog, it's all very romantic."

I stepped over and put my arm through his. "Thank you," I said.

We continued to walk, and he didn't look at me, but I saw him smile. "Thank you back."

So many things had gone so spectacularly wrong since I met him; it was, on the surface, a distressing inventory. I had sold my soul to a manufacturer of cat toys, and then to a woman who tried to set me up with a supplement guy and a guy who didn't tip. I'd watched my closest friend move away so that we didn't see each other every day anymore. I'd watched the company where I spent six years get gobbled up like a pig in a blanket, consumed by someone I knew personally, who had already raided my reserve of good ideas once, and who continued to give interviews where they called him a visionary until, six months after they hired him, he left Caravan "by mutual agreement."

Eliza had temporarily suspended new applications for the Platinum Goddess Package (and the Diamond Goddess Package, and the Girl in a Hurry Crash Course). It appeared that she was focusing on her collabs these days. I was still on her mailing list, so I knew the bottled cocktail had been revealed—it was a Cranberry Crush, but hers was going to be "lower in sugar and formulated to boost your energy." She'd started doing occasional guest spots on a Caravan podcast called *This Is the Life,* where she'd answer questions. Somehow, they had persuaded her that there was an audio project that would not be Nowheresville.

My parents liked Will, even though so far, they'd only met him over Zoom. His mother liked me, too; I'd gone to her birthday party and she sent me home with a huge wedge of apple cake and a deli container full of chicken and dumplings. I texted almost every day with Maggie, and Will came over every couple of weeks to eat with Mol and Pete.

Julie was working on a show at Tappan about the moon landing. Every time I talked to her, she divided our time. Half was spent on stories of Bella learning to ride the subway and say "pardon me" when she bumped into people. Half was spent on breathless recitations of the pleasures of working for a boss who not only was not ridiculous or duplicitous, but was working on transitioning the company into an employee-owned co-op. I was envious but ravenous; I made her tell me everything, every detail down to the color of the walls in their break room (sky blue). She insisted they had their own strange rules and regrettable patterns and as many unmet goals as anybody, they just didn't make her feel terrible in the same way. "All jobs have some degree of bullshit," she told me, "but it is so refreshing just to have *new* bullshit."

As for everybody else, I had made calls to practically everyone I knew in audio on behalf of Charlie and Abby, and Melissa, and everybody else who asked me. Getting them all resettled was the one connection to that job I allowed myself to keep.

All this, all this. But somehow, everyone I loved still loved me. I still opened up audio files on my laptop and pulled out other people's voices stumbling, other people's phones suddenly beeping, other people's first answers to a question that had been followed by better ones. And at night, sometimes I opened up a fresh document and typed out one idea at a time: an eight-episode show. A daily show. A news show. An interview show. Some I would host. Some I would not. It would all shake loose if I wrote it down and left it alone. I, too, needed new bullshit.

I looked over to see Buddy taking deep sniffs of a bush that was dotted with snow. When he reemerged, he had snow stuck to his face as he came over to Will, who brushed it off for him. "Aw, Buddy," he said. "We've got you."

"We've got you," I repeated, and I leaned my head on Will's shoulder.

He turned to me. "You okay?"

"I'm perfect," I said. "For the moment, I'm perfect."

Acknowledgments

If you came here to read this part first, or even if you are just always careful to read this part at all, then you are my kind of person. Just about everything we create is a team effort in one way or another.

I have been lucky enough to work with the same superteam for three books in a row, including my agent, Sarah Burnes; my editor, Sara Weiss; and publicist Emily Isayeff. They are a good part of the reason I have loved my experiences in publishing.

I am grateful to the entire team at Ballantine, including Kara Welsh, Kim Hovey, Jennifer Hershey, Kara Cesare, Natalie Hallak, and Sydney Collins. Elena Giavaldi really understands how to present the back half of a dog and make a book cover sing. (Speaking of which, Buddy was inspired by my dog Brian's daycare friend Jude. So thank you to Jude for being irresistible and gorgeous.) Many thanks to Loren Noveck and the copyediting team, without whom this book would suggest I do not know whether Tuesday comes before or after Wednesday.

I am indebted to everybody who has ever produced a segment or a show that I have been on. I particularly have trusted, for many years, Jessica Reedy and Mike Katzif, and everything I know about producing anything, I probably picked up from them. (Anything I got wrong was the result of not listening to them diligently enough.) The entire *Pop Culture Happy Hour* team is a delight, and they are among my most important allies.

My friends are always a primary support for me, and while I was working on this book, I had the privilege of leaning on people like Molly Backes, Jen Miller, Vicci Ho, Marc Hirsh, Stephen Thompson, Maureen Ryan, Kat Kinsman, Margaret Willison, Alan Sepinwall, Jesse Thorn, and plenty of other folks anybody would be lucky to know. No list could be exhaustive.

A big thanks to my dog for being consistently delightful, including at times when very little else is.

Thank you, of course, to my tremendous family. I love you very much.

about the author

LINDA HOLMES is the *New York Times* bestselling author of *Evvie Drake Starts Over* and *Flying Solo,* a pop culture correspondent for NPR, and one of the hosts of the popular podcast *Pop Culture Happy Hour*. She appears regularly on NPR's radio shows including *Morning Edition, All Things Considered,* and *Weekend Edition*. Before NPR, she wrote for *New York* magazine online and for *TV Guide,* as well as for the groundbreaking site *Television Without Pity*. She lives with a dog who is fine with fireworks but terrified of ceiling fans.

thisislindaholmes.com
Instagram: @lindaholmes97
Bluesky: @lindaholmes.bsky.social